Read
the Merrychurch Mysteries by
K.C. Wells

Truth Will Out

"…an enjoyable, feel good cozy mystery. Great for a trip, or a rainy fall afternoon where you can curl up with your furry four-legged buddy and a cuppa something hot. I'm looking forward to the next in the series."

—Gay Book Reviews

"I loved it and cannot wait for the next one, and I highly recommend it!"

—The Novel Approach

"*Truth Will Out* is a rather quintessential British mystery…. I look forward to more adventures in Merrychurch."

—Joyfully Jay

Roots of Evil

"It's a good mystery, but with fun, snark and sassiness that only K.C. can provide in her way."

—Love Bytes

"A good mystery, a murder, a list of potential killers, and Mike's and Jonathon's minds. It was captivating and funny."

—OptimuMM

By K.C. WELLS

BFF
Bromantically Yours
First
Love Lessons Learned
Step by Step
Waiting For You

DREAMSPUN
DESIRES
The Senator's Secret
Out of the Shadows
My Fair Brady
Under the Covers

LEARNING TO LOVE
Michael & Sean
Evan & Daniel
Josh & Chris
Final Exam

LOVE, UNEXPECTED
Debt
Burden

MERRYCHURCH
MYSTERIES
Truth Will Out
Roots of Evil
A Novel Murder

SENSUAL BONDS
A Bond of Three
A Bond of Truth

With Parker Williams

COLLARS & CUFFS
An Unlocked Heart
Trusting Thomas
Someone to Keep Me
A Dance with
Domination
Damian's Discipline
Make Me Soar
Dom of Ages
Endings and Beginnings

SECRETS
Before You Break
An Unlocked Mind
Threepeat
On the Same Page

Published by DREAMSPINNER PRESS
www.dreamspinnerpress.com

K.C. WELLS

A NOVEL MURDER

Published by
DREAMSPINNER PRESS

5032 Capital Circle SW, Suite 2, PMB# 279,
Tallahassee, FL 32305-7886 USA
www.dreamspinnerpress.com

This is a work of fiction. Names, characters, places, and incidents either are the product of author imagination or are used fictitiously, and any resemblance to actual persons, living or dead, business establishments, events, or locales is entirely coincidental.

A Novel Murder
© 2020 K.C. Wells

Cover Art
© 2020 Paul Richmond
http://www.paulrichmondstudio.com
Cover content is for illustrative purposes only and any person depicted on the cover is a model.

Mass Market Paperback ISBN: 978-1-64108-168-9
Trade Paperback ISBN: 978-1-64405-573-1
Digital ISBN: 978-1-64405-314-0
Library of Congress Control Number: 2020933301
Mass Market Paperback published November 2020
v. 1.1

Printed in the United States of America
∞
This paper meets the requirements of
ANSI/NISO Z39.48-1992 (Permanence of Paper).

For my husband, Andrew, who is so good at planning a murder that he is making me nervous....

Acknowledgments

Thank you to my beta team, as always. I couldn't do this without you.

CHAPTER ONE

February 14, 2018

JONATHON DE Mountford relieved the circulating waiter of two champagne flutes and handed one to Mike Tattersall. "Here. You look like you need another one."

Mike leaned in close. "What I *need* is to get out of this tux and into a bath. Preferably with you."

Jonathon was glad he wasn't sipping his champagne. "Don't say things like that when I can't react." They were in the ballroom of the Grosvenor Hotel in London, two of perhaps a thousand guests at an exclusive charity ball. The entertainment was over and the dancing had begun, with champagne flowing like water.

Considering the price of the tickets, that was the least Jonathon expected. The Valentine's Day ball was to raise money for children in need, and so far, the total amount for the event was in the millions.

For him, however, the highlight was not the five-course dinner, or the celebrity acts, or even their magnificent surroundings, but the sight of Mike in a tux. That was a first, and the only downside was that

Jonathon couldn't make it obvious he was drooling. There were enough photographers mingling with the guests to make him wary of being caught on camera, although ironically that was the purpose of their attendance.

Right on cue, Ruth Ainsworth sauntered over to him, holding her own glass of bubbly. "Don't you think it's time we danced?" She flashed Mike a smile. "If Hubby doesn't mind, that is."

Mike huffed. "Hubby. Yeah, right." He waved his hand. "Go on, enjoy yourselves. Someone has to." He put down his glass on a nearby table, then held out his hands for theirs. "I'll mind the champagne. Just don't expect there to be anything left when you're done. I need all the alcohol I can get to survive this shindig."

Jonathon gave him a warm smile. *Thank you,* he mouthed before leading Ruth by the hand to the dance floor. He put his hands on her waist, she looped her arms around his neck, and they glided to the music, joining the hundred or so couples who were already similarly engaged.

"Not a same-sex couple in sight," Jonathon said sadly as they circled the room.

Ruth sighed. "Then you're not looking hard enough. I saw two men dancing together ten minutes ago." She caressed his cheek. "It wouldn't matter if half the couples dancing were LGBTQ. That still wouldn't mean you could dance with Mike." She glanced over in the direction of Mike's table. "He hates this, doesn't he?"

"He's not the only one," Jonathon assured her. "And as for hating it, which part? He's met some people who think having a lot of money is an excuse for a lack of manners. Others who'd look down their noses at him if they knew he owns a pub. Yet more who've only come here to be seen." Jonathon could understand Mike's discomfort. This was not his usual terrain. Merrychurch seemed a long way away.

"Is that what we're doing?" she said quietly. "We've attended two charity balls in two months. So we've contributed to charities. Big deal. That's not why we've come. We're here so your father gets to see photos of Jonathon de Mountford dancing with the Honorable Ruth Ainsworth in the society pages. So he can think he's won—for the time being, at least."

It was Jonathon's turn to sigh. "Do you think we can call it a night after this number?"

Ruth gave a mock gasp. "Am I that bad a dancer?"

He laughed. "You're a wonderful dancer. But I'd rather have Mike in my arms. No offense."

"None taken. The idea was to buy us some time while you came up with a plan. Are you saying you have one?"

"Unfortunately, no, not yet." Jonathon looked across the room to where Mike sat, steadily draining his glass. "I asked him to come because I couldn't bear the thought of him not being with me. But it's torture. Not sitting too close to him. Not staring at him when he looks so…."

"Edible?" Ruth's lips twitched.

Jonathon chuckled. "You know me far too well."

"Why do you think I told Clare she couldn't come? I knew how much willpower I'd need, and frankly, I haven't got that much. But I want her here. I want to dance with her, hold her, laugh and joke

with her like all the het couples are doing right now."
Ruth's face tightened.

"You're getting tired of it all too, aren't you?"
Jonathon hated all the subterfuge.

"Yes," she replied promptly. "I loved the idea
back at Christmas, when we talked about being seen
together to let your father think we were actually considering his stupid suggestion, but now? I'm not sure
how much longer I can keep up the public smiles and
fending off questions from friends who want to know
if wedding bells are in the future."

Jonathon snorted. "If they were really your
friends, they wouldn't be asking such idiotic questions. Unless they want to know when you're marrying Clare, which is totally acceptable."

"Have you asked him to marry you?"

Jonathon's gaze was once more on Mike. "Not
yet, no. I didn't want to propose, then keep him waiting for years. If I'm going to get down on one knee,
it'll be because I already have a date in mind."

She chuckled. "Sorry. I'm picturing you kneeling in
Merrychurch's tea shop, proposing over the coffee and
walnut cake with all the old dears clucking around you."

He widened his eyes. "Oh, I like that." He leaned
in close and whispered, "I already have the ring."

Ruth gaped. "You dark horse. When did you get
that?"

"When I went shopping after the New Year's Eve
ball. Mike stayed at the hotel." Jonathon grinned. "I
guess I wiped him out."

She rolled her eyes. "Spare me the details of your
sex life."

Jonathon smirked. "We were dancing. Not *every-thing* that comes out of my mouth is dirty."

"No—only a mere 99 percent of it." Ruth frowned. "Wait a minute. You were dancing with me all night. Mike sat and watched. How did that wipe him out?"

Jonathon bit back a smile. "We were dancing in our hotel room."

Ruth arched her eyebrows. "Ah-ha. And now we have the truth. *Horizontal* dancing."

He wasn't about to deny it. At that moment he caught sight of a photographer getting closer. "Paste on your smile. We've got company."

"I was thinking of something more along these lines." Ruth gave him an adoring look.

He snickered. "Don't overdo it, or my father real-ly *will* be expecting imminent wedding news."

"Too much? Got it." Ruth smiled at him as they danced past the man with the camera, both she and Jonathon turning their heads in his direction. Once he'd taken his photo, Ruth leaned in. "Now dance me over to where Mike is, and the three of us can sit, drink, and talk—providing he hasn't finished off all the champagne."

"That works for me." Jonathon steered them in Mike's direction, loving how Mike's face lit up when he saw them approaching. He took in the state of the glasses and signaled to a nearby waiter for more champagne.

They had plans to make, and a council of war re-quired sufficient alcoholic lubrication.

MIKE PROPPED himself up on the pillows and watched Jonathon undressing. "So what am I missing at the Grosvenor? Because I thought we were staying there. What's it like?" Not that he was complaining about Jonathon's choice of hotel. The bed was as supremely comfortable as the last time they'd stayed there, and the unexpected bottle of champagne chilling in an ice bucket was a pleasant surprise. The Soho Hotel had been his treat for Jonathon's twenty-ninth birthday, and they'd had a wonderful weekend.

"Swanky. Expensive. You'd hate it." Jonathon flashed him a grin. "Besides, we had a great time when we were here last. I thought you might like to relive the experience."

"Which part? The bath? The shower? The bed? The carpet? The lack of sleep?" Mike looked Jonathon up and down as the clothing fell away to reveal his lean form. "As handsome as you look in a tux, I much prefer you out of it."

Jonathon's phone buzzed, and he groaned. "I thought I'd put it on silent. It had better not be my father."

"Then don't look," Mike suggested. "Whoever it is can wait. This is our first Valentine's Day together, and I've spent most of the evening not being able to touch you. I want to make up for lost time." He gazed at the red roses standing in a vase on the table. No one had ever bought him flowers on Valentine's Day, let alone roses, and the romantic gesture was perfect after spending an evening keeping Jonathon at arm's length.

Jonathon glanced over at his phone, then climbed naked onto the bed and crawled over to him. "It was a great dinner, wasn't it?"

"It was," Mike agreed, temporarily distracted by Jonathon's obvious arousal. His own erection was already tenting the soft white sheet that covered it.

"And the entertainment was top-notch?"

"It was." Mike smiled. "But all I could think of was the finale when I finally got you to myself."

"I'm sure Clare was thinking exactly the same thing. She had to wait until the ball was over before she got to see Ruth."

Mike's eyes glittered. "And I'm sure *they're* not wasting time answering texts or talking." He crooked his index finger. "Now come here and kiss me."

"Don't you want more champagne?"

Mike shook his head. "All I want to taste is you."

Jonathon's face glowed. "As if I could refuse an invitation like that." He straddled Mike's lap, and their lips met in a soft, tender kiss. He looked Mike in the eye. "Love you."

"Love you too. Now switch off your phone before it interrupts us again. Because I have plans for this gorgeous body."

Jonathon stretched his arm toward the bedside cabinet where his phone sat. "I like the sound of these plans. Do I turn out the light too?"

"Leave it on. I don't want to deprive myself of the best part."

"And what's that?" Jonathon asked as he molded his body to Mike's.

Mike lifted Jonathon's chin with his fingertips. "Looking into your eyes while I make love to you."

The time for talking was past.

JONATHON HAD no idea what had awoken him or what the time was, but it was still dark outside. He eased himself across the mattress, not wanting to disturb Mike as he reached for his phone. Then he lay on his back, stuffed pillows under his head, and switched it on. The screen lit up the white sheets with an eerie glow.

"Can't sleep?"

Jonathon gave a start. "Don't do that. I thought you were asleep. And I was only checking the time."

Mike gave a sleepy chuckle. "Well, you've checked it. Now turn off the phone, get over here, and I'll snuggle you back to sleep."

"Just a sec. I've got a few emails." Jonathon clicked on the bedside lamp.

"Which can wait until morning."

He sighed. "One look, okay?" He glanced at the screen, frowning. "Who is Heather Caldicott, and why is she emailing me?"

Mike sat up beside him, rubbing his eyes. "Heather runs the Merrychurch library. And I have no idea why she'd be emailing you."

Jonathon had seen the library in the village. Someone had taken the ground floor of a thatched house and turned it into the cutest little library, with gleaming wood floorboards and dark wooden bookshelves. The selection of books wasn't huge, but Jonathon guessed it met the villagers' needs.

Mike peered over his shoulder. "So what does she want?"

Jonathon scanned the text. "She's organizing the first Merrychurch Literary Festival this June."

"Great! That still doesn't answer my question."

Jonathon switched off his phone. "Have you ever heard of Teresa Malvain?"

Mike widened his eyes. "God, yes. She's like a modern-day Agatha Christie. She writes murder mysteries set in this quaint little village. The amateur sleuth is the doctor's receptionist." He cocked his head. "You *must* have heard of her."

Jonathon bit his lip. "I don't read murder mysteries. And until this moment, I had no idea *you* did."

Mike made a snuffly noise, and Jonathon managed to make out the words "guilty pleasure." Jonathon thought it was an adorable reaction. Mike gave him a halfhearted scowl. "Get to the point. It's way too early to be talking about this."

"The *point* is, Heather was going to hold the event in the library. Readings by authors, Q and A sessions, et cetera. But today she received an email from Teresa Malvain's agent. It seems Ms. Malvain wants to attend the festival."

Mike gaped. "That's quite a feather in Heather's cap if she can get Teresa there."

Jonathon nodded. "It seems Teresa used to live in Merrychurch. But Heather now feels the library is way too small for such an event, and she wants to ask—"

"If she can hold it at the manor house," Mike concluded.

Jonathon grinned. "You're fast. Teresa Malvain as the guest of honor will undoubtedly increase the number of people attending the festival. But there's plenty of room at the hall."

"Good. I'm glad that's all decided. Now turn off the light and cuddle me."

Jonathon chuckled. "Bossy." He clicked off the lamp and shifted across the mattress to snuggle against Mike's firm, warm body. They lay in silence for a while, Mike's arms around him, Mike's scent filling his nostrils. "Tonight wasn't so bad, was it?" he asked after a while.

Mike sighed heavily. "No, it wasn't. I just hated that I'd gone there to be with you, only I had to act like you were nothing more than a friend. Don't get me wrong. I know why you and Ruth were doing it. But it felt...."

Jonathon laid his head on Mike's furry chest. "If it makes you feel any better, I don't want to do that again. We've made my father happy for a while. But tonight made me realize something. Making him happy makes both you and me *un*happy, and I don't like that."

"But what's the alternative?" Mike stroked Jonathon's head. "You *know* what he wants. You married to Ruth, producing little de Mountfords, with me in the background, your dirty little secret."

"He can want that as much as he likes, but he's not going to get it. And if he pushes me too far, he won't like the consequences." Jonathon kissed Mike's chest, loving the hitch in his breathing. "And now we're going to stop talking."

"You got some other activity in mind?" The rawness in Mike's voice was a definite turn-on.

Jonathon laughed softly. "I was thinking of going back to sleep." Mike let out a low growl, and Jonathon found himself flipped onto his back, his heartbeat increasing. "Okay. Maybe not."

Sleep was overrated.

CHAPTER TWO

June 2018

HEATHER CALDICOTT consulted her list again, and for the tenth time since their meeting had begun, Jonathon wished she'd relax.

"Heather, everything is running like clockwork. The caterers will arrive tomorrow afternoon to set up the ballroom, we've got a small army of volunteers ready to set up the tables once the dinner is over, and the banners got here this morning. They're fantastic. The first Merrychurch Literary Festival is going to be a roaring success."

With a heavy sigh, she closed her notepad. "Sorry. It's just that ever since Teresa Malvain announced she was going to attend, this event has blown up out of all proportion. I thought we'd sell maybe fifty or so tickets when I first envisaged this. But now we're talking hundreds." She gave him a grateful smile. "Thank you so much for organizing the dinner the night before it kicks off. It was a wonderful idea. Seating the authors with their fans… brilliant. Of course, everyone wanted to be at the top table."

"There's a top table?" Mike grinned. "Sounds more like a wedding than a literary dinner." He picked up the coffeepot. "Another?"

Heather held out her empty cup. "Thanks. I need all the caffeine I can get. And God, yes, there's a top table. They all want to have dinner with Teresa." She sighed again. "We've sold every ticket for the dinner. The ballroom will be packed. I still can't thank you enough for agreeing to hold the festival here. Such beautiful surroundings."

"I take it all the authors have confirmed their attendance?" Mike asked.

"Every last one of them. And not just authors. We've got publishers attending, not to mention Professor Harcourt."

"That name rings a bell." Mike stroked his beard thoughtfully. Jonathon loved how he did that. Almost as much as *he* enjoyed stroking Mike's full beard. Of course, he also loved it when Mike used it in more creative ways. Then he realized Mike was staring at him, his lips twitching.

He reads my mind far too easily.

Mike widened his eyes. "Got it. He's a forensic pathologist. The Met used him as an expert witness loads of times. How did you get him to come?"

"He's going to give a talk on autopsies. He said it would be a great opportunity to show that the crime shows on TV get it all wrong." Heather chuckled. "Sounds like it'll be interesting. As long as he doesn't bring visual aids. I don't want the readers throwing up."

"Why am I picturing Doctor Who's hand floating in a jar?" Jonathon snickered.

Mike rolled his eyes.

"And as for getting him to come, he didn't take much persuading once he knew who the main speaker was. Apparently he's a fan." Heather finished her coffee. "If you're sure we've covered everything?"

Jonathon gave her a hopefully reassuring smile. "I'm sure. Try not to worry. I know this is your baby, but trust me, it's going to run like a well-oiled machine. Before you blink, it'll be Saturday and the readers will be lining up on the driveway, ready to collect their programs and tote bags."

She stared at him. "The tote bags! I forgot about them."

Mike laughed. "Will you stop panicking? Everything is under control. The volunteers spent yesterday filling them with all the swag that was sent to us, as well as all the free books. I never saw so many boxes." He took hold of her hand. "Breathe, Heather. The bags will be in the entrance hall on two long tables. Once a reader shows their registration details, they'll be given a bag. Every author was sent details of accommodations, here and in nearby towns. And the guest of honor arrived today. She's already in her room at the pub, though why she wanted to stay there and not a hotel, I'm not sure."

"And Mike is treating her like royalty," Jonathon added. He didn't tell her how Mike had gone into panic mode when Teresa requested a room, but he knew that had mostly to do with Mike wanting to make a good impression. He needn't have worried. The room looked amazing. And besides, Teresa knew it was a room above a pub, not in a plush hotel, so she couldn't really complain.

"You two have been so wonderful." Heather stood and collected her bag from the back of her chair. "Still, I'll be relieved when it's Sunday night and this is over. *Then* I'll relax."

"Before you start planning the 2019 Merrychurch Literary Festival, you mean." Mike grinned. "Because you *know* this one is going to go so well, you'll have to do it again. Your only task will be going one better than Teresa Malvain."

"Think big," Jonathon suggested. "Stephen King. Neil Gaiman. Nora Roberts."

Heather snorted. "Getting Teresa was a fluke. I doubt I can improve on her. Unless she loves it so much, she wants to come back."

Jonathon rose to his feet. "I'll show you out. And we'll see you tomorrow afternoon so you can check over the ballroom."

Heather gave him an unexpected hug. "Thank you. I couldn't have done this without you." She released him and grabbed Mike. "You too."

Mike let out an *oof*. "Wow. When you hug, you really hug. Glad we could help. Now go get some sleep. It's already past ten o'clock."

They walked her through the manor house until they reached the entrance hall. Heather stared at the tables laden with bright red tote bags, all bearing Teresa Malvain's logo and the black-and-white cover of the latest Summersfield book, her murder-mystery series. Posts with arrows pointed the way to the ballroom.

"There'll be a big seating plan for when the dinner guests arrive tomorrow night," Jonathon informed Heather. "So when they enter the ballroom, everyone will know where to go. The menu is on each table, and the catering staff is aware of all the allergies." He patted her shoulder. "Now stop worrying and go home."

Heather gave them a tired smile. "Okay, you've convinced me. My baby is in safe hands."

Mike opened the door for her, and she walked out to her car. They waved her off, then came back inside. Mike locked the door. "I could go back and relieve Abi for the last hour or so."

Jonathon sighed. "You know she hates it when you leave her in charge, then come back. She doesn't get to be in charge that often."

"She's running the pub tomorrow night while I'm at the dinner, isn't she?"

"Yes, and I'm sure that makes her very happy. Now let her do her job."

Mike frowned. "But Teresa—"

"Teresa is probably in the bar having a drink, or more likely in her room, on her laptop or her phone. And if she needs anything, Abi is there to provide it. Besides…." Jonathon grinned. "Which would you rather do? Go back and work behind the bar until closing, or stay the night with me?"

Mike let out an exaggerated sigh. "When you put it like that…." He grabbed Jonathon's hand. "Janet's gone to bed, right?"

Jonathon gazed at him suspiciously. "Why?"

Mike pulled him close, his beard tickling Jonathon's neck, his breath warm on Jonathon's skin. "Because I want to screw you on the couch, and I really don't want your housekeeper walking in on us. I don't think she'd ever recover from the shock."

"I appreciate your consideration. I don't want to lose her." Jonathon caught his breath when Mike slid his hands down Jonathon's back and squeezed his jeans-clad arse. "Now stop talking about Janet and take me to the living room so we can get naked."

He hated wasting naked time.

THEY LAY beneath the sheets, cuddling. Mike had never thought he was much of a cuddler until he met Jonathon. Having him in his arms was one of Mike's favorite ways to spend time, and as much as he loved their sex life, cuddling was a close second. He enjoyed the intimacy of it, of feeling so close that it was hard to tell where one ended and the other began.

"Can I ask you something?"

Mike loved the sleep-heavy sound of Jonathon's voice. "You can ask me anything." He was warm, sated, and blissfully content.

"How do you feel about… children?"

"I like them. I just couldn't eat a whole one."

That earned him a whack on the arm. "I'm being serious here."

"So was I. Have you any idea how tough those things can get?" Mike kissed Jonathon's bare shoulder. "Okay. Now I've got my serious head on. Are you asking if I want to have kids?" It wasn't as if the subject hadn't come up before, but always as a slight reference. This had a different feel to it, and the thought sent a tremor through him, as though their relationship had slipped into a higher gear.

What really surprised Mike was that he liked the idea.

They'd been together almost a year, and he loved the way things were progressing. Thomas de

Mountford was the only fly in the ointment, but he'd been quiet of late, so maybe Jonathon's idea of being public with Ruth was paying off. But children?

Jonathon rolled over to face him. "I'll be honest. I gave little thought to having kids. I was happy going around the world, taking photos, getting them published…. I never thought of settling down, having a family. Then I met you. Don't get me wrong. I still want to travel, but now I want you with me. Which is why it's a good thing to get Abi used to running the pub, because if I decide to ask you to come to Vietnam with me…."

Mike stilled. "Vietnam?" He stretched over and switched on the light. Jonathon blinked and rubbed his eyes. Mike settled back on his side, facing him. "How long have you been thinking about this?"

"A while, I suppose. Probably as long ago as November last year. It just felt too soon."

"And now?" Yeah, this whole conversation was suddenly a *lot* more serious.

Jonathon's hand was warm on his chest. "I've been thinking a lot about the future. I think that's down to my father. But what shocked me is that I want a family. So yes, I'm asking… do you want kids? More specifically, do you want to have kids with me?"

"You mean it." Like he couldn't hear the sincerity in Jonathon's voice.

Jonathon nodded. "We can talk about the logistics at a later date. Right now I want to know if you like the idea in principle."

Mike took a deep breath. "I love the idea. I think you'd make a wonderful dad. Watching you with Rachel's granddaughter showed me that."

Jonathon smiled. "She's adorable, isn't she? And so tiny."

"You do know they get bigger, right?"

"Why no, I had no idea." Jonathon chuckled. "And what about you? I love seeing you and Jason together. He really looks up to you."

Mike enjoyed it when Jason Barton came over. Since the shock of learning Mayor John Barton wasn't his biological father, Jason's life had settled down again. He and the ex-mayor were still close. However, he spent a lot of time with Jonathon in the photo editing room, learning more about photography. And when he wasn't there, he was chatting with Mike about all kinds of things. Mike liked having him around, and it was obvious that the eighteen-year-old had a strong case of hero worship going on. Not that Mike minded that at all. Since Jason had come out the previous year, he'd had a lot of questions, and both Mike and Jonathon wanted to be there for him.

"So we're agreed. We'd both make great fathers." Mike kissed the tip of Jonathon's nose. "But kids and traveling are not a good combination."

"Okay. Travel first, *then* have kids." Jonathon sounded so confident. Mike felt it was one of his most attractive qualities.

"You know your father will freak, right?"

It was Jonathon's turn to kiss the tip of Mike's nose. "You leave my father to me. As long as I know we're on the same page, that's enough for now." He shifted closer. "I think having a baby with you sounds amazing." His voice was husky.

Mike thought having a baby with Jonathon sounded more than amazing. It yelled *commitment*, and that made his heart soar. *Me and Jonathon. Kids. A family.*

Mike didn't think he'd ever been happier.

Jonathon's warm fingers encircled Mike's dick, and Mike chuckled. "As long as you're not planning on me getting you pregnant. Because I foresee a problem with that."

Jonathon kissed his neck, and a shiver ran through him. "Just think of all the fun we'll have trying."

Mike sighed happily when Jonathon threw back the sheets and sat astride him, already reaching for the lube. "I take it we're starting now."

Jonathon nodded before bending over to kiss him on the mouth. "No time like the present."

CHAPTER THREE

JONATHON TOOK one last look around the ballroom.
The fifteen or so large round tables were all set up,
covered in white tablecloths, with ten place settings at
each. Wine and water glasses gleamed, and for each
place, there was a bag containing a gift from the author who would be sitting there. Jonathon loved that.
He'd already met a few of the authors, who seemed
thrilled to be there. And at one of those tables would
be one of his dearest friends, Melinda Talbot. Weeks
before, when he'd shown Melinda the list of attending
authors, she'd given her husband, Lloyd, a beseeching
glance. With a sigh, Lloyd had inquired about getting
her a ticket. Jonathon wasn't all that surprised to find
Lloyd not interested in the festival—he doubted the
vicar had much time for fiction.

"It looks wonderful." Heather appeared at his
side. "And the dinner guests are starting to arrive."
She glanced around. "Where's Mike?"

"Bringing Teresa. They should be here any
minute."

"What's she like? I've never spoken to her. We've
communicated so far via email."

Jonathon was not about to reveal Mike's initial impressions. After spending five minutes with her, he'd sent Jonathon a text.

God, she loves herself.

"I haven't met her yet," Jonathon said truthfully. He gazed at the large easel where the seating plan was balanced. Each table had a large number at the center, clearly visible. He stepped closer to peer at the list below Table 1. "I'm sure you have your reasons, Heather, but putting you, me, *and* Mike all on one table with Teresa? Wouldn't it be better to spread us around a little?"

Her cheeks flushed. "Probably, but I wasn't thinking logically. It was more along the lines of 'I want you there for moral support.'"

He could understand that. It was Heather's first major event, and she was barely keeping her nerves in check. "Fair enough. I just hope Teresa doesn't feel overwhelmed." He took another look at the list. "Have you met any of the other authors at our table?"

Heather shook her head. "The only people I know at the table are you, Mike, and Fiona McBride. I haven't met the other authors yet, and the additional guests aren't even from Merrychurch. They've come for the festival." She smiled. "Every B and B and guesthouse in the village must be at bursting point, there are so many visitors."

Jonathon had wondered about the unfamiliar names at their table. "Fiona McBride. She's a villager, isn't she? Doesn't she live near the water mill?"

"That's right. And we had to put her at the top table. She's Teresa's number one fan."

Jonathon chuckled. "Okay. Shades of *Misery* here. As long as she doesn't do a Kathy Bates number on her."

Heather tut-tutted. "Fiona created the Teresa Malvain Fan Club. It's a huge undertaking, because Teresa has fans all over the world. The Summersfield books have been translated into several languages. Fiona runs the website for the club. She keeps readers posted on everything Teresa is doing, new releases, social media links…."

"Then I can understand why you'd put her on our table. It wouldn't be right to seat her anywhere else." Jonathon took another glance at the board. "And we've got Professor Harcourt too. That could make for some interesting dinner conversation." He grinned. "Don't you agree?"

"Oh sure. Murder and forensics. I can see it now. Teresa will be talking about killing people, and the professor will be talking about what he does when the bodies end up on his table." Heather shuddered. "Please tell me I placed them next to each other, so the rest of us don't have to listen to their grisly conversation."

Jonathon burst into laughter. "I hardly think their discussions will be grisly." He peered at his watch. "We'd better get out there." He'd arranged for waiters to be in place in the entrance hall, serving glasses of wine or juice.

They left the ballroom and were immediately immersed in a crowd of people drinking and talking animatedly. Jonathon caught sight of Mike as he entered the hall, an immaculately dressed woman with a discontented expression at his side. The first thought to cross Jonathon's mind was that Teresa needed to look like she was happy to be there. He walked toward them, his hand outstretched.

"Welcome to de Mountford Hall."

Teresa took it briefly. "Then you must be our host, Jonathon de Mountford. I remember your uncle, Dominic. He seemed a fair man, if a little aloof."

For a moment Jonathon was shocked into silence by the sharp remark. He quickly recovered. "Strange. I never found him to be like that. But maybe that's because I knew him better than most." He bit back the words *including you*. It wouldn't do to offend the guest of honor before the festival had begun, even one who appeared not to care whom she offended. "I've been informed you were once a resident of Merrychurch. Has it changed much?"

Teresa gave a little snort. "Hardly. But then, Merrychurch always felt like it was stuck in a different era." She didn't make it sound like that was a good thing.

Mike cleared his throat. "Are they ready for us in there?"

Jonathon really hoped so. Polite small talk with Teresa was not his idea of fun. In as few as two exchanges, she'd succeeded in putting his back up. "Let's find out." As he walked toward the ballroom door, it opened and a waiter appeared, dressed in black.

"We're ready for you and your guests, Mr. de Mountford."

Before Jonathon could thank him, Teresa's sharp voice interjected. "Mr. de Mountford? I'd have thought living in the manor house, you were at least a lord or something."

"The de Mountfords are one of the oldest families in England," a female voice exclaimed suddenly. They were joined by a middle-aged woman in a dark blue dress and jacket. "The title may have died out, but thankfully the family has not."

Teresa arched her perfectly sculpted eyebrows. "Thank you for the history lesson, Mrs.....￼"

"McBride. Fiona McBride." Fiona gave a polite smile that didn't reach her eyes. "I'm surprised you don't remember me."

Teresa stared. "We've met before?"

Fiona nodded. "I've lived in Merrychurch many years. And I remember you before you were Teresa Malvain."

Teresa stilled, her expression impassive. Then she nodded slowly. "Fiona McBride. Of course. You're the one who runs that little club."

Fiona gaped, but then regained her posture. "Seeing as it currently has over four thousand members, I wouldn't call it little."

Mike coughed. "I don't know about you, but I'm hungry. Let's go in." He gave Jonathon a compassionate glance, then gestured to the ballroom door. "After you, Ms. Malvain."

Jonathon waited until everyone was inside before entering. He smiled to himself when he caught Mike's clear voice, announcing to the waiting crowd that dinner would be served shortly and for everyone to take their places. *Leave it to the ex-copper to take charge.* When Jonathon felt a pat on his arm, he turned to find Heather at his side, the only person remaining.

"Let me repeat what a wise man said to me last night. Breathe, Jonathon."

Jonathon chuckled. "Is it that obvious?" He held out his arm. "Allow me to escort you in to dinner, Miss Caldicott."

"Delighted, Mr. de Mountford." As they strolled through the ballroom doors, she leaned in. "Dinner is going to be more interesting than I anticipated."

Jonathon sighed. "I've got a bad feeling about this."

Heather laughed. "It probably won't be as awful as you think." She cast a glance in Teresa's direction. "Although…."

They made their way to the top table, where Mike had seated Teresa. Most of the seats were already occupied. A tall, thin man with a shock of brown hair and gold-rimmed glasses stood as Jonathon approached, his hand held out.

"Mr. de Mountford, I'm delighted to meet you. Phil McCallister."

Jonathon shook his hand. "I recall your name from the program. You also write murder mysteries." He didn't miss the appreciative gleam in Mike's eyes.

Phil nodded enthusiastically. "I'm on the fourth book in a series."

"Though whether *he* writes them is debatable," Teresa muttered under her breath.

Phil flashed her a scowl but quickly schooled his features. "I'm really looking forward to the festival. It's the first time I've attended one." He retook his seat.

"And we're glad to have you." Heather beamed. She smiled at the petite woman next to him. "You must be Melody Richards."

Melody returned her smile. "It's my first literary festival too. I'm quite excited. It's going to be—"

"When you've done as many conventions and book signings as I have," Teresa interjected, "it gets to be old hat, especially when you meet so many fans. Although I don't suppose you have that problem, do you, dear?"

Jonathon blinked, as did a couple of the seated guests. He threw Mike a puzzled glance, but Mike gave a quick shrug. Apparently, he found Teresa's behavior as bewildering as Jonathon did.

"I'm not late, am I?" An elderly man with thinning white hair joined them.

"Not at all," Jonathon said warmly. "And you are…?"

"Professor Lionel Harcourt." He extended his hand and gave Jonathon's a vigorous shaking. "I would have been here earlier, but my taxi was delayed for some reason."

Mike smiled. "There aren't that many taxis in Merrychurch, and I'd bet they've been kept busy this evening." He held out his hand. "Mike Tattersall, professor. We've never met, but I'm aware of your reputation. I used to be in the Met."

Professor Harcourt beamed. "Oh, how wonderful. An ex-colleague."

"Hardly that, but I did hear you giving evidence in several trials."

He chuckled. "I may have done that on a few occasions."

"Nice to see you again, Professor." Teresa gave him a polite, tight smile.

Professor Harcourt reciprocated with a courteous nod. "Ms. Malvain." He glanced around the table, smiling. "Well, this is delightful." He pulled out a chair and sat down. "So how many other people at this table are authors?" Phil and Melody raised their hands, and Professor Harcourt beamed again. "Since my retirement, I've become an avid reader. I look forward to chatting with all of you." He sighed. "You have no idea how many times I've been approached by publishing companies with a view to writing about my career as a forensic pathologist, but I'm afraid I have no such aspirations. I don't know how you writers do it. I used to hate writing my *reports*." The professor peered at Fiona. "Your face is familiar. Where do I know you from?"

"I run the Teresa Malvain Fan Club."

He nodded. "That's it. Your picture is on the site."

"You're a fan?" Mike appeared surprised.

"Certainly. I love a good murder mystery. Not that authors get it right all the time." His eyes sparkled. "But I'll talk more about that at the festival."

"What's that, Ms. Malvain?" One of the guests pointed to a large book sitting on the table next to Teresa's place setting.

She patted it. "*That* is my notebook. It goes where I go, and with good reason. When you have a memory as cluttered as mine, it pays to write everything down."

"Isn't that what phones are for?" Melody inquired. "I just make a voice recording if I get an idea."

Teresa's smile was nothing more than a stretching of her lips. "Which is all well and good, but can we rely on technology? Batteries run out. Phones stop working. As Mark Twain said, 'The dullest pencil is better than the sharpest memory.' Which is why my notebook never leaves my side. One never knows when inspiration will strike, when a new idea for a book will suddenly flash into one's mind."

Melody Richards cleared her throat. "You shouldn't believe everything you read on Twitter. Mark Twain didn't say that—it's actually a Chinese proverb. 'The faintest ink is more powerful than the strongest memory.'" Her smile matched Teresa's perfectly.

Teresa's eyes flashed, but she said nothing. Mike's gaze met Jonathon's, and he mouthed *ouch*.

The waiters appeared, armed with the starters, and for a while the conversation dried up a little as the guests ate. Yet more waiters circled, pouring wine.

Beside him, Heather nudged Jonathon. "This is wonderful," she said quietly.

"I'm glad you like it," he replied warmly. She seemed more relaxed than the previous evening, thankfully, although she kept glancing in Teresa's direction, the faintest frown in evidence.

Jonathon could understand that. There was an atmosphere around the table, and he had no doubt as to what—or rather, *who*—had caused it. He made a mental note to discuss it with Mike later that night.

"I'm sure you must get asked this all the time," Mike began, looking at Teresa. "Where do you get your ideas from?"

Teresa wiped her lips with her napkin and sat back in her chair. "You're right. I do get asked that a lot." Polite laughter rippled around the table. "Do you know what the hardest part of my job is? Weaving plot lines. And I'll let you into a little secret." She leaned forward conspiratorially, and Jonathon was amused to watch most of the people seated around her mimicking her action. "I *hate* writing plots."

Chuckles broke out at this, while waiters collected plates and whisked them away.

"But isn't that part and parcel of being a murder-mystery writer?" Fiona inquired.

Teresa shrugged. "Yes, but I'm basically a lazy person. Besides, I don't have to come up with new ideas all the time." She flung out her arm. "There's a rich vein out there in the real world. Cold cases. Real cases. One has only to find them."

"But then… it's not original." Mike was frowning.

"Oh, I don't write all my books based *exactly* on real-life cases," Teresa remonstrated. "In fact, I've only ever done that once. Or should I say, I've *planned* to do that. Isn't that right, Professor?" Before he could respond, she plowed ahead. "I do a lot of research into police cases. In fact, sometimes I feel my research is more thorough than the original investigation."

"The police might disagree with you on that point," Mike muttered. He took a sip from his wine-glass and leaned back, regarding her thoughtfully. "Let me ask you something. Supposing in the course of your research, you turn up something that the police missed. Maybe there was a miscarriage of justice. Maybe they got the wrong man. What would you do? Would you have a moral obligation to share it with the police? Because if they reopened the case, it would be all over the media, and there goes your book." He tilted his head to one side. "Or would you just write it and be damned, letting the criminal walk free?"

Jonathon knew Mike well enough to know he wasn't happy about the latter. He regarded Teresa with interest, awaiting her response.

Teresa ran her finger around the rim of her wineglass. "I've made more than enough money with my writing. Six years of successful murder mysteries adds up to quite a lot, especially when they continually top the bestsellers list. In fact, if I never wrote another book, I'd still be very comfortable." She looked Mike in the eye. "That kind of wealth allows you to do the right thing." She drained her glass, then picked up the wine bottle, pouting slightly.

Mike heaved a sigh that was clearly of relief. "Then you'd share your information with the authorities."

She nodded slowly. "Justice must be served, after all." Her face brightened as the waiters arrived with the main course. "Is there more wine coming? Because this bottle is empty."

Jonathon had a feeling they were going to need a lot more wine on their table before the evening was finished.

CHAPTER FOUR

BY THE time dessert arrived, Mike had had his fill of Teresa Malvain. Every remark aimed at Phil, Melody, and Fiona seemed to have a barb attached, which only reinforced his initial impressions. Bestselling author or not, Teresa was an unpleasant person. Professor Harcourt had tried to engage her in conversation about topics not related to writing, but with little success. And the more she drank, the sharper her comments became. Fiona had given up trying to initiate conversations and had seemingly retreated into herself, while Heather looked on, clearly appalled by her guest's behavior.

Teresa is a nasty piece of work. What made it worse was that Mike loved her books. The dinner had given him an insight into the author that had left a sour taste in his mouth. It seemed to him that Professor Harcourt was the lucky one. He'd emerged unscathed, as Teresa had hardly exchanged more than a couple of words with him. Phil, Melody, and Fiona had not been so lucky.

The waiter placed the dessert plates on the table, and as he went to fetch more, Fiona caught his arm.

"Please make sure Ms. Malvain doesn't get anything with nuts in it. She's allergic."

Teresa gave her a frankly amused stare. "I'm pretty sure they already have my allergies on file. I filled out the online form, same as you probably did." Despite the several glasses of wine she'd imbibed, her speech remarkably showed no signs of slurring.

"I think Fiona is just being careful," Mike said smoothly. "We wouldn't want anything to happen to the guest of honor." Except at this point, he couldn't have cared less. Throughout the meal, Phil and Melody had answered questions from the two guests who were obviously fans of their work, responding with interest and genuine enthusiasm. Professor Harcourt had regaled them with interesting tales, thankfully none of them as grisly as Heather had feared, and Mike had enjoyed listening to him.

"So, Melody." Teresa filled her wineglass before giving Melody a bright, false smile. "Won any awards lately?"

Mike had no clue what *that* was about, but judging by the way Melody's face tightened, it was obvious the question was loaded with malice.

Melody straightened in her chair. "Not lately, no." She bit her lip, as if trying to prevent herself from saying more.

"Tell me more about your next book," Fiona said quickly, addressing Teresa. "I saw your post on Facebook. It sounds really interesting. I can't wait to read it." Her eyes gleamed. "Will you be talking about it in the Q and A tomorrow? I know you said it would be a surprise, but I'd love to share more details with your fans. From the horse's mouth, as it were."

Teresa grinned. "And I promise to answer all questions—stopping short of revealing who the murderer is, of course." Polite chuckles broke the silence that followed her announcement. Teresa patted her A4 notebook. "What I have in here is going to please a lot of readers, though perhaps not those in Merrychurch. It's rather fitting that I should reveal details about it in my former village." Her eyes were bright. "There's a reason murder mysteries work well in a small village setting. There's such an abundance of secrets. Everyone thinks they know everyone else, but do they, really? You have no idea what your neighbor gets up to behind closed doors." She grinned at Jonathon. "Or your tenants." Teresa gave Mike a sideways glance. "Or your patrons."

Professor Harcourt chuckled. "I can see I need to attend your sessions, Teresa. They promise to be highly entertaining. As a former GP of a small village, I can attest to the accuracy of your statements. Village life may look peaceful on the surface—all fetes on the green, homemade jams, and WI meetings—but if you look closer, there is always something lurking in the shadows."

Mike said nothing. As a former policeman, and having had two murders committed in Merrychurch in the past year, he knew they spoke truthfully. He only knew he preferred to look into the sunlight, and leave the shadows alone.

"But this is where I should add that the plot of my next Summersfield novel isn't going to be the only surprise," Teresa announced, her eyes sparkling. "I'm about to dip my toes into a new, lucrative market."

"And will you be talking about that at the festival?" Fiona asked eagerly.

Teresa tapped the side of her nose. "That will have to remain a secret a little while longer." A waiter leaned in to place a dessert in front of Teresa, and she beamed. "That looks delicious. And nut-free, which I'm sure will please our hostess. Heaven forbid her main speaker should be unable to attend the festival, carried off due to an allergic reaction. I imagine the entire event would collapse." And with that, she took a forkful of lemon-and-lime cheesecake and ate it with gusto.

"Is your allergy that severe?" Jonathon asked.

Teresa nodded. "I've had a few encounters with the dreaded nut during my life. Of course, each time the reaction is stronger, faster. I dare say another would see me off completely. That's why Mike is right. It pays to be careful." She pointed to the cheesecake with her fork. "This really is delicious."

Mike realized it was the most cheerful Teresa had been all evening.

I wonder if I've got cheesecake on the menu in the pub. It would certainly be one way of keeping her happy. Because he was already learning that very little made Teresa Malvain happy.

Across from him, Heather grimaced. "Okay, that's weird." She put down her fork.

"What's the matter?" Mike inquired.

Heather peered closely at her dessert. "For some reason, my cheesecake is dusted with ground almonds. Now, while I do like almonds, they don't really go with a lemon-and-lime cheesecake."

Jonathon frowned. "That is weird. There are no almonds on mine." He glanced at Mike's plate. "Or Mike's either."

Heather chuckled. "Someone in the catering company is having an off day." She took a look at Teresa, who seemed oblivious to the entire exchange. "Thank God it was my plate and not hers," Heather said in a low voice. "She'd be threatening legal action by now."

Mike had a feeling Heather's assessment was probably correct.

MIKE GLANCED at his watch: nine o'clock. Coffee had been served, and a large number of the guests had already departed.

Jonathon touched his arm. "Go on. Go back to the pub. It's likely to be a busy night, with all these attendees staying in the village. Poor Abi will be rushed off her feet."

Mike gave him a grateful smile. "You sure? I don't want to leave you to deal with all this."

Jonathon laughed. "Deal with what? The waiters will clear the tables, the volunteers are already lining up outside to set up for tomorrow, and Janet is going to lock up when everyone has left. They don't need me—which is a good thing, because I'll be in the pub, helping you."

If they weren't sitting at a table in a room full of mostly strangers, Mike would have leaned over and kissed him. "You're wonderful," he said softly.

"Is there a number I can call for a taxi?" Teresa asked loudly.

"There's no need," Mike assured her. "I'm going to the pub myself. I'll take you."

She waved her hand. "I don't want to impose. Just give me a number for a taxi."

"Here, I'll call one for you." Professor Harcourt removed his phone from his pocket, then scowled at the screen. "Damn thing's dead. The battery must have run out."

"See?" Teresa sounded almost gleeful. "What did I say about technology?"

Jonathon coughed. "Except in this case, having a notebook wouldn't help you find a taxi."

She gave him a hard stare.

"How about I drive *both* of you to the pub?" Mike announced. "Only, can we leave now?" He had visions of Abi struggling to cope on her own with a packed pub.

"That works for me," Professor Harcourt said cheerfully. "I'm staying in a B and B in the village. But I wouldn't say no to a nightcap. Would you like a drink, Teresa?"

"Make that a coffee and you're on. There are a few things I'd like to discuss with you." Teresa rose to her feet, grabbed her notebook, and shoved it into her large shoulder bag. "Well, come on if we're going."

Mike muttered under his breath as he led them out of the hall and toward his 4x4. Jonathon came too, chuckling to himself. As he opened the car door, Mike spied Heather. "Want a lift to the pub?"

She shook her head. "I've got my car, thanks. And to be honest, the only place I'm going is my bed. I want to be bright-eyed and bushy-tailed for tomorrow."

"Then I'll say good night." He gave her a wave, then got behind the wheel.

"I thought you were in a hurry?" Teresa murmured from the back seat.

Mike was going to be so happy when the pub was closed and he finally got into bed, hopefully with Jonathon staying the night.

A short while later, he pulled up in front of the pub and everyone got out.

"You go and park the car. I'll take them inside." Jonathon squeezed his arm. "Then I'll get behind the bar and help you."

"Thanks." Mike left them and drove around to the rear of the pub. From the sounds that emerged, it was a very busy night. He hurried into the building through the back door, his eyes widening when he saw the mess in the kitchen. It looked like Abi had been inundated with food orders. When he stepped into the pub, he was glad Jonathon had come along too.

The pub was the busiest he'd ever seen it. Every table was occupied, every chair was taken, and many patrons were standing around, drinking. Thankfully, Jonathon had secured a table for Teresa and Professor Harcourt, thoughtfully tucked away in a quiet corner. Except it didn't stay quiet for long. As soon as people saw who had arrived, they made a beeline for Teresa.

Mike could see it was going to be a long night.

Jonathon had already started clearing tables, bless him, and was loading the glass washer. Abi looked like she needed a break, so Mike told her to take one. He got stuck with the task of pouring pints and glasses of wine. Anyone wanting one of Jonathon's cocktails would have to lump it.

Jonathon approached the bar. "Can you do two coffees for Teresa and Professor Harcourt? One black, one with cream." He grinned. "When you have a minute, that is."

Mike rolled his eyes. "Oh, I think I can manage that." He set about his task, filling the receptacle with ground coffee. Then he was back to the bar to pour more pints. He could just about glimpse Teresa, obscured by a crowd that had gathered around her table. He recognized some of the people from the meal.

"Hey, do you want to know what's weird?" Jonathon was at the bar again, this time collecting orders to deliver to tables. "Take a good look at the people around Teresa."

Mike peered at the throng. "What about them?"

"There isn't one villager among them." Jonathon pointed to the other end of the pub. "Most of the villagers are sitting over there. It's like there's an invisible wall between them and her."

Mike shrugged. "Or maybe they can't get near her for all her adoring fans." He snickered. "And there are certainly a lot of them."

"Haven't you done those coffees yet?" Jonathon's eyes gleamed with mischief.

"Watch it or you'll find yourself walking back to the hall tonight."

With a last laugh, Jonathon picked up a tray of pints. "Where are these going?"

"Seth's table."

"Got it." Jonathon headed in that direction, and Mike poured the coffees. Before he could deliver them, more people surged toward the bar, and he knew Abi's break was over.

"Is it always this busy?" Phil McCallister appeared at the bar, holding a ten-pound note in his hand. Melody Richards was with him.

From his stool at the bar, Paul Drake chuckled. "I've not seen Mike this flustered since he got here." He gazed around him. "Course, I've never seen the pub this busy either."

"I call this the Teresa Malvain Effect," Mike said with a grin. "Can't complain, even if I do need another pair of hands."

"I don't come in here often." Fiona joined Phil and Melody, staring at the crowded pub. "Now I know why."

"This is not usual." At that moment, Abi reappeared, and Mike kissed her on the cheek. "Excellent timing."

She laughed. "Yeah, I had a feeling I'd be wanted. I'll deal with that end of the bar—you deal with this one."

"Perfect." Mike poured a pint for Phil and a white wine for Melody just as a fresh wave of drinkers hit. For the next five or ten minutes, he didn't have time to think as he poured drink after drink. It wasn't until Professor Harcourt appeared that he remembered the coffees. "My apologies," he said as he pointed to where the two cups sat on the bar. "I should have brought those over. They'll be cold by now. Let me make some fresh coffee."

He turned to set up the machine, but Professor Harcourt stopped him with a hand to his arm, giving him a reassuring smile. "They'll be fine. And if Teresa should complain—although I'm sure that's not in her nature—I'll buy her another one." His blue eyes twinkled with good humor.

Mike had to work really hard not to snort. "Is she coping with the onslaught?"

Professor Harcourt bit his lip. "She's being polite. I think that's a bonus at this stage." He picked up the cups. "I'll be right back if she has a problem with the coffee." He walked slowly back to their table, carrying the two cups with great care.

"When does this festival end?" Abi asked as she reached up for a clean glass.

Mike laughed. "It hasn't even started yet." His bank balance would be healthy by the end of it. He wasn't so sure about his energy reserves.

"Mike?" Jonathon dashed over to the bar. "Something's wrong."

Mike jerked up his head and scanned the pub. There seemed to be a commotion over in the corner where Teresa and Professor Harcourt were sitting. He caught Teresa's raised voice. "No, now!" Something hit the wooden floor with a loud clatter, and suddenly the crowd parted and Professor Harcourt emerged, his arm around Teresa's waist.

"I'm taking her upstairs to her room," Professor Harcourt called out. "She needs some medication." Teresa appeared confused, lurching dizzily toward the door that led to the private part of the pub where the guest room was located, along with Mike's room.

Mike nodded, his heartbeat speeding up. "Call me if you need anything."

"I will." Professor Harcourt helped Teresa to the door, and it closed behind them.

"What's wrong with her?" Mike asked Jonathon.

"No idea. But she looks terrible. Do you want me to go up there?"

Mike shook his head. "She's in the best possible hands. Didn't Professor Harcourt say he was a GP once?"

"That's right." Jonathon peered toward the corner where they'd been seated. "Oh, they must've knocked one of the cups off the table. It's broken. I'll clear it up."

A thud above their heads stilled Mike instantly. "Okay, that wasn't good."

Seconds later, Professor Harcourt reappeared, his face pale, his breathing rapid. "Call for an ambulance! Now!" Then he disappeared again.

Mike was out from the behind the bar in a flash. "Call an ambulance," he yelled to Jonathon. "I'll go and see what's happened." Not waiting for a response, he dashed toward the door, his customers getting out of his way. He took the stairs three at a time, then ran full pelt into the guest room.

Teresa lay on the floor, her feet propped up on the bed, and Professor Harcourt was clearly in the middle of chest compressions, his hair unruly, his breathing harsh. He paused and looked up as Mike approached.

"What happened?"

Professor Harcourt sighed heavily. "Anaphylactic shock, I'd guess." He applied two fingers to her wrist, then her neck.

"Don't stop!" Mike stared in horror at Teresa's still form.

Professor Harcourt's quietly spoken words confirmed what he already knew. "Too late. She's gone."

He sat back on his haunches, looking exhausted. "I couldn't help her. The reaction was too strong."

"Reaction to what?" This couldn't be happening.

"Well, we know she was allergic to nuts. I guess we'd better start looking downstairs for a source."

Cold washed over Mike. "Oh my God. I think I know where we can start."

"What do you mean?"

All the energy seeped out of him. "Peanuts. There are peanuts on the bar. I meant to ask Abi to remove them, but I forgot." This was a nightmare.

He'd killed Teresa Malvain.

CHAPTER FIVE

PROFESSOR HARCOURT stood carefully. "I hardly think that was the cause of death." He gazed at Teresa's body, his expression sorrowful.

"Think about all those people she met downstairs tonight. All it would take would be a few of them with peanut oil on their hands. They transfer it, she touches her lips…." Mike cursed himself for not remembering to say something to Abi.

Professor Harcourt patted Mike's arm kindly. "Mike, this was fast. So fast that she had difficulty breathing. Maybe if she'd had her EpiPen, things might have been different."

Mike frowned. "But… surely she'd have carried one with her everywhere. That's just common sense."

Professor Harcourt nodded. "Which is why what happened is so strange. I…." He sighed. "Can we go downstairs? There's nothing I can do here, and to be quite frank, I need a brandy." His face was drawn and tired.

Mike put his arm around Professor Harcourt's shoulders. "Sure. The ambulance is on its way, although it may take a while. The nearest hospital is Fareham." He glanced at the still body. "Not that it matters now when they get here." He still wasn't convinced the peanuts hadn't played a part in Teresa's death.

They left the room, and Mike closed the door behind them. Silently they went down the narrow staircase and into the bar, which was surprisingly quiet. The pub's patrons cast glances in their direction, murmuring quietly. Professor Harcourt joined him at the bar, taking an empty stool.

Jonathon walked over to them, his brow furrowed. "Where's Teresa?"

Mike issued a heavy sigh. "She's dead. Allergic reaction, Professor Harcourt thinks." He glanced at the bowls of peanuts.

Jonathon widened his eyes. "Oh my God." Around them, more mutters and murmurs rose up from the crowd. "Someone should inform Heather. As well as Teresa's next of kin."

"She doesn't have any." Fiona appeared shocked. "There's an ex-husband somewhere, but he hasn't been around for ages."

Mike shook his head. "How do you know all this?"

Fiona raised her eyes to the ceiling. "You'd be amazed the things you learn from reading interviews and posts on social media. And she was on social media a *lot*. I'm surprised she found time to write, to be honest." She bit her lip. "Sorry. That was uncalled for, especially in the circumstances."

A siren's wail started in the distance, growing louder.

Jonathon sighed. "I'll show them where to go." He headed toward the door.

"Thanks," Mike called out to him. He poured two glasses of brandy and set one down in front of Professor Harcourt, who immediately took a drink. An unearthly quiet had settled over the pub's occupants, and it disturbed him. "Okay, folks," he announced loudly. "Yes, we've had a death on the premises. Can I ask that you stay in here until they've removed the body? Thank you."

Paul Drake joined him at the bar. "She's dead, then? That writer?" When Mike nodded, Paul shook his head. "You couldn't make it up, could you? Murder-mystery writer dies the night before a book festival." He peered closely at Mike. "Are we talkin' suspicious circumstances?"

Mike sincerely hoped not.

"So would someone like to tell me what's going on?" Graham Billings's deep voice cut through the mutterings that had followed Mike's announcement. Graham approached the bar, his police helmet in his hand. "Mike? Want to tell me why there's an ambulance outside?"

"That would be because they're removing a dead body from my guest room," Mike explained matter-of-factly.

Graham arched his eyebrows. "Well, of course it would be here," he said dryly. "Trouble seems to follow you around." He scanned the pub's interior. "Where's Watson?"

"If you mean Jonathon, he'll be here shortly. He's showing the ambulance crew where to go."

Graham snorted. "I knew he'd be here somewhere."

"You're going to need your notepad." Mike pointed to the table where Teresa and Professor Harcourt had been sitting. "Take a seat. I'll be right over."

Graham nodded and headed for the corner.

Abi came up to Mike and squeezed his shoulder. "I'll take care of the bar. You go deal with Graham."

Mike thanked her, then stepped out from behind the bar, his glass of brandy in his hand. "You too, Professor."

The professor nodded and got off his stool with a wince. "I fear I've strained something. Maybe my chest compressions were too vigorous." He walked slowly to Graham's table, with Mike following him.

As soon as they'd sat down, Graham got out his notepad. "Okay. What happened? And who's the deceased?"

"Teresa Malvain." Mike sipped his brandy, relishing its warmth.

Graham's eyes widened. "Wow. You managed to kill off the first Merrychurch Literary Festival's main speaker before it has even begun. Nice going." He glanced at Professor Harcourt. "And you are…?"

"Professor Lionel Harcourt." His eyes were flinty. "And I don't appreciate either your tone or your choice of words, Constable."

Graham swallowed, stiffening. Mike patted the professor's hand. "This is probably where I should add that Graham is a friend, as well as a good copper who's been a real help to us on a couple of similar… occasions."

Professor Harcourt blinked. "Do you have a lot of sudden deaths in this village?"

Graham snickered. "You'd be surprised. There's a reason I call these two Sherlock and Watson. And speak of the devil...."

Jonathon came over to their table. "They've gone," he said, his tone subdued.

"You'd better join us." Graham inclined his head to the empty chair, then plucked a pen from his breast pocket. "Okay. Who's going to start?"

Mike gestured to Professor Harcourt, who sighed. He clasped his wrinkled hands on the table. "We'd just returned from the meal Jonathon hosted up at the manor house. Teresa and I were going to have a coffee before retiring. Except the pub's occupants appeared to comprise a vast number of Teresa Malvain fans, who all wanted to talk to her."

Graham nodded, taking notes. "Then what happened?"

"When we eventually got our coffees, we drank them while continuing our discussion. I noticed Teresa seemed flushed, and her breathing was a little erratic. She said, 'This is an allergic reaction,' then grabbed her bag."

"She had allergies?" Graham's writing sped up.

"To nuts, apparently," Mike informed him.

"So this was a reaction to something she'd eaten at dinner?"

Jonathon shook his head. "The menu didn't contain any nuts. We made sure of that."

What came to Mike's mind in that instant was the dusting of ground almonds, but they'd been on Heather's dessert only, and as she'd been sitting across from Teresa, there was no way they could have ended up on Teresa's plate.

"And besides," Professor Harcourt added, "although anaphylaxis can take up to thirty minutes to start, that is unlikely in this case, given the severity of her reaction. So we're looking for a source here in the pub."

"There are peanuts on the bar." Mike pointed to the bowls. "But Professor Harcourt thinks that's unlikely as well."

"Could she have been allergic to lactose? Maybe the milk or cream in her coffee?" Graham asked.

"If she was, then she'd hardly have asked for coffee with cream," Professor Harcourt commented.

"Could she have been injected with something? If there were a lot of people milling around her...."

"Someone deliberately injected her?" Professor Harcourt frowned. "Again, that's unlikely. I'd have seen them do it. She was sitting beside me the whole time. And if someone had done that, she'd have felt it. No, the swiftness of her death points to a food allergy rather than medication."

"You mentioned her EpiPen while we were upstairs. You said maybe if she'd had one.... Wasn't that in her bag?" His words about something being strange had troubled Mike.

"As soon as she started feeling unwell, she clearly knew it was an allergic reaction. But when she opened her bag to find her EpiPen, it wasn't there. I even looked myself." His frown deepened. "That was when she told me to help her upstairs, because she had a spare in her suitcase. By that point, her breathing was more labored, and she was a little dizzy. I told her I'd run upstairs and get it, but she grabbed my arm tightly and demanded I help her out of there. What else could

I do? I helped her to her feet, told Mike I was taking her upstairs, then did just that, as fast as I could." He gave Mike an apologetic glance. "Sorry about your cup, by the way. Teresa sent it flying when she got up from the table."

Mike gave a wave of his hand. "Don't worry about it."

"But the spare EpiPen obviously didn't work," Graham continued, still taking notes.

"That's what was strange. There was no EpiPen in her suitcase. I pulled out everything in my search for it, but it definitely wasn't there. And when she gasped out 'ambulance,' I looked in her bag for her phone to call for one. Her phone was missing too. I emptied the bag's contents onto the bed, looking for it and the EpiPen in case she'd missed it. That was why I had to leave her briefly to come down here and ask Mike to call for an ambulance."

Graham slowly raised his head. "Why didn't you use your own phone? Surely that would've saved time."

"Yes, and I would have done, except for the fact that the battery had died at some point during the evening," Professor Harcourt explained patiently.

"That's right," Mike added. "He was going to call for a taxi when he noticed."

"I was stupid," the professor said with a heavy sigh. "I should have got Mike to call for an ambulance immediately. She'd have needed to go to A&E anyway, even after using an EpiPen. But I wasn't thinking clearly, obviously."

"And how was she when you got back to the room?" Graham resumed his note-taking.

"Her condition had worsened considerably, and she was fighting to breathe. When she went into cardiac arrest, I elevated her feet and started chest compressions, but she was too far gone." Professor Harcourt's face fell. "There was nothing I could do."

"He was still doing compressions when I got to the room." Mike placed his hand on Harcourt's back to comfort him.

"Is that a normal reaction in such cases?"

Professor Harcourt nodded. "When no epinephrine is administered, breathing becomes almost impossible and cardiac arrest follows. So strictly speaking, she died of a heart attack, but the cause was undoubtedly an allergic reaction. I was virtually carrying her up the stairs. She complained of nausea, her tongue was swollen, which is what made speech so difficult, and she was obviously weak and dizzy. Loss of consciousness was expected. I had hoped the chest compressions would keep her alive until the ambulance got here, but no."

"Teresa was always super careful when it came to her allergy. That's why she always carried two EpiPens." Fiona stood beside Jonathon, a glass in her hand.

Graham frowned. "And how do you know all this?"

Fiona shrugged. "Teresa gave a lot of interviews. It's well-documented. She always talked about stuff like this."

"Professor, will there be a postmortem?" Jonathon asked. "Once her allergy is confirmed, I mean."

Professor Harcourt nodded. "There's been a register of deaths by anaphylaxis here in the UK since

1992. Not that many deaths, to be honest—maybe around twenty a year."

"So yes, there'll be an autopsy." Graham closed his notebook. "Let's wait and see what it comes up with." He got to his feet. "I think I've got all I need for now. Thank you, Professor. Are you going to be in the village for a while?"

"Seeing as I'm speaking at the festival, I'd say that's affirmative. If you need me to stay after the weekend, that can be arranged."

Heather appeared, looking flustered. "Tell me it's not true. Tell me she's not dead." She wore a long overcoat, under which were pajamas.

Jonathon's expression was glum. "I take it you've heard."

"I got a call from Phil McCallister. She really is dead?"

Mike got up and put his arms about her. "Sorry, Heather. I know you wanted everything to go smoothly." She leaned into him, her face downcast.

"Who's Phil McCallister?" Graham demanded.

"An author attending the festival," Jonathon explained. "He's—" He glanced around, frowning. "He was here. Along with another writer, Melody Richards. When did they leave?"

Mike shrugged. "No clue. I didn't see them go, but then I did have my mind on other more urgent issues."

"Hmm." Graham made a note. "I'll need to speak to them."

"Maybe I should cancel the whole thing," Heather murmured, still leaning against Mike.

"Don't do that," Jonathon urged her. "Play it by ear. You have all these readers who've come here just for the festival. Not to mention the authors. Make an announcement when you open the festival in the morning. But don't be surprised if the national news picks up on the story."

"Which is all publicity, right?" Mike tightened his arm around her. "I agree with Jonathon. Don't do anything tonight."

"Okay." She rubbed her eyes. "In that case, I'm going back to bed. See you all in the morning."

"I'll go out with you." Graham replaced his helmet, shoved his notepad and pen back into his pocket, and accompanied Heather to the door.

Mike took another drink from his brandy. *Please, God, let it be an accidental death.*

He hoped the Almighty was listening.

GRAHAM'S DEPARTURE appeared to be a signal for everyone to go to the bar, including Mike.

Jonathon chuckled. "And he thought running a country pub would be a quiet life after the Met."

"I still can't believe she's dead." Professor Harcourt stared into his brandy.

"You and me both," Fiona added. She gave Jonathon a wry smile. "I'm now the organizer of a fan club whose *raison d'être* has just disappeared."

"Did you know Teresa well, Professor?" Jonathon inquired.

"Barely. Even if we did both live in Merrychurch at some point, although not at the same time."

Jonathon gaped. "You lived here? When?"

"I was the village GP from 1985 until 1989. Teresa arrived after that. Not sure when, exactly." He gave Fiona a sideways glance. "You probably know when, though. You certainly know everything else about her."

Jonathon frowned. "But at dinner Teresa said it was nice to see you again."

Professor Harcourt took another sip of brandy before continuing. "We did meet once, Teresa and I. A police officer recommended that she meet with me to discuss research she was doing for a book."

"What did she want to know?" Jonathon tilted his head to one side.

"What every author wants to know when they talk to a pathologist. 'Tell me there's an undetectable, untraceable poison out there that no one's ever used before.'"

"And is there?" Fiona's eyes sparkled.

Professor Harcourt laughed softly. "If there is, it hasn't reached my ears yet—or my autopsy table." He glanced around the pub and shivered. "I didn't like the atmosphere tonight. At the dinner *and* in here."

"What do you mean?" Except Jonathon already had an idea of what was coming.

"It felt like there was a lot of malice in the air, if that doesn't sound too melodramatic, given the present circumstances."

Fiona huffed. "That's not really surprising. Teresa didn't gain herself a lot of friends while she lived here. And by the sound of it, she didn't improve once she'd left Merrychurch."

Professor Harcourt stared at her. "I see."

Fiona took a large drink from her wineglass. "I may be the organizer of her fan club, but even I have to admit she had her moments." Then she, too, shivered. "Okay, that's enough. One shouldn't speak ill of the dead, right?" She finished her wine. "I'm going to call it a night. Will I see you both at the festival tomorrow?" When both Jonathon and Professor Harcourt nodded, she smiled. "Good. Then I'll say good night." And with that, she got up and walked to the door, pausing to greet a few people on her way.

"I should get going too." Professor Harcourt finished his brandy. "Please say good night to Mike for me?"

Jonathon nodded. "Do you want me to see you to your B and B?" He stood up, then collected the empty glasses.

"Oh no, I can manage. Besides, I need to read over my notes for my session."

Jonathon was burning with curiosity. "What's your topic? Oh—wait. I know. Heather said you're talking about autopsies."

Professor Harcourt beamed. "That's right! And I'm also going to point out that the crime dramas everyone is so fond of—*CSI*, et cetera—are *not* the gospel when it comes to forensic procedure."

"I look forward to hearing you." Jonathon had a feeling Mike would enjoy that one. He bade Professor Harcourt good night, then rejoined Mike at the bar, where the pub's patrons appeared to have rediscovered their thirst.

Jonathon couldn't wait until it was closing time. He wanted to get Mike on his own and hear his thoughts on the evening's events.

Another death in Merrychurch. At least it's not a murder this time.

CHAPTER SIX

JONATHON WALKED slowly up the stairs, feeling weary. The night had taken its toll, and he was bone-tired. Below, he could hear Mike locking the door. When Jonathon reached the landing, he gazed at the closed door of the guest room. On impulse, he crossed the floor and opened it.

The room was a chaotic mess. Teresa's suitcase lay open on the floor beside the bed, its contents strewn over the rug, no doubt the result of Professor Harcourt searching frantically for the spare EpiPen. On the bed lay Teresa's capacious bag, its contents disgorged due to another search. It took Jonathon a moment to realize something was missing.

"Mike?"

A minute later, Mike entered the room. "What's up?" He glanced at the chaos. "I'd better put this right in the morning."

"Come here a minute." Jonathon pointed to the bed. "What don't you see?"

Mike joined him and gazed at the heap of items. He rubbed his beard. "Okay, you've lost me. What am I missing?"

"Her notebook. Remember? The A4 notebook that goes with her everywhere?" Jonathon scanned the room. "Well, it isn't here." His gaze alighted on the small table by the window. "What's that?" An open cardboard box sat there. He went to it and peeked inside. "It's a hardback copy of one of Teresa's books." Jonathon reached in and withdrew it. "*Murderous Intent,*" he read aloud.

"That's her latest release," Mike informed him.

Jonathon turned to face him with a wry smile. "Okay. Exactly how many of Teresa's books do you possess?"

Mike blinked. "Er... all of them?"

Jonathon chuckled. "The things I'm still learning about you." He leafed through the book. "Is it any good?"

"I liked it."

"Do you find yourself reading them with your ex-copper's head on?"

Mike groaned. "All the time."

That was funny. "Why can I see you shouting at the book, 'But that wouldn't happen in real life!'" Jonathon said with a grin.

Mike huffed. "Not all the time, you understand. Just now and again. Which is strange, especially as she claimed to do so much research. You'd think she'd have a friendly copper on call for checking what she'd written."

"Or maybe she wasn't as diligent in her research as she'd have us believe." A flash of yellow caught Jonathon's eye, and he went back a page or two. "This is weird."

"What is?"

Jonathon held up the opened book for Mike to see. "A word has been highlighted in here."

Mike leaned over and peered at it. "*Never*. Okay, that *is* weird. Are there any more?"

Jonathon went back to the start of the book. "Let's have a look." He thumbed through the pages, noting each highlight. When he got to the end, he closed it slowly. "I don't like this." His stomach clenched.

"What did you find?"

Jonathon took a breath. "A phrase. *The past never goes away*." He put down the book and glanced at the box. "This was addressed to Teresa here. Why send it to the pub?"

"Maybe whoever sent it figured as the festival was going to be in Merrychurch, it would find its way to her eventually."

"Or else they knew she'd be staying here," Jonathon mused. "Did she tell everyone where she was staying?"

"I'd have thought that unlikely, except after listening to Fiona, I'm beginning to think Teresa was one of those people who shared everything on social media. And she did reserve the room ages ago." Mike reached for the book, but Jonathon stopped him with a hand to his arm. "What's wrong?"

"Don't touch it."

Mike's brow knitted. "Why not? You just touched it."

"Yes, as did Teresa—and whoever sent it."

Mike cocked his head to one side. "What are you thinking?"

"That maybe her death isn't as accidental as it might appear." The uneasy feeling in his stomach worsened. "Mike… can you cause anaphylactic shock?"

Mike stilled. "You mean…."

Jonathon nodded slowly. "It's possible, isn't it? Either she came into contact with whatever caused the reaction by accident, or else someone made sure she did." He stared at the mess of clothing and other items. "Maybe the same person who came up here and stole her EpiPen from her suitcase. They knew she was staying here, right? How easy would it have been to sneak upstairs tonight, when the pub was so full? *You* certainly wouldn't have seen anyone do that. Me neither, for that matter."

"Yes, but someone else might have. It would be a risk. And what about the EpiPen in her bag? How did that disappear?"

Jonathon stroked his chin. "If I remember correctly, her bag was under the table. Think about how many people were clustered around her, asking questions, demanding autographs. Maybe someone snuck it from her bag in all the commotion."

Mike glanced at the clock beside the bed. "It's too late to call Graham. This will have to wait until morning."

Jonathon swallowed. "Then you think I'm right?"

Mike sighed. "I think it's a possibility. We'll see what he says. Maybe the book and her allergic reaction aren't connected, but…."

"But it is suspicious." Jonathon shivered. "Let's get out of here. And we don't touch anything else, all right?"

Mike gave him an amused smile. "Just which one of us is the ex-copper here?" He headed for the door, with Jonathon right behind him. When they were outside, Mike closed the door and locked it. "I don't want anyone going in there until Graham has seen it."

Jonathon nodded. "He'll need my prints and Professor Harcourt's, to eliminate them from any others he might find." Much as he hated the idea, he was starting to think that Teresa had been murdered.

The postmortem would tell them how.

"Bed," Mike said quietly, tugging his arm. "I don't know about you, but I'm exhausted. All I want to do is curl up with you under the sheets and forget about all this."

Jonathon had a feeling switching off his brain might not be so easy a task.

JONATHON WAS in the middle of his second cup of coffee when Graham walked in. "Are you all done up there? There's coffee in the pot if you want some." Mike had taken Graham upstairs as soon as he'd arrived.

Graham sat down at the wide wooden table, placing his helmet on it. "Thanks. I'd love one. Mike's still upstairs." He huffed gloomily. "Great way to start my day. Seven thirty on a Saturday morning, my phone rings. 'Good morning, Graham. Can you come to the pub? We think we've got another murder.'" He narrowed his gaze. "What is it with you two? Does death follow you around or something?" Graham folded his arms. "Out with it, then. Let's hear what that sleuthing brain of yours has come up with. What makes you think she was murdered?" His eyes gleamed. "Unless we're talking about *another* dead body you've managed to rustle up during the night?"

Mike entered the kitchen at the tail end of Graham's remark and made a beeline for the coffee. "One dead body is more than enough, thank you very much."

Jonathon got up and handed him another mug from the cabinet. "For Graham." Then he sat back down and ran through their findings, while Mike poured the coffee.

Graham's face fell. "Seriously, though, after taking a look at her room, I have to agree with Jonathon. This points to a suspicious death. We'll know for sure after the autopsy, of course, if it turns up something that definitely shouldn't be there." A heavy sigh rolled out of him. "Y'know, I used to have a quiet life before you two got together. A bit of illegal parking. A rowdy party or two. Someone complaining about their neighbor's dog barking all the time. Nice, simple stuff. And now, in less than a year, we're talking three murders."

"We don't know for sure that Teresa was murdered," Mike reminded him as he placed a mug in front of him.

"But it's adding up that way." Graham took out his notepad and scribbled a couple of lines.

"And I'm not sure I like the implication," Jonathon added. "You make it sound like all these murders are taking place because we got together. As if we've somehow caused them to happen."

"Well, you've got to admit that's how it looks. Three suspicious deaths? It's beginning to feel like one of those detective series on TV. You know the ones, where the dead bodies start piling up." Graham tapped his notepad with his pen. "And now I have to report this." He sipped his coffee. "Now I remember why I came over at this hour. Your coffee is way better than the stuff at the station."

"The festival begins today. Should we say anything to Heather about our suspicions?" Jonathon asked.

Both Graham and Mike shook their heads. "Say nothing," Graham urged. "She can announce Teresa's death, of course. It's not as if she could hide that, given the number of people in the pub last night." He rubbed his chin. "But you know what? You two could prove useful."

Jonathon widened his eyes. "In what capacity?"

Mike chuckled. "I think I know the answer to that one. He wants us to keep an eye out for anything suspicious. Maybe someone at the festival had it in for her. They might relax now that she's dead, thinking no one suspects foul play."

"Relaxed enough to reveal motives, you mean?" Jonathon shrugged. "It's possible, I suppose."

Mike finally sat down, a mug in his hand. "I hate to throw a spanner in the works, but something has just occurred to me. If it *was* murder, then all those people in the pub last night could be witnesses. And most of them aren't from around here. So when the festival ends tomorrow evening, they'll leave."

"Never mind witnesses—one of them might have done it." Jonathon stared at Graham. "And then it'll be a case of person or persons unknown. Especially as the postmortem results won't be out until after the festival finishes."

Graham scowled. "Not on my watch." He leaned back in his chair, his expression thoughtful as he drank his coffee. No one said anything for several minutes. Finally, Graham sighed. "Okay. There's only one course of action. I'll have to make an announcement at the festival opening."

"What kind of announcement? 'There's been a murder. Please raise your hand if you did it'?" Jonathon snickered. "I can see *that* going down well."

"The thing is, you're right. We won't have the postmortem results until at least Monday, so I need to get details from everyone who was here. That means I have to say we're treating her death as suspicious for the moment. Then I ask anyone who came into contact with her that evening to please come forward and give me any information they feel might be relevant." Graham peered at Jonathon. "Is there a room I can use at the manor house?"

He nodded. "I can set you up in the study."

"And I can give you a hand," Mike added. "I can take down names and details for you. It's not like I don't have the experience, right?"

Graham gave them a grateful glance. "Thanks. The last thing I want is for the postmortem to prove this was murder and not to have records of who was there."

"Half the village was here last night, only most of them kept their distance," Jonathon commented. "Paul Drake was in his usual spot at the bar. He might have seen something."

"Unless it turns out he's the murderer," Graham said with a grin.

"He can't bear to slaughter his own pigs, let alone a human being," Mike observed.

"I think Paul gets on better with his pigs than with the rest of us mere humans," Jonathon added. All three of them laughed at that.

"Fiona can probably give you a lot of information too," Mike said, before draining his mug.

Graham snorted. "If I have any questions about Teresa, it's Fiona I'll be consulting. That woman knows all there is to know about her." He glanced at the wall clock. "I'd better get a move on. When does the festival kick off?"

"It opens at ten in the ballroom. Then the panels start in there and in the music room, so there'll be movement between the two. Refreshments are being served in the entrance hall."

Graham got to his feet. "Then I'll be there at nine to set up in the study. I take it one or both of you will be there?"

"Both of us. Abi is running things here this weekend."

Jonathon couldn't resist. "Mike wanted to make sure he attended the festival. I thought he was there to support me, but *now* I find he's a closet Teresa Malvain fan and murder-mystery reader."

Mike glared at him. "You say that like it's a bad thing. What's wrong with reading?"

Jonathon held up his hands defensively. "Nothing. I'm just saying that I've known you almost a year, and I'm only learning about your reading habits now. It's as if you didn't want me to know." He loved teasing Mike.

"I hate to break up this lovers' tiff, but we've got work to do." Graham stuffed his notepad and pen into his pocket. "I'll see you both up there." And with that, he left them.

Mike collected the mugs and plates. "He's right. We've got work to do."

"This is certainly going to be the most memorable literary festival ever." Jonathon felt bad for Heather. All the effort she'd put into preparing for it, and the one thing everyone would remember would be the death of the guest of honor.

"As long as we only have one death to deal with," Mike said dryly.

Jonathon shivered. "Amen to that."

CHAPTER SEVEN

GRAHAM REPLACED his notepad in his breast pocket. "Thank you for your attention, ladies and gentlemen. And if any of you do remember something you
feel would be vital to this investigation, please find me
in the study. And one final note...." He gave a broad
smile. "Enjoy the festival. I know that might be difficult, given the circumstances, but the organizer has put
together a great line-up of speakers, so make sure you
get the chance to listen to them. And if you want to but-
tonhole them after, or tell them what a fantastic author
they are, do that too. This is your chance to thank them
personally for all those great books." He stepped away
from the mic, amid subdued applause, and the crowd
began to disperse, some taking seats in preparation for
the next speaker, others exiting the ballroom.

Jonathon patted him on the back. "Thank you.
That was nicely done."

"Heather set the tone." Graham gave her a nod.
"That minute's silence was a good idea."

Heather sighed. "It seemed the respectful thing to
do." She glanced around. "Where's Mike?"

"Setting up the study for Graham. He says he'll
stay as long as he's needed." Jonathon consulted the

printed agenda. "And I was going to stay in here and listen to the murder-mystery panel. Phil McCallister is on it."

"That should be a popular one." Heather's expression grew solemn. "Even if it has lost its main speaker."

Graham chuckled. "In which case, I might tell Mike to join you. Especially as he's got a thing for murder mysteries. I can cope without him." He gave them a polite nod, then left the ballroom in search of Mike.

Jonathon spied Fiona among the already-seated attendees and went over to join her, placing his agenda on the empty chair next to him for Mike.

She gave him a warm smile. "Have you ever been to one of these panels before?"

Jonathon shook his head. "This is my first book festival."

"Well, it starts with general introductions, and then the authors share a little about what they're working on. *Then* it's time for questions, and that's the best part, as far as I'm concerned." She gave a gleeful smile. "You never know what some people will ask."

There was an expectant air about her that Jonathon found intriguing. "You're planning something."

Fiona opened her eyes wide. "Me? I just have a couple of questions ready, that's all." Her eyes gleamed.

Jonathon had a feeling one or more of the authors was in for a grilling.

MIKE WAS thoroughly enjoying himself. He'd asked questions about the authors' research when it came to accuracy concerning police procedures, and it had become apparent that most of them knew their stuff. A couple had seemed uncomfortable, however, to have their work questioned by a former detective, but he'd made it clear he was asking from the standpoint of fiction reflecting reality. The audience had listened with rapt attention, and Mike had received a ripple of applause when he retook his seat.

The microphone was passed to Fiona, who rose to her feet. "I have a question for Phil McCallister. I'm sure you were saddened by the unexpected death of Teresa Malvain."

Phil gave a solemn nod. "As we all were. Teresa was an exceptional writer who will be sorely missed." Applause followed his words.

Fiona's eyes shone. "But surely in your case, that sadness was tinged with relief."

Phil frowned. "I… I don't quite understand."

"Well, surely with her dead, the lawsuit dies with her." Fiona tilted her head to one side. "Doesn't it?"

Phil blinked, his mouth opening and closing like a fish out of water, no sound issuing forth.

Fiona's brow furrowed. "She *was* suing you, wasn't she? She claimed you plagiarized *Murder Most Hideous*, the fifteenth book in the Summersfield series."

"A claim which I most strenuously denied," Phil declared loudly. Mike watched him with interest, noting the flush on his cheeks and the widened eyes.

"Of course you did," Fiona remarked. "You'd hardly admit it, right? But the word out there is that fighting the accusation in court is about to bankrupt you." She smiled. "But you don't have to worry about that anymore. No more Teresa, so no more court case. And you can deny it to your heart's content."

Phil stared at her, his pallor increasing. "There was never any basis to her accusations."

"Obviously her lawyers felt differently, if they decided to proceed with the case." Fiona's smile widened. "But we'll never know now, will we?" She sat down, passing the microphone back to the helper amid stunned silence. A moment later, another reader stood to ask a question, and the tension dissipated. Phil shuffled the papers on the table in front of him, then poured himself a glass of water, his hand trembling slightly.

Mike glanced across Jonathon to meet Fiona's satisfied gaze. "Wow. You really rattled him."

"That was my intention." She let out a contented sigh. "I'm sure I'm not the only one who was thinking that."

Jonathon tapped Mike's knee. "*Now* that barb of Teresa's at dinner makes sense."

"Which barb? She fired so many." The memory of that dinner hadn't left him.

"Remember when Phil said he was on the fourth book of his series? Teresa muttered something about how it was debatable that he wrote it."

Mike smiled. "You would've made a great police officer. Your memory is excellent."

Jonathon gave him a warm smile. "Glad to know I have my uses."

Mike laid his hand on Jonathon's knee. "Mind you, you have other skills that I value just as highly." He grinned. "But the less said about those skills, the better. At least in public, at any rate."

Fiona erupted into a loud cough, and Jonathon gave him a mock glare. "Behave."

Mike snickered. "I *am* behaving. Badly." He turned his attention back to the panel. Phil was nodding in all the right places, but his gaze kept flickering in Mike's direction. Judging by the way he was nibbling on his lip and touching his collar all the time, Phil was nervous.

Mike found that very interesting indeed.

When the panel came to an end and the applause had finished, Mike glanced at his watch. "I'm going to see how Graham got on. Hopefully he's had a few witnesses come forward."

"I'll get us some coffee and meet you in the study. I'll bring one for Graham too." Jonathon leaned in, as if to kiss Mike on the cheek, then checked himself and withdrew.

Mike was done hiding. He shifted closer and kissed Jonathon lightly on the cheek, which drew an aww from the lady behind them. Mike caught Jonathon's gaze. "I'm getting too long in the tooth to care about offending people," he said quietly. "I love you, and I don't care who knows it."

Jonathon's eyes glistened. "Love you too. Now go see Graham, while I see to topping up our caffeine levels."

Mike laughed. "Yeah, we can't neglect them." He nodded to Fiona, then got up and walked out of the ballroom, heading for the study. What he couldn't shake was the look in Phil's eyes.

That man was scared of me. Then it struck him that if Phil had had something to do with Teresa's death, no doubt having an ex-detective around would make him extremely nervous. He made a mental note to investigate Fiona's statements. *Is the possibility of being made bankrupt enough of a motive for murder?* Then he reasoned that if Teresa had been right, Phil would have been ruined. No one liked a plagiarist.

Graham was alone in the study, making notes. He glanced up as Mike entered. "What is it with this place?"

"What's up?" Mike closed the door behind him.

"That! *That* is what's up." Graham pointed to the wall behind Mike. "Do you know how long it took me to find the bloody door?"

Mike chuckled. "Hey, don't knock it. That was how we rumbled a murderer, remember?" The door with its linen fold panels had been made to blend into the wall, and there was a knack to knowing how to open it.

"Oh yeah. I'd forgotten that." Graham leaned back in his chair. "Well, this has been an interesting morning."

"Have you had many people coming forward?"

"Not many, but what they lacked in number, they made up for in quality." Graham gave a low whistle. "She wasn't a nice lady, was she?"

"You've just worked that out?" Mike snorted. "I'm surprised no one bumped her off before this. Oh, and I think I've got a suspect who needs considering. Phil McCallister." He summed up what had gone on at the panel.

Graham scribbled a line in his notepad. "I agree. I'll look into that. He was on my list of people to question anyway, seeing as he did a convenient disappearing act in the pub last night. Thanks for pointing that out, by the way." He grinned. "See? I was right. You're a handy man to have around."

"So what have you learned?"

"I've got a fair-sized list of who was near her table, for one thing." Graham peered at his notes. "That'll come in handy. Plus, I know who was at the bar. Apart from Paul, of course." They both chuckled. Paul was always at the bar. He'd once joked about having his name engraved on a plaque on the barstool where he usually sat. "From what I've gleaned so far, Teresa and Professor Harcourt were trying to talk but were constantly interrupted. People wanting autographs, asking questions...."

Mike frowned. "I thought the professor would be here today."

Graham gave a knowing nod. "Ah. Yes. Well, he would've been, except I happen to know he got a phone call, asking him to go to Fareham. Seems the coroner learned he was involved in the case and asked him to sit in on the postmortem. Apparently she wanted his involvement while he was in the vicinity. I can understand that. When you've got someone with Professor Harcourt's caliber on tap, as it were, a second pair of eyes is always a good thing. But he'll be back later."

The door opened and Jonathon entered, carrying a cardboard tray with three large polystyrene cups. "So was it murder?" He set the cups down on the desk.

Graham rolled his eyes. "Gimme strength! They haven't even sent me any preliminary results of the postmortem yet." He sniffed the air. "Thanks. I need this."

"Does that mean you haven't drawn any conclusions?" Jonathon sat in the chair facing Graham.

"Well…."

Mike arched his eyebrows. "You have. Come on, then. Share."

Graham grumbled under his breath about nosy amateurs but then sighed. "You're not gonna leave me alone, so I might as well tell you. Whatever caused the reaction is more than likely to have been in the coffee." He consulted his notes. "No one saw her eat anything. She only handled a pen and the coffee cup."

"Could someone have coated the pen in something?" Jonathon suggested. "Peanut oil, maybe?"

Graham frowned. "I like the idea, but it's not likely. For one thing, she'd have noticed as soon as she touched the pen."

"And for another?" Mike asked.

Graham snickered. "It was her pen. She got it out of her bag. And about that missing notebook. She didn't have it on the table, but a couple of people saw it when she went into her bag for that pen. So at some point between then and getting up to go to her room, someone swiped it." He glanced at Mike. "It's definitely not in her room?"

Mike shook his head. "I've been all over it. Nothing under the beds, nothing hidden in drawers or in the wardrobe. Any place where an A4 notebook could be stashed, I've searched."

"Well, we know someone was in her room, because the EpiPen from her case was missing," Jonathon commented. "Are we assuming the same person also removed the notebook from her bag? As well as her phone and EpiPen?"

Graham rubbed his chin. "That notebook sounds a bit big to hide. I mean, it's not like it could've been hidden under a coat or something, because who wears a coat in June? And surely it would've been obvious if someone tried to hide a notebook, EpiPen, and phone on them."

Mike had to agree. Then his thoughts went back to the coffee, which was looking more and more likely to be the source. "So does that mean we should be looking at whoever was at the bar? Because those cups sat there for a while before Professor Harcourt had to come get them. Anyone could have put something in them." He widened his eyes. "Wait a minute. How would they know which one was for Teresa?"

Graham put down his pen. "Right now this is nothing but speculation. Let's wait and see what the postmortem comes up with. And if it was in the coffee, we've got no evidence. I assume the cups were washed that night?"

"One of them was. The other got broken when Teresa bumped into it and sent it flying. So no, there's no evidence," Mike concluded gloomily. He looked across at Jonathon. "I think we might be out of our league on this one."

"Hallelujah!" Graham threw his hands into the air. "You were out of your league on the previous two cases, but what you did have was an awful lot of luck. Maybe this time you'll follow my advice and stay out of it? You know, police business and all that?"

Mike stared at him in amazement, surprised by his outburst.

Jonathon glared at him. "Hey. You wanted our help, remember? 'Keep your eyes and ears open,' you said."

"Keeping your eyes and ears open is one thing— actively investigating is another." Graham closed his notebook. "If no one else turns up before lunch, I'll call it a day and go back to the station to wait on the postmortem results."

"Meanwhile, we carry on being your eyes and ears here, right?" Mike scowled. "As long as we don't act on anything we find out, of course." Graham's exclamation still rankled. Whatever they'd turned up the last couple of times, they'd made sure to share it with Graham.

Then he reconsidered. *How would I have felt if it had been me investigating those cases, and a pair of amateur sleuths had been constantly sticking their oar in police business?* Graham had been extremely patient thus far. And if this did turn out to be murder, that would doubtless mean an inspector from Winchester would be in charge of the case. Graham would hate that.

"You do know why I don't want you involved, don't you?" Graham said suddenly. When Mike gave him a quizzical glance, he smiled. "One of these days, you're going to go too far and end up on a killer's radar. I would hate it if anything happened to you. Both of you."

"We like you too, Graham." Jonathon grinned. "And we'll be good. Honest."

Mike glanced across at Jonathon, biting his lip when he took a closer look at Jonathon's innocent expression. Graham might not be acquainted with that look, but Mike certainly was.

Jonathon clearly had no intention of being good.

"There is one thing you could do for me." Graham's expression grew serious. "What did you do with the broken cup?"

"The pieces went straight into the bin." Mike stilled. "You want me to take them out, don't you?"

"Only if you didn't clean them first. But who cleans broken crockery before they throw it away? Besides, you don't strike me as the particularly anal type." Graham smirked. "Although I suppose that's not really the right word to use where you're concerned."

"Oh, I don't know." Jonathon's eyes twinkled with amusement. "I think it suits him perfectly."

Mike gave him a stern look that he hoped promised retribution later.

CHAPTER EIGHT

"WHAT'S ON next?" Mike said as he returned from getting rid of their lunch wrappings. "Graham's gone, so the rest of the day is ours."

Jonathon gave Mike a hard stare. "Maybe if you kept hold of the agenda Heather gave you this morning, you'd know without having to keep asking me."

Mike grinned. "Yeah, but then I wouldn't have so much fun bugging you."

Jonathon had to laugh. "It's a good thing I love you." He was ashamed of his earlier hesitation. He'd leaned in to kiss Mike's cheek, and what had come to mind was some unknown person snapping them together and putting it online.

This is down to my father. Before Mike had come along, Jonathon hadn't given a flying leap who saw him doing God knows what to whomsoever he wanted. But since Mike's arrival and his father's interventions, something had changed. He was less inclined to upset the apple cart, more willing to consider his father's views.

But why? Where has it got me? Afraid to show affection to my own boyfriend in public. This is not who I am. This is not who I want to be.

"Jonathon?"

He blinked. Mike was staring at him, his forehead slightly scrunched up the way it always was when something concerned or worried him. "You okay?"

Jonathon gave him a hopefully reassuring smile. "I'm fine. Just zoned out for a second there."

"Where did you go to?" Mike's hand was gentle on his back.

Jonathon went with a version of the truth. "Thinking about how much I love you."

Mike's breathing hitched. "I'd love to show you how much those words mean to me." His eyes sparkled. "But I think we'd scare the normal people." He tapped the agenda in Jonathon's hand. "So how about you tell me where we're going next instead?"

Something had been niggling Jonathon. "Do we need to go to the pub and retrieve the broken cup pieces from the bin?"

Mike shook his head. "We know where they are. And the bins won't be emptied for another three days, so they're not going anywhere." When Jonathon didn't respond but simply gave him a hard stare, he sighed and pulled his phone from his pocket. He tapped the keys, then put the phone to his ear. "Hey, Abi? Do me a favor, will you? I know it sounds weird, but go to the bin in the bar and find the pieces of that broken cup from the other night. I put them in a green plastic bag. … Yes, I said it would sound weird. Just do it, okay? Now? I'll wait." Mike rolled his eyes. "Can't believe I'm doing this. It's not like they could—hello? You found them? Okay. Now put them somewhere safe. … I don't know, somewhere they can't be mislaid or lost. … Thank you.

See you tonight." He disconnected the call and gave Jonathon a pointed stare. "Happy now?"

Jonathon gave him a quick kiss on the cheek. "Very. Thank you." He scanned the page of the agenda. "There's a panel on reviews. How authors deal with bad ones, the importance of them…. That might be good."

Mike smiled. "Okay, that's the one we'll go to. Ballroom or music room?"

"Ballroom."

Mike held out his hand. "Then let's go."

Without hesitation, Jonathon laced his fingers through Mike's, and they walked through the milling crowd toward the ballroom, where attendees were already going in, talking animatedly. Heather stood at the door, smiling.

"It's going really well," she said quietly. "I thought everything was ruined after last night, but everyone seems to be enjoying it, and I've had people come up to me and say it's been great so far."

Jonathon gave her a brief hug. "I'm so happy for you. I know how much effort you put into this." He smiled broadly. "Looks like there might be a Merrychurch Literary Festival 2019 after all."

Her eyes widened in obvious alarm. "Don't jinx it! We've got a long way to go yet." She glanced through the door. "I'd better get in there. I'm emceeing this one."

"Have I missed much?" Professor Harcourt approached them at a brisk pace as Heather left. "Any more excitement?"

"As in, excitement of the dead body variety?" Mike inquired. "No, thank goodness. Although I hear you got roped in to assist in a postmortem."

Professor Harcourt nodded. "And before you ask, I can't share the results with you. That constable of yours would have my guts for garters if you learned them before he did. Official channels and all that."

Jonathon opened his mouth to protest, but Mike squeezed his hand. "He's right. Think about it. Graham would never let us see evidence again, and we want to keep Graham sweet. Don't we?" He gave Jonathon a focused stare.

Jonathon sighed. "You're right. Although it will be torture having to wait. When will Graham get the results?"

"I have no idea. I expect he won't be long in telling you, especially as you're on such good terms with him." Professor Harcourt smiled. "The coroner was very complimentary. She even asked her assistant to take a photo of us in our scrubs. Not with the body in view, of course. She merely wanted a record of the occasion."

Mike grinned. "So it's not just authors who have fans."

Professor Harcourt waved his hand modestly. "As if I'd refuse her. And I suppose all those high-profile cases do push one into the limelight. My son says he frequently meets people who instantly recognize his name."

"Your son? What does he do?" Jonathon inquired.

Professor Harcourt's face glowed with pride. "He's following in his father's footsteps. He's training to be an oncologist, and he has a bright future ahead of him." He cleared his throat. "Anyway, enough about me." He pulled his agenda from his shoulder bag. "I want to get back into the swing of things. I'm attending the reviews panel."

Mike gestured to the door. "Then let's go in and get seats."

They walked into the ballroom and found most of the rows of chairs already occupied. Apparently, reviews were a popular topic. Jonathon pointed to three chairs toward the rear and rushed over to grab them. By the time they were seated, Heather was at the mic, introducing the panelists. The only author Jonathon recognized was Melody Richards.

"Got room for one more?" Fiona appeared next to Jonathon, carrying a chair. "I wanted to sit near you." She set it down next to him, then sat.

"That depends." Jonathon smirked. "Are you going to grill the panelists the way you grilled Phil McCallister?"

Fiona laughed. "Not this time, no."

It was a lively session, with lots of interaction between authors and readers. Jonathon liked the fact that it was a lighthearted hour, with bouts of laughter as authors shared reviews that had amused them. Toward the end of the session, however, the mood grew more serious.

"Let's talk about negative reviews," Heather said, facing the panel. "Can such reviews ever have a benefit? For instance, can they point to something an author missed, or something an author might want to focus on in future books?"

"I've had negative reviews that were actually quite constructive," one author, Paula Fowler, said with a smile. "But that's not very common. There are people out there whose only pleasure in life appears to be tearing authors to pieces."

"Not to mention the occasional sock puppet," another author added.

Heather frowned. "Sock puppet?"

"Bad reviews put out there by fake accounts, usually for nefarious purposes," the author explained. "For example, supposing a very popular—but thoroughly unscrupulous—author wanted to eliminate the competition. Maybe they have a new release and they don't want other such releases to detract attention from it. So they have reviewers set up who purposefully go about giving poor ratings and poor reviews, whilst praising *their* release to the heavens."

A reader put up her hand. "You don't mean that actually happens? That's dreadful."

"Of course it happens." Melody turned the nearest mic toward her. "It happened to me. I brought out a book that was attacked by an army of rabid fans. They wanted my book to fail, pure and simple. And every subsequent book I released, the same thing occurred. It's very distressing. There have been times when I've almost given up on the idea of pursuing a career in writing."

The discussion continued, but Jonathon was intrigued by the comments. "Do you know what Melody was talking about?" he whispered to Fiona.

She nodded. "A couple of years ago, Melody was one of the finalists for the Speakman Award. It's an award for outstanding fiction that is given out every year. Well, this was Melody's debut novel, and there was a lot of buzz about it. Teresa was up for the same award, and ultimately it went to her."

"But what does that have to do with reviews?" Jonathon was puzzled.

"When the award was announced, Melody kicked up a huge fuss. She claimed that it had been an unfair process and that Teresa had bribed the judges. Apparently Melody had got to meet one of the judges and claimed her book had been out in front, but then some of the judges suddenly changed their minds, and it went to Teresa. Then Melody went on social media, protesting that Teresa had set her fans onto Melody, telling them to review her book negatively."

"Is any of this true?" Jonathon was appalled.

"We have no clue as to how the judges voted. But yes, Melody's debut book was suddenly on the receiving end of a slew of bad reviews. We're talking hundreds of them, within the space of a couple of weeks. Not to mention her subsequent releases. And yes, they probably did have an effect on sales. But as to whether Teresa orchestrated it?" Fiona shrugged. "Who knows?"

At that point, Heather speared her with a pointed stare, and Fiona lapsed into silence. Jonathon didn't follow the rest of the discussion. His mind was on Melody Richards. From the sound of it, she blamed Teresa for the failure of her books. Whether this was true or not, it explained the tension between the two of them during the dinner.

It could also be a solid motive for murder. A bruised ego, a career blighted? As a talented photographer, Jonathon knew creative people could sometimes suffer from heightened emotions, and people *had* been killed for less.

At the end of the panel, Heather thanked the authors, and the audience applauded before getting up to approach the table or to leave the room.

"Well, that was illuminating." Professor Harcourt cleaned his glasses. "My panel won't be nearly as riveting."

"You're speaking tomorrow, aren't you?" Jonathon asked.

Professor Harcourt nodded. "I'm a little nervous, to be truthful. I'm more accustomed to lecturing medical students on the intricacies of forensic pathology. Their questions tend to be purely technical and free from emotion. I'm not sure what to expect from this audience."

"Trust me, they'll be riveted," Mike assured him. "There's a reason TV shows like *CSI* and *NCIS* are so popular. People want to know how crime detection works."

"Are you going to talk about cases you've worked on?" Jonathon asked him.

"Yes. I'm also going to go through the basic terms so people are more familiar with them. Different types of lividity, how we determine time of death...."

"We did a little of that ourselves last year," Mike commented with a wry smile.

Professor Harcourt blinked. "Truly? We must talk about this at some point. Perhaps this evening in the pub? I should like to hear more." He smiled. "You two fascinate me."

"We aim to please." Jonathon consulted his agenda. "And now I'm going to grab a coffee before the next session."

"And what's that on?" Mike asked.

"Conflict within romance."

"As in, how to avoid it or create it?"

Jonathon grinned. "Maybe a little of both?"

THE EVENING pub crowd was a good deal smaller than the previous night, but Jonathon was secretly pleased about that. He didn't want Mike run ragged, especially when Jonathon had plans for once the pub had closed. He aimed to shut out the world and lose himself in Mike's arms.

Bliss.

His phone buzzed in his pocket, and Jonathon removed it to peer at the screen. *Dammit.* It had been a few months since his father had called—not that Jonathon had minded that in the slightest. With a sigh, he signaled to Mike that he had a call, then stepped outside into the warm evening air. Despite it being past nine, the sun hadn't fully set yet and cast long shadows over the village green.

"Hello, Father."

Thomas de Mountford cleared his throat. "Ah. So you *are* alive. I was beginning to wonder."

"What can I do for you?" With his father, it was always best to get straight to the point.

"It's been a while since we last spoke. I was wondering how things are progressing."

"Things?" Jonathon wanted to laugh. His father was never one to speak in such vague terms. "Care to be more specific?" As if he didn't know what was coming.

"I saw the photos from the ball at the Grosvenor."

Seeing as that had been the whole point of the exercise, Jonathon said nothing, waiting for more.

"So I'm calling to see if there have been any developments between you and Ruth. Do you have any news for me?"

"No, I don't. We're not engaged. We haven't even spoken of it." Though strictly speaking, that was a lie—they'd talked about *an* engagement, after all.

"Then maybe you should speak of it. You're going to be thirty this year. Time is trickling through your fingers, especially if you intend starting a family. You don't want to be much older with small childre—"

"I think you need to stop right there." Jonathon was suddenly bone-tired of hearing the same old refrain.

"Excuse me?" Ice crept into his father's voice.

Jonathon gave in to the weariness that pervaded him. "Dominic's death brought a few things home to me. Life is too short, for one thing. None of us know how long we've got. And I truly believed you losing your brother would… mellow you somehow, but I can see now that was wishful thinking."

"I think you're the one who needs to stop before you say something you regret."

"Oh, I'm past that stage." Jonathon took a deep breath. "The last ten years of Dominic's life were spent in secret. He couldn't share the fact that he had a male lover because he knew how you'd react. How you felt society would react—well, the society *you* move in. And I vowed I would never live like that.

Hell, I *didn't* live like that—until you started pushing me to marry for the sake of the family's future."

"Do you want our bloodline to die out?" his father demanded.

"No, but that doesn't mean I think yours is the way to go to prevent that." Jonathon sighed. "Maybe Dominic's death made me less self-centered. More open-minded. More willing to consider the views of others. And so with you, I strove to find some middle ground. To achieve some balance in my life."

"Which is why we discussed—"

"No," Jonathon interjected. "You proposed your way, and I went along with it. And that is the problem. With you, there *is* no middle ground. Everything has to be your way. And unless you are willing to put aside your own ideas and plans, there will never *be* any middle ground. So…." He was shaking. "I've been reassessing my life, and I've come to the inexorable conclusion that your way and my way conflict. If I follow your plan, you'll have your next generation, sure, but *I* will be miserable as hell. And that raises a question in my mind. What kind of father would wish such abject misery on his son?"

"Jonathon, I—"

"And so I've made a decision," he announced.

There was a brief silence so tangible that it had weight. "What kind of decision?" The cautious note in his father's voice was so unlike him it stilled Jonathon for a moment.

"Pretty life-changing, actually. I'll make sure you hear it from me first, rather than by any other means." There was someone else who needed to hear it first. And without delay.

Before his father could utter another word, Jonathon said his goodbyes and ended the call. He was still trembling as he fought to breathe. When he'd regained a little more control, he went back into the pub and crossed the floor to where Mike was serving behind the bar.

Mike looked up from his task of pouring a pint. "Who called?"

Jonathon ignored the question and held out his hands. "Can I borrow your car? There's something I need to pick up from the manor for tonight."

From his usual spot, Paul Drake cackled. "'Ere, you wanna watch out, Mike. He's goin' to pick up the handcuffs he keeps next to his bed."

Around him, raucous laughter burst out.

Jonathon glared at Mike. "You told!"

Yet more laughter erupted.

Mike rolled his eyes, shoved his hand into his jeans pocket, removed his keys, then tossed them to Jonathon. "Don't drive it like you drive that Jag, okay?" His eyes twinkled. "I know what you get like when you're behind the wheel."

Jonathon said nothing but dashed out of the pub and around to the rear car park to Mike's 4x4. He drove through the village as fast as he dared, his heart pounding at the thought of what he was about to do. It was scary as hell, but he knew deep down it was the right thing.

He left the engine running as he ran into the hall and up to his bedroom, going straight to the top drawer where he'd stashed his quarry. After shoving it deep into his pocket, Jonathon ran down the stairs and back to the car. He headed up the driveway, swerving to avoid Ben Threadwell, the gardener, who was wheeling his barrow across it, obviously clearing up after his day.

Jonathon hit the brakes. "Sorry!" he yelled through the window. "Why are you still working at this hour?"

Ben scowled at him. "I'm getting my jobs done that I couldn't do today, 'cos there were hordes of people everywhere. When does this shindig finish?"

"Tomorrow evening. Then it's back to normal, I promise."

"Good," Ben grumbled before resuming his trek, slowly pushing the wheelbarrow. Once he was safely out of the way, Jonathon raced down the driveway, turned into the lane, and headed toward the village. He'd never made the journey so quickly.

When he reentered the pub, Mike was chatting with Paul, and the air was filled with the buzz of talk. Many of the locals greeted Jonathon warmly, which gave his confidence a much-needed boost. He stopped dead in the middle of the crowded pub and addressed Mike.

"Could you come out from behind the bar for a minute?"

Mike grinned at him. "What are you up to?"

Jonathon said nothing, but simply pointed to the floor in front of him.

Shrugging, Mike lifted the flap and joined him. "Okay. I'll play along."

Jonathon's breathing sped up, his pulse racing. "I'm sorry if I ever made you feel that you weren't a key part of my life. Because you are."

Mike stilled. "Where's this going, Jonathon?"

Around them, voices fell silent.

He took another breath. "And I'm also sorry I took so long to come to my senses. I've felt this way for months, and I should have acted sooner."

"You're worrying me," Mike said quietly. Jonathon could feel the gazes fixed on them.

He gave Mike a warm smile. "Nothing to worry about." He removed the ring box from his pocket and got down on one knee. "Mike Tattersall… will you marry me?"

Mike stared at him in stunned silence, and Jonathon's heart was beating out a military tattoo. Then Paul Drake yelled, "What are you waitin' for? It's hardly a surprise, is it? It's not like we haven't seen the two of you canoodlin' this past year. And it's not like we didn't all see it coming."

His exclamation seemed to be the impetus Mike needed. He took a deep breath. "Yes, Jonathon de Mountford. I will marry you."

"Oh thank God." Then all words ceased when Mike hauled him to his feet, the ring box forgotten for the moment as he took Jonathon in his arms and kissed him.

CHAPTER NINE

THE APPLAUSE came from every direction, and suddenly there were villagers clustered around them, patting them on the back and shouting out their congratulations.

It still hadn't sunk in when Jonathon freed himself from Mike's embrace, took hold of his left hand, and slipped a white gold band onto his ring finger. Mike stared at it.

"Do you like it?" Jonathon asked with an obvious note of anxiety.

"I love it. And it fits. How did you manage that?" Mike couldn't stop looking at the gold band, as if breaking eye contact with it would somehow make it disappear and the whole magical moment would become nothing more than a wonderful dream.

"I took a chance that your ring finger was the same size as its opposite number. Remember when you had to fix your bike after Christmas and you got oil all over your hands? When you took off your signet ring to clean your hands, I did a quick measure." Jonathon grinned. "I put it on a piece of paper, then drew around its inside."

That stopped him dead. "Christmas? When did you buy this?"

"After New Year, in London." Jonathon smiled. "It's been hidden under my briefs ever since."

Mike stared at him in wonder before placing his hands on either side of Jonathon's sweet face and kissing him tenderly. A chorus of *aww*s rippled around them.

"Where's the champagne?" Paul joked.

Mike broke the kiss. "You know what? You're right. If ever a situation called for champagne, it's this one." He released Jonathon and dashed behind the bar. "Who wants to join us in a glass of champagne?"

Jonathon burst out laughing. "You expect any of this crowd to say no to that?"

Mike chuckled as he pulled bottles from the fridge. "Yeah, that was dumb. Help me set up the glasses?"

Jonathon joined him behind the bar and started placing champagne flutes in rows, while the villagers gathered, the air full of laughter and chatter.

Mike gave Jonathon an inquiring glance. "So... wanna tell me what brought this on?"

Jonathon laughed. "That call? Was from my father. You can blame all this on him."

Mike gaped at him. "I don't believe for a second it was his idea. Remind me to thank him next time I see him." He popped the first cork, and everyone cheered. Mike poured, and Jonathon handed out the glasses, until there were four or five empty bottles in the recycling box below the bar and everyone who wanted a glass had one.

Mike raised his glass. "To us."

Jonathon clinked with him. "To us." The sound echoed around the pub, and the villagers fell silent as they drank. Then the noise level hiked back up as people resumed their seats, taking their champagne with them.

"You've had the ring since January?" Mike was dumbfounded.

Jonathon nodded slowly. "I was waiting for the right moment, until I realized this evening that I didn't want to wait any longer."

Mike took a sip of champagne. "So... any idea when you want to do this?"

"As soon as possible?" Jonathon sighed. "Like I said, I don't want to wait. What would be perfect would be the church, with Lloyd performing the ceremony, but I know that's not going to happen. In which case, Plan B is at the manor, in the Italian garden." His smile reached his eyes. "I was thinking about the two of us standing between those two statues. You know, the ones I always used to think were trying to grab each other. The sound of the fountain, the open air... with any of the villagers who want to join us to celebrate."

Mike couldn't think of a more perfect setting. He wanted to ask about Jonathon's parents, but that would put a dampener on the mood, so he pushed that aside.

"Okay, what have I missed?" Graham strolled into the pub, dressed in his jeans and T-shirt, a denim jacket slung over his shoulder. Beside him was Professor Harcourt, dressed more formally in a jacket and tie over dark pants.

"There's gonna be wedding bells," Paul announced, pointing toward Mike and Jonathon. "They're finally getting hitched. About bloody time."

Mike poured out the last of the champagne and handed it to the two men. "And what you missed was the lord of the manor getting down on one knee."

"Damn. I'd have paid good money to see that." Graham glanced around the pub. "Did none of you video it?"

Judging by the loud exclamations that erupted, it seemed no one had been on the ball. Secretly, Mike was glad of that. He didn't think Thomas finding a video of his son's proposal online would go down too well. As much as he'd hated the man's meddling, Mike felt it was better that he heard the news from Jonathon's lips.

I think we ought to try to stay on his good side—if he has one. After all, he's going to be my father-in-law. That thought brought with it a small measure of apprehension. He couldn't see Jonathon's parents welcoming him with open arms.

"Congratulations." Professor Harcourt raised his glass. "May you both have many happy years together. Speaking as someone who has been happily married for the last twenty-seven years, I can highly recommend it."

Graham raised his glass too, but no sooner had he drunk from it than his face fell.

An uneasy feeling settled in the pit of Mike's belly. "What's wrong?"

"I'm pleased for you both, honest I am…."

"There's a 'but' coming," Jonathon remarked, putting down his glass on the bar.

Graham sighed. "I hate to be the one to spoil the occasion but… I just heard back from the coroner." Then he gave Professor Harcourt a quick glance. "Unless you've already shared the details with them?"

Professor Harcourt shook his head briskly. "It wasn't my place to do so."

Graham gave a satisfied nod. "Okay." He sat on the nearest empty stool and leaned closer, lowering his voice. "This can't go any further than you two, all right? I'm only telling you because you've already guessed the outcome, more or less."

"Then it was murder?" Mike's pulse quickened. "What did you find?"

Graham indicated Professor Harcourt, who also leaned in close. "There was evidence of peanut oil in the digestive tract," the professor said in a low voice. "And the only reason we found it was because we specifically went looking for it, based on our speculations." He met Mike's gaze. "Definitely not the peanuts on the bar. And it had to have been in the coffee. Pity we don't have the cup to analyze its contents."

Mike cleared his throat. "Actually? We do."

Professor Harcourt blinked. "We do?"

"I asked them to retrieve it from the rubbish," Graham said with a smug smile.

Professor Harcourt beamed. "That's marvelous, especially as the cup Teresa sent flying was hers. In which case, we need to send the pieces off for analysis."

"I'll see to that first thing Monday," Graham assured him. "Which leaves us with one conclusion. Someone in the pub Friday night killed Teresa. And it had to be premeditated, because who just happens to have peanut oil on them?"

"I'm afraid I must concur," Professor Harcourt added. "If you add to that the missing notebook, EpiPens, and phone, it all points to murder."

"And that means I'm not allowed to investigate it," Graham pointed out gloomily. "Even if I now have one accidental death and two murders under my belt, them upstairs still feel that a humble constable can't cut the mustard."

"What does that mean?" Professor Harcourt inquired.

"It means the powers that be are sending a detective inspector from London to be in charge of the case." Graham took another long drink from his glass.

"As long as it's not Gorland," Mike joked. When Graham's miserable expression didn't alter, he froze. "Oh my God. It is, isn't it?"

Graham raised his glass. "Guess who's coming to dinner."

Beside him, Jonathon groaned. "I hoped we'd seen the last of him."

Mike's heart sank. "When does he get here?"

"My guess is Monday," Graham replied. "And you know how he feels about you two 'meddling,' as he puts it. So you'd better leave this one to the professionals." Mike caught sight of Jonathon's fixed stare and added his own. Graham sighed. "Yeah, it was worth a try, but I didn't expect any other reaction, to be honest. Please… try to be inconspicuous? And don't launch into it right away. Have a night off. You just got engaged, for God's sake. I'm sure you've got better things to do with your evening than sleuthing." He grinned.

Professor Harcourt coughed. "That name seems familiar. Gorland.... Gorland...." He took a sharp intake of breath. "DI John Gorland, from the Met?"

"The very same." Graham indicated Mike with a nod of his head. "And he and Mike aren't exactly bosom buddies."

Jonathon let out a derisive snort. "Understatement of the year."

Professor Harcourt had a twinkle in his eye. "What did Graham mean about you two meddling?"

Graham burst out laughing. "Like I said, Sherlock and Watson, these two. Mind you, they've been very useful. They helped solve a murder at the tail end of last year, and another during the summer."

"Helped?" Mike huffed. "Who called you to say who the murderer was? Who put you on the track of—"

"Yeah, all right, you *may* have provided some valuable assistance." Graham rolled his eyes. "Amateurs."

"But Mike is hardly that," Professor Harcourt said with a smile. "A former DI, who would have gone places if not for unfortunate circumstances." Mike arched his eyebrows, and Professor Harcourt shrugged. "I looked you up when the coroner recognized your name. A promising career."

Mike gestured to his prosthetic foot. "Until I lost this. But you know what? It brought me here, to Merrychurch." He gazed warmly at Jonathon. "To you."

The light in Jonathon's eyes....

"Oh, get a room," Paul groaned from his seat at the bar. "I suppose we'll have nothing but wedding plans from here on in. Hurry up and tie the knot, for God's sake."

Jonathon laughed. "Funny you should say that. I'm not a fan of long engagements. So I was thinking… how does September sound?"

Mike could live with that.

WHEN THE door was finally locked and bolted for the night, Jonathon heaved a sigh of relief. "I swear tonight dragged more than usual." He'd looked at the clock so many times, willing the evening to be over so they could talk.

Except he planned to do a lot more than talk.

"Well, it's not every night you get engaged." Mike shook his head. "I certainly didn't see this in my future. Not in this village, at any rate."

"And then I turned up, pulling my suitcase, looking lost and forlorn."

Mike snickered. "Hardly." He took a last glance around the pub, then went to the light switch. "Go on up. I'll be right behind you."

Jonathon went through the door that led to the narrow staircase. When he reached the upper floor, he paused, staring at the guest room.

So it was murder.

What troubled him most was that if ever anyone deserved to be bumped off, it was Teresa Malvain.

"What are you thinking?" Mike said softly from behind him.

Jonathon sighed. "That if this was one of your murder mysteries, readers would be hoping that

Teresa was going to be the victim long before she drank that coffee."

"Well, we've already got a few suspects."

Jonathon chuckled. "I think we've only got started. I'm sure more will appear once we start looking into the case." He paused. "We *are* going to look into it, aren't we? Even if Gorland is in charge?"

"I think we just do our usual thing and talk to people. It's worked well for us so far."

Jonathon turned to face him. "But this feels different from the last case, and I'm not sure why. No one set out to murder Mrs. Teedle, did they? They simply took advantage of finding her incapacitated. This was premeditated. Someone came to the pub with peanut oil and deliberately put it in her coffee."

"We *think* that's what happened," Mike corrected. "We'll know for sure when the pieces are analyzed."

Something else had niggled him, a thought that had flashed through his mind, only to leave as quickly as it had arrived. The notion that they'd missed something vital….

Mike reached out and stroked Jonathon's cheek. "No more talk of murder for tonight. Not when we have much more delightful things to discuss." Mike lowered his hand and pointed to his room. "Bed. Now."

Jonathon laughed. "Bossy." He walked over to Mike's bedroom and entered, with Mike following behind. Once inside, he closed the door, then gently backed Jonathon up to it, kissing him on the lips. Jonathon responded, his arms around Mike's neck.

When they parted, Mike looked into his eyes. "You're sure about this? Us getting married, I mean."

Jonathon smiled. "I wouldn't have bought the ring if I hadn't been sure. The call with my father crystallized my thinking, and I knew finding the so-called perfect moment wasn't worth prolonging the wait any more."

Mike took his hand and led him over to the bed. "Can I ask you something? What did your dad say that got you so riled?" Jonathon ran through the conversation, not missing out anything. Mike listened intently, and when Jonathon was done, he squeezed Jonathon's hand. "So he doesn't know about the engagement?"

"No. You had to be the first one to hear about that."

"Well, of course," Mike said with a smile. "So when will you tell him?"

Jonathon stood at the foot of the bed, unbuttoning his shirt. "I'm not going to waste any time. He has to know from me before he gets wind of it from another source. And there's something else you and I need to discuss, but that can wait. Right now we need to celebrate."

Mike grinned, easing Jonathon's shirt off his shoulders, his fingers skating over Jonathon's bare flesh. "What did you have in mind?"

Jonathon got busy freeing Mike from his shirt. "You might want to text Abi and tell her to open the pub tomorrow."

Mike opened his eyes wide. "And why's that?"

"Because there's no way you're going to be alert enough, seeing as you're not going to be sleeping tonight."

Mike laughed quietly. "Hey, I'm almost forty-three. What makes you think I can go all night long?"

Jonathon grinned. "What makes you think you'll be doing all the driving?"

CHAPTER TEN

JONATHON DIVIDED his time between eating his eggs and bacon, and consulting his short list of suspects. *Well, so far it's short.*

Mike got up from the table to pour more coffee as Abi bustled into the kitchen.

"This is the last day of the festival, isn't it?" she asked as she deposited her shopping bags on the table.

"Yup." Mike placed the mugs on the table. "And thanks again for running the pub during the day. We've really appreciated it."

Abi beamed. "Hey, no problem. You know me, always happy to do a few shifts. The money comes in handy, especially as my holiday is coming up next month." Her eyes widened. "So is it true, what I've been hearing in the village? Jonathon proposed last night?"

"In front of all the regulars, down on one knee," Mike confirmed, smiling broadly. "And I said yes, as if you didn't already know that."

"Fantastic!" Abi sighed. "A gay wedding. I've never been to one of those."

"I think you'll find they're just like het weddings," Jonathon remarked. "Except for the fact that we'll be naked, and instead of a wedding reception, we'll be hosting a gay orgy."

"Seriously?" Abi's jaw dropped, but then she rolled her eyes. "Yeah, right." She glanced at the clock on the wall. "Aren't you two usually up before this? Running late, are we?" Her lips twitched. "And no, I don't want to hear why. I can probably guess. I'll be back in a bit." She left the kitchen.

"Why does everyone around here seem to think we spend all our time having sex?" Jonathon demanded.

Mike snorted. "Er... because we do?" He pointed to Jonathon's notepad. "I see you've progressed from using Post-its. Who's on the list so far?"

"Phil McCallister, for one. I think he has to be on it. Then I've added Melody Richards." Jonathon leaned back in his chair. "Do you recall what Fiona said, the night Teresa died? Something about her not gaining a lot of friends when she lived here and how things didn't improve once she'd left. I wonder what Fiona meant."

"Then we either need to talk to Fiona or else find someone who knew Teresa when she lived here. The prof's out. Teresa came here after he'd left." Mike rubbed his beard before breaking into a smile. "Melinda."

Jonathon nodded eagerly. "I'll call her and ask if we can come to tea this afternoon." He'd been meaning to contact her anyway, once he realized he hadn't spotted her once at the festival. *Some friend I am. I didn't even notice.* Then he sighed. He *had* been rather occupied.

"It's Sunday," Mike reminded him. "Won't she be rather busy?"

"Not in the afternoon. But it does mean we'll miss the closing of the festival. The last panel ends at five o'clock."

"Then we'll have a cup of tea with Melinda and Lloyd at four before nipping up to the hall to see the end of the festival."

Jonathon liked that idea. Then another thought occurred to him. "We mustn't forget that book package. We need to trace it. Because either the killer sent it to put Teresa on her guard, or it was sent by someone else wanting to deliver a message."

"Good thinking. I'll go to the post office tomorrow morning and see what I can find out. I did take a look at the postmark, though. It was mailed from Winchester."

Jonathon sighed. "I was hoping it had been posted locally."

Mike gave him a stern glance. "And if it was from a local, surely they'd want to cover their tracks. They'd hardly be likely to walk into the village post office, would they?" He gestured to Jonathon's phone, sitting next to his notepad. "Now give Melinda a call."

Jonathon folded his arms. "I may not have been born here, but I know enough to realize that the vicar's wife is not going to answer calls at this hour on a Sunday morning. Not when there's this little thing called Sunday morning service." He smirked. "I'll text her. She can read that whenever she gets a moment. Although I suspect reading texts when your husband is in the middle of delivering a sermon might be frowned upon by the congregation."

Then he reasoned that Melinda wouldn't care about the frowns of her fellow worshippers. She was a formidable woman.

He glanced at the time. "We'd better get up to the hall. Professor Harcourt's session starts at eleven, and I don't want to miss it." He genuinely liked the elderly gentleman and was looking forward to hearing his tales.

"As long as Fiona hasn't come prepared to give *him* a grilling as well." Mike finished his coffee. "I must admit, she really is the fount of all knowledge when it comes to Teresa."

Jonathon chuckled. "Be careful. So was Kathy Bates's character in *Misery*. And look how that ended up."

"I think, given the situation, we're quite safe. It's not as if she can hobble Teresa, right?"

No, Jonathon thought forlornly. *Someone else has already beaten her to it.*

"THANK YOU for agreeing to this," Mike said as he poured the tea. "We didn't give you a lot of warning."

Melinda waved dismissively. "If I hadn't been baking yesterday, I would have told you to come some other time. But as you can see," she said, gesturing to the table heavily laden with cake and scones, "I was rather busy in the kitchen." She picked up a knife and sliced into the carrot cake. "And I know exactly what to give Jonathon."

Mike laughed. "She knows you too well."

Jonathon took the proffered plate with a smile. "I'm just sorry we can't stay long." Seconds later, Jinx the cat was winding in and out of his ankles, purring loudly.

Mike grinned. "Someone is after your cake."

"And he's not going to get any," Melinda declared. "That cat is already too fat for my liking. No wonder he hasn't caught a mouse in years." She gave Jonathon a wistful glance. "Was the festival wonderful? I'm sorry to have missed it, but I'd double-booked myself. When I checked my diary, I had meetings all Saturday morning, and then I had the baking to do. I was still kicking myself for missing the dinner. That was down to a migraine, unfortunately."

"I did wonder why I hadn't seen you," Jonathon said quietly.

"I thought the two of you might be here to ask for advice," Lloyd said, after sipping his tea. "I am correct, aren't I, in thinking that congratulations are in order?"

"Word gets around fast," Mike commented. "Yes, we got engaged last night."

"Wonderful news," Melinda enthused. "So that's why you're here? To discuss the wedding?" Her eyes glittered. "Or is the purpose of this visit of a more morbid nature? A little sleuthing, perhaps?"

"You really do know us far too well," Jonathon murmured. He removed his notepad from his pocket. "We wondered if you could give us any background information about Teresa Malvain, seeing as she used to live here."

Melinda nodded eagerly. "She arrived in… 1992, I think it was. Of course, *then* she was Teresa Thompson. She and her husband lived in a cottage near the village hall."

"What was she like? Did she get on with her neighbors?" Mike wanted to know.

Melinda gazed at him thoughtfully. "I suspect you already have some idea about that. Well, to be truthful, I—or should I say, we—felt sorry for her husband, Richard."

"Poor man," Lloyd muttered. When Mike stared at him in surprise, he sighed. "My sympathies will always be with a man who is continually on the receiving end of his wife's sharp tongue. And poor Richard was frequently in that position. One wonders how he put up with it for so long." He gazed adoringly across the table at Melinda. "Some of us were far luckier."

Mike loved the fact that they'd been married for so many years and were still plainly in love.

"So what happened?" Jonathon asked.

"Richard lasted until 1998, and then he left her. I think it fair to say that most of the villagers were probably cheering him on in secret. Teresa decided to remain in Merrychurch, and she got a job as the doctor's receptionist."

"That's what her sleuth does in her Summersfield books," Mike exclaimed.

Melinda's thoughtful gaze hadn't altered. "Then maybe that's not the only similarity. Maybe you need to take a closer look at her books."

"Mike has all of them," Jonathon announced with a grin.

Mike coughed. "Yes, but I don't remember *everything* about them. I think the obvious person to ask is Fiona. She knows Teresa's books inside and out."

Melinda stilled. "Fiona McBride? She's helping you? Hmm."

Jonathon met Mike's gaze before leaning forward. "Is there something we should know about her?"

"Well...." Melinda appeared reluctant to continue.

Lloyd gave a dry chuckle. "What my dear wife is trying so hard *not* to say is that Fiona helping you solve Teresa's murder might be more like Dracula helping you work out who is leaving those little holes in people's necks."

Mike blinked. "You mean she should be a suspect? But why?"

Lloyd cleared his throat. "You need to look at what happened to her husband. That might be considered by some to be a motive. Not that I think for one minute that Teresa had as much to do with his death as Fiona would like to believe, but—"

"But coming back to the purpose of your visit—Teresa...." Melinda took a drink of tea before continuing. "I'm going to be blunt."

Jonathon bit his lip. "When are you ever anything but?"

That raised another wry chuckle from Lloyd.

Melinda sighed heavily. "I have no wish to speak ill of the dead, but... she was a gossip. I think you'll find that if you interview the older members of Merrychurch, there will be quite a few who remember what Teresa was like. She may have left the village ten years ago, but some of us have long memories." She glanced at the clock on the mantelpiece. "Now, if you're going to make it to the closing of the festival, you need to drink your tea and eat your cake." Melinda gestured to the plate of sultana scones. "Do try one."

Mike figured that was all they were going to get out of Melinda on the subject. He helped himself to a scone with butter, strawberry jam, and a dollop of thick cream. Jonathon's eyes gleamed, but he said nothing. Mentally, Mike made a note to write a list of Merrychurch's oldest inhabitants. It was beginning to look like their inventory of suspects was about to grow.

"Although...." That twinkle was back in Melinda's eyes. "Should either of you wish to discuss wedding plans, may I offer my services as wedding planner? I could advise you on the service, the reception...."

Lloyd erupted into a fit of coughing, and when Melinda gave him a sharp look, he said in a most apologetic tone, "Sorry. Crumb went down the wrong way." Then he leaned closer to Jonathon and whispered, "Run, dear boy. Run away. Before she really gets started."

It was all Mike could do not to choke on his mouthful of scone.

HEATHER WAS in the middle of her closing speech, in which she thanked Jonathon for opening up the hall for their use, when Mike noticed Graham toward the rear of the ballroom. He nudged Jonathon. "He's looking very official."

Jonathon glanced in Graham's direction. "Hmm. I wonder why he's here."

No sooner had the final round of applause died down than Graham made his way purposefully through the crowd toward Phil McCallister and

Melody Richards. Mike tried not to stare as Graham addressed them, his notepad in his hand. From their expressions, it was obvious that the two authors were not happy. Graham made notes, then gave a quick nod before walking in Mike's direction.

"Well, my first literary festival is at an end." Professor Harcourt joined them, his bag over one shoulder. "I must say I enjoyed it immensely—with one exception, of course." He gazed anxiously at Jonathon. "Was my session all right?"

Jonathon smiled widely. "It was more than all right. It was fascinating. I'm sure everyone liked it."

"Ah, Professor Harcourt. Just the man." Graham reached them, notepad still in hand. "I need to ask what your immediate plans are, sir. I've been asked to speak to a couple of the witnesses, to ask if they could stick around a few days. I realize this may be inconvenient, but—"

"Nonsense, Constable," Professor Harcourt replied affably. "I understand completely. You have a case of murder to investigate. And to be honest, I have no qualms about delaying my departure." He smiled, his eyes twinkling. "I may have difficulty making my wife see it that way, but I'm sure she'll understand too." He lowered his voice. "Although I suspect she'll be happy to have me out from under her feet for a while longer."

Mike inclined his head in Phil and Melody's direction. "I take it they're not so happy to be staying."

Graham snorted. "What gave it away?" Phil's expression was sullen as he stared at them. "The DI called me at home this morning to tell me to make sure any witnesses didn't leave before he had a chance to interview them."

Mike huffed. "As if he's going to learn something that you haven't already."

"Or maybe he thinks the murderer will fall on his or her sword and confess as soon as Gorland so much as looks at them." Jonathon scowled. "Pompous little—" Graham coughed violently, and Jonathon clammed up.

Mike snickered, then gave Professor Harcourt an apologetic glance. "Sorry. There's no love lost between us and DI Gorland."

"I'd surmised that much," the professor said dryly. "It sounds as though things will become more interesting once he's in charge."

"And in the meantime, Jonathon and I have a task to complete." Mike gave a quick glance around before leaning forward and speaking in a low voice. "We're building up a picture of Teresa when she lived here."

Professor Harcourt's gaze narrowed. "I see. You think there might be one or more persons in the village with a motive for murder."

"Right now it's only a hunch," Mike admitted.

Graham snickered. "Except your hunches have a habit of paying off. I'm not gonna tell you *not* to continue, but I will suggest that you get your *task* done before the DI gets here. Because you *know* what's gonna happen as soon as he finds out you're up to your usual tricks." He fixed Mike with an intense gaze. "And I don't have to remind you to share whatever information you manage to glean, do I?"

Jonathon grinned. "We said we'd be good, didn't we?"

Graham raised his eyes heavenward. "I'm gonna regret this, aren't I?"

Mike barely registered Graham's rhetorical question. He was already devising his list of people to approach. And he had a good idea where to start.

"Fancy a visit to Rachel's for a cup of coffee tomorrow morning?" he asked Jonathon in as nonchalant a manner as he could muster.

Jonathon's eyes glittered. "I think that sounds like a great idea."

Coffee, cake—and questions.

CHAPTER ELEVEN

RACHEL MEADOW stared at them as they entered her tea shop. "I'm not sure I want to talk to you two," she declared with obvious mock indignation. She cleared the table that some customers had vacated, placing the teapot, cups, saucers, milk jug, and cake plates onto her tray.

"What have we done now?" Jonathon demanded.

Rachel straightened. "Excuse me? You got engaged on Saturday night. How come I had to find out about it from a customer? I'd have hoped to have gotten it from the horse's mouth at least."

"That's fine. We'll just take our gossip elsewhere," Mike announced with an evil glint in his eyes.

She stilled. "Gossip? Are we talking Teresa Malvain–type gossip?"

Jonathon tried hard to keep a straight face. Mike knew how to push Rachel's buttons. "Possibly," Jonathon said, drawing out the syllables.

Rachel glanced around the tea shop, then pointed to a table in the window. "Sit there. I'll bring out your usual. Coffee, two slices of cake?" And before they could say a word, she'd disappeared through the door that led to the kitchen.

Jonathon sat at the round table. "This is where we were sitting the first time you brought me here." He loved the brasses on their high shelf, the pretty watercolor paintings of local scenes, and the frothy lace curtain that covered the top half of the bow windows.

But the best part was sitting on a tray Rachel carried through the door. A tall, elegant coffeepot, accompanied by two china cups, a white milk jug, and two plates, each barely visible beneath the slab of delicious-looking cake that covered it.

"I swear, you always manage to come in the day I bring in a freshly made walnut cake. How do you do that?" Rachel set the tray down on the white tablecloth.

"What can I say? It's a gift." Mike picked up the plate and sniffed.

Jonathon had to laugh. "I've never seen someone inhale a cake before."

Rachel chuckled. "You leave him alone. It's his favorite." She placed her hands on their shoulders. "This is on the house. Call it my way of saying congratulations. And when I get a moment to breathe, I'll see if Doris has any decent engagement cards in her shop."

"I had no idea he was going to propose," Mike explained. Then he added with a smile, "Although to be fair, Jonathon had no idea he was going to propose that night either."

There was no way Jonathon could argue with that.

She bent down, her head between theirs. "Now, about this gossip…," she said conspiratorially.

Jonathon burst into laughter. "Grab a chair and join us. It's not as if we didn't come here with the express purpose of picking your brains anyway."

"Oh, goodie." Rachel pulled up another chair and sat facing them. "Okay. The word on the grapevine is, it's murder. Someone induced anaphylactic shock."

Jonathon was seriously impressed. "Wow. Your grapevine is amazing."

She preened. "Only the best gossip reaches these ears. So is that right?"

"Only if this goes no further," Mike advised. Then he rolled his eyes. "Who am I kidding? You probably get to hear more than we ever do."

Rachel's expression grew more somber. "I don't share what you tell me. You know that."

Jonathon reached over and squeezed her hand. "We do. So… yes. Someone made sure she ingested peanut oil."

"To which she was highly allergic, according to the internet." She frowned. "Does that mean you're looking for suspects in the village?"

Jonathon had been giving the matter some careful thought. "We want to know if there's anyone in particular from her past in Merrychurch who might have reason to want her dead. Because the word reaching our ears is that Teresa—"

"Pissed off a lot of people," Mike said, finishing his sentence. He aimed a grin in Jonathon's direction. "You're too much of a gentleman to say 'pissed off.' I, however, am not."

Rachel's frown deepened. "Well, a few things come to mind. She was certainly adept at putting people's backs up. But whether what she did was sufficient reason for them killing her, that's another matter."

"Tell us and let us decide." Jonathon got out his pen and flipped open the notepad.

"Okay," she said slowly. "You might want to look at the Bradings, to start with."

Mike gave her an inquiring glance. "The name isn't familiar."

"Maybe they're before your time. The Bradings were a family who moved into the village in 2013, and they rented Teresa's former cottage. She'd moved to London years before, but she'd held on to the house. Well… the Bradings weren't that wealthy. They had a little girl, Sophie, who had some sort of debilitating disease, and the doctors were doing lots of tests, trying to cure her." Rachel's face tightened. "She was six."

"Aw, the poor kid." Mike poured the coffee.

Rachel sniffed. "Anyway, they'd been in the house maybe a year or more when Teresa put the rent up. I mean, it skyrocketed. She wasn't alone, by any means—house prices rose dramatically in 2015, especially for properties in desirable areas." Rachel gestured to the window. "Welcome to Merrychurch, one of the most desirable villages in the UK, apparently. But back to my story. Teresa obviously felt she could get more for the place, and although it was a struggle, Mr. and Mrs. Brading paid the increase, because they wanted to stay here. I don't blame them. It's a great place to bring up kids."

"What happened?" Jonathon forked off a piece of carrot cake.

"Teresa put up the rent again. What with the cost of Sophie's treatment, which was private because they couldn't find an NHS specialist for her, and the hefty rent increases, the Bradings had to move. They just couldn't afford to live there anymore. So at the beginning of 2016, they left. Not long after that, Teresa sold the house for a tidy sum." Rachel's face fell. "Then it became obvious why she'd put the rent up. She wanted her tenants out of there so she could sell it when the market price was at its highest. But they had a lease, so she found a way to make them want to leave."

"But did the terms of the lease allow her to do that? Hike up the rent?" Mike appeared horrified.

Rachel nodded. "Mrs. Brading told me the lease made provision for rent increases. Very cleverly, it made no mention of how high the rent might possibly go."

Jonathon suddenly had a sinking feeling in his stomach. "What happened to Sophie?" When Rachel's eyes glistened, he knew. "She died, didn't she?"

Another nod. "Not long after they'd left. Now, no one can say that Teresa caused Sophie's death, but…."

"But her parents might think otherwise," Jonathon concluded. "Especially if they're distraught and looking for someone to blame." He cocked his head to one side. "Where did they end up?"

"They found a place in Fareham, which was closer to the hospital. There was no money left for treatment, although they tried crowd-funding for a while—not with much success, I might add." Rachel wiped her eyes. "Poor Sophie. Her death really knocked the stuffing out of them." Her eyes widened. "Oh God. Rebecca…."

"Who's Rebecca?" Mike inquired.

"Sophie's older sister. She'd be about eighteen now."

"What about her?"

Rachel took a deep breath. "I saw her only a few weeks ago in the village. She's got a job, here in Merrychurch. She's a cleaner at the Cedars, that residential home on the road to Lower Pinton." She stared at them, aghast. "You don't think she could've had something to do with Teresa's death, do you? I mean, she adored Sophie. We all did."

"As to whether she had something to do with it, that will depend entirely on whether she was in the pub Friday night." Mike frowned. "And although I was run off my feet, I don't recall seeing an eighteen-year-old girl at the bar, but—"

"Which means nothing," Jonathon interjected. "She might have felt she was too conspicuous, in which case it would have been easier to ask someone to help her."

Mike widened his eyes. "Anyone 'helping' her, as you put it, would be guilty of murder. Who would willingly do that, knowing what the charge would be if they were caught?"

Jonathon met his gaze. "Someone who knew the family. Someone who felt as strongly about Sophie's death as she did."

Rachel's breathing hitched. "Jonathon's right. Rebecca had a lot of friends, and they're still in the village. And like I said, everyone adored Sophie. That child simply… drew people to her. She might have been seriously ill, but she was a ray of sunshine around here. So yes, while Rebecca might not have been in the pub that night—and you'll need to check that out—someone could've been there on her behalf."

"Then she goes on the list until we can prove she had nothing to do with it." Jonathon shivered. "I didn't expect anything like that was lurking in Teresa's past." Although it did fit in with what he'd learned about her thus far. He had to wonder, was there more to come?

"Thank you, dear." The two old ladies who'd been seated on the other side of the tea shop got up from their table and walked sedately toward the door, waving cheerily.

"Thank you!" Rachel called out. When the door shut behind them, leaving only the three of them in the shop, she stood. "Let me clear away their cups, and then we can talk some more."

Jonathon waited until Rachel was in the kitchen before letting out a sigh. "This is awful. That poor family." He pushed his plate away. "I think I've lost my appetite. And if I were Rebecca, I wouldn't think twice about putting something in Teresa's coffee. Maybe not with the idea of killing her, but possibly with a view to making her really ill."

"Except that theory doesn't hold water, not when you take into account the missing EpiPens. If they only wanted her to be ill, they wouldn't have stolen them."

Jonathon frowned. "I see what you mean. The two things have to be connected."

"We need to find Rebecca, even if it's just to eliminate her from our list of suspects."

"And if she did do something? She's eighteen." Jonathon's heart ached for her. He was an only child, but that didn't mean he couldn't empathize with her.

"And eighteen-year-olds have been known to commit murder, especially where family is involved."

"I've been thinking," Rachel said as she approached their table and sat down. "There are other examples of people who might bear Teresa a grudge, but I'm not sure it would be a motive to kill her."

"Well, let's hear about them."

"You might want to consider the Merrychurch Reading Club."

Mike blinked. "Is there such a thing?"

Rachel smiled. "It consists of eight or nine ladies who meet up once a month to discuss a book. They did ask me to join them, but hey, since when do I have time to read?"

"So what happened with the ladies?" Jonathon wanted to know.

"They asked Teresa to speak to them, as a former resident. You know, talk about her books, her writing, her career. The only reason they approached her was because she used to live here."

"Let me guess." Mike snorted. "She told them where they could put their invitation."

"Not quite," Rachel said with a wry grin. "She sent a frosty reply—or rather, her PA did. She didn't bother to reply personally."

"Yeah, that sounds about right." Mike shook his head. "Which only goes to confirm my impressions of her. But you're right. I can't see some little old lady slipping peanut oil into her coffee simply because she couldn't be bothered to answer their letter."

"Are there others?" Jonathon asked.

Rachel nodded. "Some of her former neighbors were in London at Foyles for a book signing. Teresa was one of the authors. But when they got to see her and asked how she was doing, she blanked them.

One of them told me, 'It was like we were dirt on her shoe.'"

Jonathon let out a low growl. "Okay, it's official. Teresa Malvain was a bitch, and I'm surprised no one killed her before this."

Rachel coughed. "Be careful where you say that. After all, *you* were in the pub that night, weren't you?"

Mike snickered. "And I can see John Gorland grinning in delight at the idea of you being a suspect."

They had a point. "Okay, I'll keep my thoughts to myself."

"And in the meantime, I'll keep thinking about anyone else who should be on your list." Rachel glanced at Jonathon's notepad, her eyes twinkling. "Although you might need a bigger one of those."

The way things were shaping up, Jonathon wouldn't be the least bit surprised.

CHAPTER TWELVE

THE MANOR house had been restored to its usual state, albeit with Ben grumbling about people walking all over his precious gardens. Janet, the housekeeper, was clearly delighted to have things back to normal and even more pleased at Jonathon's news of the engagement.

"So will Mr. Tattersall be moving in here after the wedding? Will he continue to run the pub?" Janet asked as she poured Jonathon's coffee Monday morning. Mike had stayed the night at the pub. Jonathon loved the fact that they weren't in each other's pockets all the time, but Janet's questions did raise an interesting point.

Things were bound to change after the wedding.

"I'll be honest—we haven't discussed that yet." But maybe it was time they did.

Of course, the first order of business would be to inform his father, but Jonathon wanted to wait a while longer. In order for that conversation to take place, a couple of vital conversations had to happen first.

No time like the present.

Jonathon got out his phone and called Mike. "Good morning."

"It is now." Mike's voice stirred Jonathon's memory, and suddenly he was thinking of a warm bed and an even warmer, lean body curled around him. "Miss me?" Mike asked gruffly.

"You know I did." Jonathon pushed aside the tempting thoughts, not that it took much to have his body reacting. Mike's voice was enough. "Listen, I wanted to run something by you. I'd like to invite Ruth and Clare for the weekend."

There was a brief pause. "You're up to something. Is this anything to do with your father? Because I thought we were past trying to placate dear old dad."

"Well, kind of…. But it's more for our benefit. I don't want to discuss this over the phone. We can talk about it later." The idea had come to him in the early hours, and he couldn't wait to share it with Mike. It was of vital importance, however, that he saw Mike's reaction to the idea.

We need to be together on this.

"So what's next? Bear in mind that Gorland could arrive at any minute, and we don't want to be seen treading on his toes, now do we?"

Jonathon snickered. "Like I care." Except he didn't want to jeopardize Graham's position. "But something occurred to me. Rachel said Rebecca was working at the Cedars, and that got me thinking. Who else do we know who was probably around when Teresa lived in Merrychurch?"

He could hear the grin in Mike's voice. "Lily Rossiter."

"Exactly. She'd love to have visitors, and she'd especially love to help us with another case. Plus, we might get to see Rebecca, thus killing two birds with one stone."

"Great idea, but you might want to call them first, to make sure Lily is up for a couple of visitors. Ninety-year-old ladies do have off days, y'know."

Good thinking. "I'll call them now. As soon as I've finished my coffee."

"Well, of course. Have to get your priorities right, don't you? Just keep me informed. If it's a go, I'll come pick you up." Another pause. "I really did miss you last night. I know that doesn't make sense, not when we see each other as much as we do, but—"

"But now you're starting to realize that getting married means a more permanent arrangement, and you want it to start as soon as possible," Jonathon ventured, finally putting into words what had been running through his mind all morning.

"Yes. You nailed it." Mike's voice softened. "In case I haven't already mentioned it, I can't wait to marry you, Mr. de Mountford."

"The feeling is entirely mutual, Mr. Tattersall." Jonathon smiled. "But now get off the phone so I can finish my coffee." And with that, he disconnected the call, still smiling.

Life was definitely good.

LILY GREETED them warmly, not rising from her chair but taking their hands in hers, an open book in her lap. "It is so good to see you again." She gestured to her surroundings. "You find me in my usual habitat, contemplating the garden, my books beside me." Her blue eyes twinkled. "And speaking of books, I hear the first Merrychurch Literary Festival knocked 'em dead. Literally." Lily peered at them over her glasses. "Death is never far behind you two, is it?"

Mike leaned forward, his forearms resting on his knees. "Which is why we're here."

"Not more codes to break, surely." Lily's face wrinkled into a smile.

"Not this time." Jonathon mimicked Mike's body language. "Actually, we're here to find out what you know about Teresa Malvain. Specifically when she was a Merrychurch resident."

Lily relaxed against the soft cushions at her back. "Ahh. Our inquisitive doctor's receptionist. She always was far too fond of putting her nose into other people's business. The problem, however, was that she had no qualms about sharing what she had learned."

Mike blinked. "Er.... Surely that wasn't allowed? Confidentiality and all that."

"Well, yes, I'm sure most GP's receptionists would abide by that basic rule, but apparently not Teresa. The trouble was, there were people in the village who lapped up whatever she told them. And, unfortunately, there were consequences. Not for her, but for the patients. One patient in particular."

Mike didn't have to look at Jonathon to know the notepad and pen had come out. "What happened?"

Lily removed her glasses and placed them carefully in their case. "Harold Tenby. A lovely, dear man. He married well, and they complemented each other. A very happy marriage. Elaine doted on him, and he adored her."

"I'm guessing something went wrong." Jonathon sat with his pen poised.

Lily nodded. "Harold went away on a business trip that he'd organized for himself and his employees. It was little more than an excuse to enjoy themselves in foreign climes. A very exotic location, excessive eating, lots of alcohol… and the latter proved to be his undoing. Not long after he'd returned, rumors began circulating in the village, implying that Harold had caught something nasty while he'd been out there. And yes, we are talking something nasty of the sexual variety."

"He had an affair?" From Lily's description, Harold didn't seem to be the type.

"Hardly that. From what he told me, it was one moment of drunkenness at a party. Harold never could hold his liquor. Except as it turned out, he wasn't entirely to blame."

"He told you what had happened?" Jonathon scribbled down notes.

Lily sighed. "He was the one who arranged all my insurance, and from that initial meeting, we became good friends. When the rumors first started making their rounds, he came to me, distraught. What made it worse was that people in the village really believed he could have an affair. If ever a man was deeply in love with his wife, it was Harold. He had no recollection of the night, but the sexually transmitted disease was evidence of his transgression."

"Let me guess. Teresa started the rumors." Mike glanced at Jonathon. Judging by his grimace, he was finding the whole thing as distasteful as Mike.

"Oh, no one ever came out and said Teresa had been the one to tell them, but we all knew. How else would they have found out? That woman was such a gossip. And of course, eventually the rumors reached Elaine's ears."

"He hadn't told her about the STI?" Mike was horrified. "But what if he'd passed it on to her?"

"Harold's intention had been to take his medication and let the infection clear up before resuming marital relations." Lily shook her head sadly. "His own profound feelings of guilt made that easier. He couldn't believe he'd let himself get into such a predicament."

"What did Elaine do when she found out?"

"She didn't view it as a one-time aberration, but as evidence that Harold had been, and was still being, unfaithful, no matter how strongly he denied it. She was the kind of woman who neither forgave nor forgot, and she left him. Unfortunately, the house and the business were in her name, for tax reasons. So perhaps it is more appropriate to say Harold was asked to leave."

"Well, even if it was a one-off, he did have sex with someone else," Jonathon reasoned.

Lily gazed at him thoughtfully. "Imagine for a moment a boss who is fairly straitlaced. He doesn't drink to excess. Then his employees find themselves on a trip with him where the alcohol is flowing freely, and yet still he doesn't relax enough to their satisfaction, because unlike them, he doesn't spend his evenings at the bar, drinking cocktails until they throw him out. So they decide to play a prank. It starts harmlessly enough with an invitation to have a drink with them. Only then, the game changes. 'What if we spike his drink? I wonder what he'll do?'"

Mike gaped. "They didn't."

"Oh, they did. And they admitted as much the following morning, along with showing him the videos they'd taken on their phones of him dancing like a lunatic with a young woman wearing very little. Presumably the same young woman who... yes, well. Harold, of course, didn't remember any of this. His employees found it all highly amusing, until Harold pointed out that they had, in fact, drugged him, and as such he had grounds to report them to the police. That soon changed their tune."

"What happened to Harold?" Mike asked quietly. If *he'd* been in Harold's shoes, he wouldn't have been so lenient.

"A friend took him in and gave him a room. He found a job, and little by little he got his life back. But he was never the same—a shell of a man, really. His life had been ruined."

Jonathon gazed at her with obvious interest. "The friend who helped him... that was you, wasn't it?"

Lily gave him a gentle smile. "You're a very perceptive young man. Mike is a lucky fellow."

"I think so too." Mike placed his hand on Jonathon's knee.

Lily glanced down, and her smile grew wider. "Oh. Oh, my dears. Do I take it there have been developments?"

"You don't miss much, do you, Lily?" Mike took Jonathon's hand in his.

She let out a contented sigh. "I wish you both every happiness."

"Where is Harold now?" Jonathon asked.

"When I moved into the Cedars, I intended to sell my house, but instead Harold lives there. He pays rent, of course, but nothing like what a rental agency would charge him. And he looks after the place for me." Lily met Mike's gaze. "I know what you're wondering. Is he the type of person who might seek revenge on the woman who blighted his life?"

"Well, is he?"

Lily clasped her wrinkled hands in her lap, staring at them. "The Harold I knew would not have sought revenge. The man he became? That is another matter."

"You know we'll have to talk to him, don't you?" Mike said softly. "And if we don't, the police certainly will, once they start putting together their own list of suspects."

Lily sighed heavily. "Jonathon, could I borrow your notepad and pen for a moment?"

"Of course." He handed them to her, and she wrote carefully in an elegant script. Then she handed them back. Jonathon peered at the page, then met Mike's gaze. "Well, we know where to find him."

Mike reached across and laid his hand over hers. "Thank you."

She nodded. "Be kind to him?"

"Of course." He released her hands and got up. "We'll let you know what we discover."

"I shall be praying that you exonerate him." When Jonathon leaned in and kissed her cheek, she flushed. "I hope you realize I expect an invitation to the wedding."

Jonathon smiled. "I hope *you* realize we both want you there."

After saying their goodbyes, Mike headed back to the reception desk, with Jonathon at his side. The receptionist was in the middle of a phone call, so they waited. When she was done, Mike gave his brightest smile.

"I was wondering if Rebecca Brading is working today. I understand she cleans here."

The woman behind the desk frowned. "Rebecca? Why on earth should you want to speak with one of our cleaners?"

"Her name came up in conversation, and we'd like to talk to her, if that's possible," Mike said smoothly.

The receptionist huffed. "Well, you can't talk to her if she's working. Let me check her hours." Then she looked over Mike's shoulder and smiled. "You're in luck. She *is* in today, but it looks like she's just finished. That's Rebecca on her way out the door."

Without waiting to thank her, Mike quickly went to the door, and Jonathon followed. A young woman was walking away from them.

"Rebecca Brading?" Mike called out.

She paused and turned. When she saw them, her eyes widened and she broke into a run.

"Wait!" Mike yelled, but she picked up speed.

"Stay here. I'll catch her." Jonathon sprinted after her, leaving Mike by the steps.

Why the hell did she run away like that? Because in Mike's book, that usually pointed to one thing only.

Guilt.

Chapter Thirteen

"Stop!" Jonathon called out as he got closer. "We just want to talk to you!"

Rebecca showed no signs of slowing as she went through the gates that marked the Cedar's boundaries, her long hair swaying. Jonathon picked up speed, wishing he was fitter. On impulse, he yelled, "We want to talk to you about Sophie!"

Rebecca came to an abrupt halt, turning to face him, panting visibly. "I know who you are. I know who he is. You're lying. Why would you want to talk about my sister?" She bent over, her hands on her knees, obviously fighting to get her breath back. "God, I'm out of shape."

"That makes two of us," Jonathon said as he cautiously approached her. He held up his hands as he got closer. "Please. Don't run off. We only want to talk. It's not like we're the police, right?"

"He was a copper." Rebecca's eyes gleamed with suspicion.

"Yes, but he's not now. If you've spent any time in the village, you know he runs the pub." Jonathon lowered his hands. "Please, Rebecca. A chat, that's all."

She glanced around her at the country lane. "Here?"

Jonathon thought quickly. "How about at the tea shop? Let us buy you a cup of tea." He smiled. "I don't know about you, but after that mad dash, I need one."

She tilted her head to one side. "You don't look like a lord of the manor."

"And how does a lord of the manor look, in your experience?"

Her lips twitched. "Like a bit of a stuffed shirt."

Jonathon chuckled. "Then I'm glad I don't. But do I look like someone you can trust? Because I'm asking you to walk back to the car park with me, and then we'll drive to the tea shop, where we can talk in comfort."

Rebecca bit her lip, tossing her hair over her shoulders. "I guess I can. I haven't heard anything dodgy about you." She walked over to him, slowly. "Okay. I'll go with you. As long as we're not gonna walk into the tea shop to find that constable waiting for us."

Jonathon crossed his heart. "I promise." He figured Graham would be too busy dealing with Gorland to be having tea and cake at Rachel's. At least, he hoped so. Jonathon gestured to the gateposts, and she nodded. They walked up the long, curved driveway to where Mike was still standing at the front steps.

Mike gave Rebecca an inquiring glance. "Why did you run like that?"

"Not here," Jonathon remonstrated. "We're going to Rachel's for tea."

Mike arched his eyebrows, then pulled his car keys from his pocket. Rebecca followed them to the 4x4, and minutes later they were on their way.

Jonathon was quiet as they drove toward the heart of the village. He had to admit, running like that wasn't the action of an innocent person, and he was intrigued to discover her motivation.

Because it really didn't look good.

MIKE POURED the tea, waiting until Rachel had left them to deal with another customer. "Now," he said as he passed Rebecca a cup, "tell us why you ran like that."

When she said nothing, Jonathon passed her a slice of cake. "Here. This is really good."

Rebecca tried a forkful, rolling her eyes. "Oh God. This is gorgeous." She took another mouthful, then regarded Mike. "You came to the Cedars to find me. Why?"

Mike made a mental note. Never mind torture for getting people to talk. What was obviously needed was cake. "Actually, we were there to see a friend of ours, Lily Rossiter."

Rebecca's face brightened instantly. "Aw. She's lovely. I always like it when I get to clean her room. She's really cheerful, and she talks to me." Her forehead furrowed. "Then why did you say my name like that, if you were there to see Lily?"

"A friend was telling us about Sophie," Jonathon said in a low voice. "We're really sorry. She sounds like she was a wonderful little girl."

"She was." Rebecca's expression tightened. She jerked her head in Mike's direction. "You think I had something to do with that writer's death, don't you? Because of Sophie?"

Mike shrugged. "It was a possibility that we had to check out." He took a close look at her. He didn't recall seeing her in the pub, either Friday night or at any other time.

"It wasn't me." She bit her lip. "I wasn't even at that dinner."

Jonathon opened his mouth to say something, but Mike flashed him a glance. "Then you know she had an allergic reaction." Rebecca was clearly under the impression that Teresa had eaten nuts of some kind during the meal, and he didn't want to correct her. He wanted to see where this led.

Rebecca nodded. "But it wasn't me," she insisted again. "So you're talking to the wrong person. And besides, it could've been an accident. A mistake."

Jonathon frowned. "What could have been an accident?"

Rebecca took another mouthful of carrot cake, ignoring him.

Obviously the cake wasn't working anymore.

Mike cut into his slice of Battenberg, relishing the thick layer of pale yellow marzipan that covered it. Marzipan was a favorite of his and always the first part of the Christmas cake to be eaten. When he was little, his mum used to make a fantastic Christmas cake, although she made a separate smaller version for his dad, who couldn't stand the taste of ground almonds.

Ground almonds....

Mike stared at Rebecca. "Okay, so you weren't at the dinner. But you know someone who was."

She jerked her head up, then froze.

Mike nodded slowly. "So who did you get to sprinkle the ground almonds on Teresa's cheesecake?"

This time there was no mistaking the flash of fear in her wide brown eyes.

Jonathon gaped. "But—"

Mike plowed ahead. "That was the plan, wasn't it? To introduce nuts into her food?"

Rebecca swallowed. "We didn't know it would kill her, honest. We just thought it would make her really ill."

"But you knew she was allergic to nuts," Jonathon confirmed. "What did you think would happen?"

"That she'd get sick!" Rebecca yelled.

A cup clattered into a saucer. Mike looked over to where Rachel stood with a customer, both staring in their direction. Then the lady cleared her throat and resumed her quiet conversation. Rachel gave them a sympathetic glance.

Rebecca took a deep breath. "Sorry about that." She took a few more seconds to breathe deeply. "My mum is allergic to penicillin. I've seen what she's like when she's taken it by accident. She gets a rash and a temperature, and she stays in bed for a few days."

"And that's what you thought would happen to Teresa?" Jonathon asked.

Mike sighed inwardly. Whatever else Rebecca—and her unknown accomplice—were guilty of, it wasn't murder. He was glad. He hated to think of her young life ruined. Then he reasoned that whatever the outcome, they had knowingly given her something that might cause her death, even if they hadn't intended to kill her.

"Who's we?" he asked softly. When she didn't reply, Mike put down his fork, reached across, and took her hand. "Rebecca. It's all right." It wasn't, of course, but that would be up to the police to decide.

She shook her head, tears spilling over her cheeks. "No, it's not. We killed her."

Jonathon put his hand on her back. "You didn't." She stared at him, wiping her eyes. He sighed. "Yes, Teresa died of anaphylactic shock, but it was the result of something she ingested in the pub. Hours after the meal."

"And besides, I think she'd have noticed something as obvious as ground almonds, don't you?" Mike added. "She was very careful when it came to her food."

She frowned. "But…."

"Whomever you got to add the nuts… they put them on the wrong plate," Jonathon announced. "Our friend Heather got them instead."

Her frown deepened, and then she stared at them with wide eyes. "Really?"

Mike nodded. "So I'm guessing you know someone who was working on the catering team." He gave her an inquiring gaze. "One of the waiters?"

The sharp hitch in her breathing told him all he needed to know. Then she sagged into her chair. "My boyfriend, Sam. Ever since we learned she'd died, he's been waiting for a knock on the door. We were sure it was the almonds that had killed her." That flash of fear was back. "We… we can't be done for that, can we?"

Mike had to be honest. "The police might view it as attempted murder, but once you explain that you thought it would cause a reaction like your mum's, they might be lenient. You just need to be honest with them."

"Go to the police station with Sam," Jonathon suggested. "Come clean right away. If you do need a barrister, I'll find one for you. A good one." He smiled. "I have some connections that might come in useful."

"But be prepared for what might happen," Mike warned her. "Will Sam go along with this?"

"Yeah. He only did it because he loves me." Rebecca sighed. "We were crazy to think we'd get away with it." Her breathing grew more even. "I'm glad it's out in the open. These last few days have been really bad."

Jonathon patted her on the back. "Now drink your tea. Then we'll find Sam."

She nodded, picking up her cup and drinking deeply from it.

Mike poured himself a second cup. At least they could cross Rebecca off the list. The only thing was, he had a feeling there would soon be more names to take her place.

"MIKE!"

"Hang on a sec," Mike called out from under the bar. "There's a problem with this barrel. The line is clogged."

"Then it will have to wait. We've got a visitor."

Something in Jonathon's tone gave him pause. "I know who it is, don't I?"

"Oh yes."

Mike got to his feet and grabbed a rag to wipe his hands. Seconds later, Detective Inspector John Gorland swaggered into the pub, wearing a dark gray suit and a sneer.

Maybe that's his permanent expression.

Mike gave Gorland a broad smile that he knew would aggravate him. "Good afternoon, John. How nice to have you back in our neck of the woods." Behind Gorland, Jonathon covered his mouth quickly, his shoulders shaking.

"You've been putting your nose in police business again, haven't you?" Gorland's eyes glinted. "And don't bother denying it. I was at the police station just now when a pair of teenagers walked in, saying they'd been advised to pay us a visit. By you." He narrowed his gaze. "And Mr. de Mountford. Which reminds me. Billings tells me congratulations are in order." His sneer was still in place. "Congratulations."

"Does the Met have to send you on another sensitivity course or LGBT awareness training session?" Mike reached for his phone. "Because I think I'll call them and recommend exactly that. You obviously need it."

The sneer disappeared, to be replaced by a scowl. "Stay out of this investigation. You were lucky the first time, and you happened to be in the right place at the right time with the last one, but not on this occasion. If I find out you've been interfering with police business, I'll throw the book at you."

Whatever else he'd been about to say was lost when Professor Harcourt entered the bar. "I'm sorry to disturb you, but the door was open, so I—" He stared at Gorland, who reacted with obvious surprise.

"Professor Harcourt, I didn't realize you were still in the village."

The professor smiled pleasantly. "I'm in no hurry to go back to London. I'm staying at a B and B in the village. Besides, since I retired, I'm a man of leisure, and my wife is always pleased to get rid of me for a while. Plus, I've had a few ideas about this case that I wanted to share with these two." He gave Mike a cheerful nod.

Gorland cleared his throat. "I am of course aware of your reputation, sir. You've worked on some important cases. Not to mention the fact that the commissioner speaks highly of you. But... please remember this is police business, and that Mr. Tattersall and Mr. de Mountford are only civilians, when all is said and done."

Professor Harcourt nodded sagely. "And right now I'm here to talk about books."

Gorland blinked. "Books?"

"Why, yes. The three of us are fans of the late Teresa Malvain." Professor Harcourt gave him a polite smile. "Think of this as an impromptu book lovers' meeting."

Mike stifled a snicker. *Like Gorland will swallow that one.*

"I see." Gorland cleared his throat. "I'll be seeing you, *Mr.* Tattersall." And with that, he strode out of the pub.

Jonathon applauded. "We've never got rid of him so fast. Thank you."

Professor Harcourt rolled his eyes. "I know the type. I'm so glad I don't have to deal with all that these days. They only call me in now and again when a case foxes them, or if I get asked to lecture. Nowadays my garden claims most of my time."

"Do you miss it?" Jonathon asked.

He sighed. "At times. It was a fascinating career."

Mike was curious. "Are you really a fan of her books?"

Professor Harcourt's eyes gleamed. "I have all of them. Reading murder mysteries might seem like a busman's holiday, but that's how I relax." He took a seat at the bar. "I don't suppose I could have a coffee before you open?"

"No problem." Mike got on with setting up the machine.

"Me too," Jonathon added.

Mike chuckled. "I'd taken it for granted that I would be making one for you too. You haven't had nearly enough caffeine today."

Jonathon laughed. "It's scary how well he knows me." He paused. "Professor, can I ask you a question? It's about something Teresa said at the dinner."

"Please, ask away."

"Teresa said she'd only once planned to write a book based exactly on a real-life case. Then she said to you, 'Isn't that right, professor?' What was the book she was talking about?"

"My word, what an excellent memory you have."

Mike turned to face them, carrying two cups. "Try living with him," he muttered. "He never forgets anything."

Professor Harcourt took a sip of coffee. "She knew from our meeting that I was a fan of her writing. Maybe she assumed I was a really big fan and knew the ins and outs of everything, like Fiona McBride.

I swear she probably knows everything about Teresa, right down to the frequency of her bowel movements." His eyes twinkled. "Pardon me. That remark was uncalled for."

"But quite apt, coming from a pathologist." Mike stilled. "You know what? Maybe we should follow Melinda's advice."

"Which particular bit?" Jonathon said with a wry smile.

"She said maybe we should read Teresa's books. Teresa kept alluding to Merrychurch when she was talking about them. About why murder mysteries work well in village settings." Mike stroked his beard thoughtfully. "So here's an idea. What if one or more of Teresa's books is based on someone in the village? She promised to answer all questions, remember. And she said she was basically lazy. So what if—"

"What if she wrote a book loosely based on something that really happened in the village?" Jonathon's voice cracked with excitement. "Obviously not a real murder, because we'd all know about it. But a death that could have been murder."

Mike nodded eagerly. "And maybe someone in the village got nervous. All this attention on her Summersfield books…."

Professor Harcourt arched his bushy eyebrows. "You think one of your neighbors might be a murderer?"

Jonathon met Mike's gaze. "It wouldn't be the first time."

"But there are twenty books in the series," the professor exclaimed. "I can't remember the plots of all of them." He regarded Mike closely. "Do you have her books here?"

Mike nodded. "They're in a bookcase on the landing."

Jonathon blinked. "I never noticed them."

Mike grinned. "Some detective *you* are."

"Then here is what I propose we do," Professor Harcourt continued. "We divide up the books between us, and we read them."

"Now?" Mike inquired.

"As soon as possible. And I also suggest that we note the bare bones of each plot. Then we get together in a day or two and compare notes."

"Then what?" Mike didn't see where this would take them. Having lived slightly less than two years in Merrychurch, his knowledge of the village wasn't sufficient for him to know which plots to investigate.

"Then we take our notes to someone who will be able to point us in the right direction," Jonathon announced triumphantly.

The light dawned. "Melinda Talbot." Mike smiled. If anyone would know which books were thinly disguised portrayals of real-life events, it would be Melinda.

Professor Harcourt cleared his throat, and Mike realized he'd zoned out. The professor gave him a patient smile. "You'd better go get those books, Mike. We have a lot of reading to do."

He had a point.

As Mike headed for the door that led to the staircase, he caught Jonathon's chuckle. "I wonder if Abi would like a few more shifts this week."

CHAPTER FOURTEEN

HIS SKIN still beaded with water, Mike pushed open the door to Jonathon's bedroom and entered. To his amusement, Jonathon was sitting in exactly the same position as he had been before Mike's shower: on the bed, pillows stuffed behind him, legs bent, and peering at a book.

"Do you know whodunit yet?"

Jonathon did a good impression of leaping out of his skin. "I had no clue you'd come into the room." He picked up a bookmark and placed it between the pages.

"Must be an engrossing read." Mike sat on the edge of the bed and bent over to remove the silicone prosthesis from what remained of his foot. A thought occurred to him. "This has never bothered you, has it?"

Jonathon shifted across the bed until he was kneeling up behind Mike. He put his arms around Mike's shoulders and kissed the top of his head. "Not once."

Maybe that was part and parcel of why Jonathon had been unlike any man Mike had met since he'd left the police force. The few guys Mike had hooked up

with had clearly found his disfigurement unpleasant.
Jonathon hadn't batted an eyelid. He hadn't ignored
it either. The first time during lovemaking when he'd
gently raised Mike's leg to tenderly kiss him there,
Mike had teared up.

"Love you," he said quietly.

Jonathon's warm breath tickled his ear. "That's
why you're marrying me, silly." Then he shifted
once more, and Mike found himself on his back,
Jonathon astride him, leaning over to kiss him again
and again.

Jonathon chuckled. "Your beard is tickling me."

"I'll shave it off," Mike said emphatically.
"Tomorrow."

Jonathon reared upright, his eyes blazing. "Don't
you dare. That would be cause for divorce before
we're even married." He stroked Mike's beard. "I like
it. Especially when you rub it over my—"

Mike covered Jonathon's mouth with his hand.
"Before you get carried away, how about you share
whatever it is you wanted to run by me?" He removed
his hand.

Jonathon climbed off and lay down on the bed
beside him, his hand making slow circles on Mike's
belly, not venturing down as far as the towel that still
covered him. "You remember we talked about having
children?"

"Sure." Then he put two and two together. "Does
this have anything to do with inviting Ruth and Clare
to stay?"

Jonathon beamed. "I hope our kids inherit your
brains. Yes, sweetheart." He paused, his gaze locked

on Mike's. "How would you feel if we asked Ruth to be our surrogate?"

It took a moment for the implications to fully sink in. "Your father suggests you marry Ruth, because she's of good breeding stock, to put it plainly. So how could he complain if she's our surrogate? Jonathon, you are a genius."

"Hang on a minute," Jonathon said, laughing. "She hasn't agreed yet."

"Do you think she will?" Mike didn't want to consider rejection.

"She might—if we return the favor."

"I don't understand."

Jonathon smiled. "She and Clare want children too. So here's my plan. I donate sperm so she can carry our baby—then at a later date, *you* donate sperm so Clare can have *their* baby." His eyes shone. "That way, everyone is happy. Including my father."

Excitement bubbled up from deep inside him. "Call them. Now. Ask them to come here for the weekend."

Jonathon laughed, a joyous sound that filled the room. "You really like this idea, don't you?"

"Like it? I love it. I only hope they do too."

"I'll call them in the morning. I don't think they'll mind a visit. They love coming here. But we won't mention the reason for the invitation until they get here. Besides...." Jonathon grinned. "I have more pressing things on my mind right now."

"Such as?"

Jonathon slid his hand down Mike's belly. "Discovering what you're hiding under this towel."

"Then maybe you should take a look." Mike caught his breath as Jonathon slowly unfastened the towel.

"Aw, for me? You shouldn't have."

JONATHON YAWNED, his hand covering his mouth. After two days of skimming through seven murder mysteries, he'd reached breakpoint. "I don't care if I never read another one of these as long as I live." He rubbed his eyes. "Who knew reading could make you so tired?"

"Have you noted the plot?" Mike asked from the other end of the couch. Jonathon had insisted on putting some space between them, especially after the first morning's reading, when Mike had gotten ideas about what comprised a break—and what activities could occupy said break.

Two hours later....

JONATHON NODDED, stifling another yawn. "I hope some of these strike a chord with Melinda. I'd hate to think we'd spent all this time reading these books without anything to show for it." He glanced across at Mike. "It was probably easier for you. After all, you've already read them at least once." He grinned and pointed to the heap of novels on the coffee table. "How many times have you read these?"

"I refuse to answer that question on the grounds that I might incriminate myself." Mike put down the book he'd been reading. "Okay. That was my last one."

"Mine too." Jonathon looked at the clock over the fireplace. "It's not that late. I'll call Professor Harcourt and see how he's doing." They'd heard nothing from him for the last couple of days, so Jonathon assumed he was as engrossed in his task as they had been.

He picked up his phone and found the professor's contact details. Professor Harcourt answered on the third ring. "Good evening. Your timing is uncanny. I was about to call you. I've just finished the last book."

"Excellent. Then I'll call Melinda to organize a meeting." He smiled to himself. "When was the last time you had an old-fashioned afternoon tea?"

"Tea *and* talk? How delightful. Yes, that sounds splendid. Let me know the time." Jonathon caught the professor's yawn. "Oh dear. I think I might have an early night. All this reading has worn me out." He bade Jonathon good night and they finished the call.

Jonathon put aside his phone. "This was a really good idea of Professor Harcourt's. I only hope it pays off."

"Well, if it does, it will mean one of our neighbors got away with murder. That's a not-so-pleasant thought."

Jonathon stared at him. "And here's another for you. We assumed all the villagers kept their distance in the pub that night because they remembered what Teresa was like. What if some of them stayed as far away as possible because they didn't want Teresa to say something that might incriminate them?"

Mike became very still. "That's a good point."

"And here's another. What if someone in the village did get away with murder but had no idea that Teresa had put it in a book? Maybe they're not a big reader. Now, all of a sudden, there's all this attention being paid to her series. Remember the leaflets Heather had made? The ones she put through everyone's door? She had all the Summersfield covers, plus a précis of each book."

Mike widened his eyes. "And someone takes one look at a particular book and thinks, 'Wait a minute. That's talking about me.'"

"Exactly," Jonathon said triumphantly. "And then they realize that for two whole days, Teresa is going to be talking about those books. That book. Which is the last thing they want. Because if they've noticed similarities, so might other people in the village. So what are the options?"

"Shut her up—for good." Mike frowned. "But how would they know about the allergy?"

"The same way Fiona knew—she read it somewhere online. Let's face it, if you're going to kill someone, you do your research, especially if you want to do it in such a way so you don't get caught."

Mike's expression grew even more troubled. "It's not a nice thought, though. One of our neighbors could be a murderer. Maybe even one of our friends."

Jonathon waved dismissively. "I'm thinking it's someone we don't know very well. Because can you see Rachel, or Paul, or Seth, or Doris, committing murder?"

Mike arched his eyebrows. "I think we've been down this route before. With the last two murders, to be precise."

Jonathon stilled. "Okay, another good point." He yawned. "Sorry. I think Professor Harcourt has the right idea about an early night."

Mike said nothing but popped open the top button on his shirt. Then the next. And the next. All the while, his gaze was focused on Jonathon, his eyes gleaming.

Jonathon held up one finger. "Hold that thought." He got up and extended a hand to Mike. "Let's take this to the bedroom. Janet hasn't gone to bed yet."

Mike grabbed his hand, and Jonathon hoisted him to his feet. "I thought you wanted an early night?"

Jonathon snorted. "Well, what do you expect when you start revealing that chest?" He led Mike to the door, pausing to switch off the lights.

It was still going to be an early night, except they might not get to sleep for a while.

"WHERE'S LLOYD?" Mike asked as they took their seats in Melinda's cozy sitting room.

"Working on Sunday's sermon." Melinda gave him a wry smile. "And seeing as today is Thursday, and he only started work on it this morning, he has a lot to do." She smiled warmly at Professor Harcourt. "It's lovely to see you again after all these years."

"You too. I remember your arrival in the village, when Lloyd was first moved to the parish." The professor's smile seemed tinged with sadness to Mike's mind.

Melinda chuckled. "Funny to think that was over thirty years ago." She gestured to the table, which was as full as ever. "Help yourself to cake or scones. There's plenty."

"There always is," Jonathon commented. "I think Melinda's afternoon teas are the reason I've put on weight since I came to this village."

"Then you obviously need to do more exercise." Melinda's eyes sparkled.

Mike was glad he wasn't drinking at that moment. "You know, it's so wrong that a vicar's wife can say those words, and I immediately think there's a hidden meaning."

Melinda snickered. "Hidden? You mean dirty. That's because you have a dirty mind." She poured tea into the cups. "Now, who's going to start?"

It took them almost an hour to run through all the plots. Thankfully, Melinda would stop them after a minute if nothing seemed familiar. Now and again, she jotted down a few notes on a slip of paper, but most of the time she was able to multitask, refilling tea cups and plates as she listened.

When they were done, the three of them sagged into their chairs and Melinda went to the kitchen to make a fresh pot of tea. When she returned, she joined Mike on the couch, her paper in her hand and a cup of tea on the small table beside her.

"My, my. Teresa was certainly prolific. When did the first of these books appear?"

"2012," Mike announced, after consulting his notes.

"Twenty books in six years." Melinda arched her eyebrows. "One would hope such proliferation didn't lead to a lack of quality."

Mike had the distinct impression Melinda was stalling. Then it hit him why that might be. "You recognized something, didn't you?" Something she was clearly unhappy to share.

Melinda said nothing but picked up her cup and drank. After a moment, she sighed. "Two of those books could very well refer to incidents that took place in Merrychurch."

"Two?" Jonathon stared at her. "Well, that's something. What can you tell us?"

Melinda put down her cup, then took her handkerchief from the pocket of her tweed skirt. She held it in her lap, twisting it in a nervous manner.

"Melinda?" Mike said softly. "What is it you don't want to tell us?"

She blinked, as though startled, then bit her lip. "The case of the old lady who died in suspicious circumstances? Where an unexpected relative inherited everything? That sounds remarkably like what happened with Meredith Roberts."

Jonathon frowned. "Does she live in the village? I've never met her." When Professor Harcourt appeared surprised by this, Jonathon explained that he hadn't been long in the village himself and didn't know everyone. "Although I should get to know more people, in all honesty."

"Yes, she still lives here. And it was her aunt who died suddenly."

"Okay. Then we can look into that. And the other case?" Mike pushed.

Melinda sighed again. "The young farmer who thought his mother had run off and left him and his father years previously. Rumors had abounded that she'd gone off with another man. But when the sleuth looks into the case, she discovers there's a field his father won't cultivate, even though they badly need the extra crops. It turns out that the older farmer had killed his wife and buried her there."

"And that sounded familiar?" Jonathon asked.

Melinda nodded slowly. "It bears a remarkable similarity to actual events. A farmer's wife did indeed leave the village without a word, and yes, there were rumors circulating for a while that the husband had murdered her. There was no son, however. That's where the story differs from reality. But then the rumors died down and were dismissed as mere fancy."

Mike regarded her closely. "Who was the farmer?" Although the thought was slowly forming in his head that he might already know the answer to that, given Melinda's reluctance.

Her troubled gaze met his. "Paul Drake."

CHAPTER FIFTEEN

JONATHON STARED in astonishment. "No. There's no way Paul could be a murderer."

"But you cannot know that with any degree of certainty," Professor Harcourt admonished gently. "One never knows how anyone will react when pushed to their limits. What if she had confronted him and there had been a dreadful argument? What if she had provoked him?" He gazed intently at Jonathon. "You cannot let your personal feelings cloud your judgment. Let me ask you this: knowing Paul as you do, would you therefore dismiss this idea and *not* investigate further?"

"We can't ignore it," Mike told him solemnly. "After all, we know from our own experience that people will constantly surprise you. Don't we?"

Jonathon said nothing, although he knew they were both right.

"I don't like the idea of Paul being involved in this any more than you do," Melinda admitted. "But Mike is correct. You can't ignore it."

"Maybe not," Jonathon said slowly. "But we can choose which of the two cases we investigate first. And I vote for looking at Meredith Roberts."

"If it helps, I don't think it's Paul either," Mike said in a low voice.

Professor Harcourt's lips twitched. "Do I take it that the local constable doesn't mind you two *investigating*, as you put it?"

Jonathon chuckled. "Seeing as we helped him solve two murders, he's inclined to turn a blind eye. Gorland is more of a problem, however."

"We have to work hard to stay under his radar," Mike added.

"So how will you go about this? You can't simply turn up on her doorstep and say you're investigating Teresa's murder and she might possibly have a motive." Professor Harcourt took a bite of madeira cake. "This is delicious."

"How long has Meredith lived in the village?" Jonathon asked. "Or maybe I should ask, did her aunt die, and was Teresa living in the village at the time?"

Melinda frowned. "Let me think. Old Miss Tremont died in 2001, so yes, Teresa was here."

"Then that makes it simple," Jonathon declared. "We go to see Meredith, telling her we're helping the local police build up a picture of Teresa Malvain's life in Merrychurch, and is there anything she can tell us. Then we can segue into the book and see what she says."

"She's hardly going to admit it, is she?" Professor Harcourt exclaimed. "She's not going to say, 'Oh, fancy that, she wrote a book describing how I murdered my aunt so I could inherit everything. It's a fair cop, Guv. I'll come along quietly.'"

Melinda stared at him, then burst into a peal of bright laughter. When she composed herself, she smiled. "With these two, one never knows. People tend to talk to them. A lot."

"It's Jonathon," Mike concluded. "They take one look at that face and instantly trust him."

Jonathon said nothing, but reached over and covered Mike's hand with his.

"Or, as in your case, fall in love with him." Melinda smiled warmly.

"Best decision I ever made, giving him a lift from the station." Mike grinned.

Professor Harcourt coughed. "I hate to break up this mutual appreciation party, but you have a murder to solve." His eyes twinkled. "And I'd *love* for you two to solve it, rather than that sneering detective."

"We'd like that too." Jonathon finished his last morsel of cake, then glanced at Mike. "And seeing as we have guests arriving tomorrow, maybe we should talk to people while we can."

He imagined there wouldn't be much time for investigating, not if the discussion went as he hoped.

As we *hope*, he amended. Mike was as excited by the prospect as he was.

"What about you, Professor?" Mike asked. "Will you be going home now?"

Harcourt shook his head. "I'm going to spend a few days longer. Besides, I haven't been given official leave yet. It seems my presence is still required here. So I intend to discover some of Merrychurch's beautiful gardens, seeing as I can't work on my own."

"Do you like gardening?" Melinda's eyes lit up. "Because you are more than welcome to join me in the vicarage garden. There is always so much to do at this time of year."

"That would be splendid." Professor Harcourt beamed. "Now I am so glad I came to tea."

Jonathon smiled. Professor Harcourt would be happily occupied, while they got on with a little sleuthing. First stop would be Meredith Roberts.

Paul Drake could wait a while longer.

"I WAS at your Bonfire party last year," Meredith announced as she poured coffee for them. "I wanted to come over and say hello, but you know how it is. Too many people around, feeling shy...."

Mike had never been shy, but he could empathize. "Jonathon is hoping to do it again this year."

Her face lit up. "Oh, that would be wonderful."

Jonathon was gazing at their surroundings. Mike had to admit they were charming. The cottage had a cozy feel to it, with low-beamed ceilings, and parquet flooring covered in thick rugs.

"This room is lovely," Jonathon said suddenly. "And I like the fireplace. There's nothing like a real fire in the wintertime, is there?" Logs were stored on either side of the chimney breast, piled up to waist height. A thick rug lay in front of it.

Meredith nodded enthusiastically. "You can't really see yourself reading by a *radiator*, can you? But there's something magical about a log fire." She gazed at the room. "And it is a lovely house. I was so lucky that Aunt Barbara left it to me. It's nothing like the poky little house I was living in. That was just a box compared to this." She got to her feet. "Come and see the kitchen."

Jonathon and Mike followed her across the wide hallway into the large square kitchen. A range dominated one wall, painted in dark olive green. The smell of freshly baked bread filled the air, and from the window came the scent of potted herbs. The floor was covered in deep terracotta tiles, and the overall impression was that of a typical country kitchen.

"Did your aunt like cooking?" Mike asked, looking at the shiny pans hanging from hooks above the range. "This looks like a great kitchen for a good cook."

"I don't really know." Meredith gave a shrug. "Auntie and I weren't that well-acquainted, to be honest."

"And yet she left you her house? She must have cared for you," Jonathon reasoned. There was no response from Meredith, apart from a noncommittal noise. He met Mike's gaze briefly, and there was the tiniest inclination of his head toward the cabinets. Mike followed his gaze and saw immediately what had caught Jonathon's attention.

A couple of large bottles of oil, the picture of a peanut on both labels.

Meredith turned to face him at that moment, and Mike looked away from the bottles. "I do like your hallway," he said, exiting the kitchen and stepping into the dark entrance hall. Paintings covered the white walls, and below one was a low bookshelf in dark oak. Mike peered at the books, recognizing some of the titles instantly.

Well, well, well. Meredith is a Teresa Malvain fan. She appeared to have every book in the Summersfield series.

Meredith gestured to the living room. "Let's go back to our coffee, shall we?" They followed her there, and Meredith sat in the wide armchair beside the fireplace. "So, you're here because you want to know about Teresa Malvain, from villagers who knew her from way back? I remember her, of course." Her thin face tightened even more. "Can't say I really liked her. She was a terrible gossip. You daren't tell her anything, for fear she'd tell the whole village. Because that's what she did."

"Well, we know now she wasn't above taking true incidents from the village and putting them in her books," Jonathon said in a conspiratorial tone.

"She never did." Meredith's eyes opened wide in surprise, but her tone was flat and unconvincing to Mike's experienced ears.

"Really," Jonathon continued. "Why, only yesterday we were discussing one of her books, and someone said it reminded them of someone in the village." He was staring at her, his brow slightly furrowed.

"Get away." That same look of surprise was there, only this time, something flickered in Meredith's eyes.

Mike had a good idea why Meredith wasn't asking about the book, but he wasn't about to let her off the hook. "It was a story about an old lady who died in suspicious circumstances, only to have all her money and property go to a relative who no one had expected to inherit. A relative who hadn't spent a great deal of time around her aunt." Mike widened his eyes dramatically. "Of course. Now I know why your name is familiar. They were talking about you."

Meredith froze. "Me? But what has that got to do with me?"

"Well, you just told us your aunt left you this house and that you didn't really know her all that well. Maybe someone thought that sounded similar to the case in Teresa's book," Jonathon suggested with a helpful air.

"But Auntie's death wasn't suspicious," Meredith declared loudly, her eyes flashing. "Why would someone say that?" She narrowed her gaze. "*Who* said that, more to the point? They can't go around spreading malicious rumors like that."

"Did you know your aunt was going to leave you everything?" Mike asked.

"I had no idea. It was a complete surprise. I was as flabbergasted as everyone else when I found out."

"Did you know she'd made a will?" Jonathon asked. His furrowed brow hadn't altered.

"No," Meredith responded immediately, although she nodded.

Mike knew what that meant. He pushed on. "Surely that's not the first time you've heard about the similarities between your circumstances and Teresa's book. I mean, you must have thought that yourself when you read it."

Meredith blinked. "I haven't read it," she said, her hand coming up to her mouth.

Mike mimicked her blink. "Really? Oh. I was sure you must have, after I saw it on your bookcase out there." He pointed toward the hallway.

"Oh. Those were Auntie's books. I'm not even sure what's on those shelves." She let out a light laugh. "I'm not much of a reader."

"Your aunt obviously was. She has the entire collection of Teresa's books."

"Now I know where I've seen you before." Jonathon gave a wide triumphant smile. "You were in the pub on Friday night."

"Me?" The word came out as a squeak. "I'm not really one for going to the pub."

Jonathon shook his head. "No, I remember you. I brought a gin and tonic to your table, and the lady you were with had a glass of sherry."

"You're mistaken." Then she stilled. "Oh. Wait. Yes, I *did* pop into the pub that night. I was meeting my friend, Emma. I didn't stay long, though. There were too many people in there." Meredith glanced at her watch. "Oh, look at the time. I must get on. So much to do." She stood. "Well, it was nice to finally meet you, and I hope I helped, but I really must get on."

Mike rose to his feet, and Jonathon did too. "Thank you for the coffee, and your time." He shook her hand, and she showed them to the door. As they reached it, Mike paused. "You know, something's been bothering me, and I just figured out what it is. Those books of your aunt's? They couldn't possibly have belonged to her."

Meredith froze. "Why on earth not?"

"Because your aunt died in 2001, right?"

Meredith gave a cautious nod.

"Well, the first Summersfield book only came out in 2012, so for your aunt to have bought it would be sort of impossible." Mike flashed her a wide smile. "Thanks again for the coffee." Without waiting for her reply, he walked out the door, with Jonathon behind him.

Once they were outside, Mike strode purposefully to the car. They got in, and Jonathon chuckled. "Nice catch. It didn't occur to me about the books until you pointed it out. And she certainly didn't look happy that you'd noticed." He shook his head. "That was stupid."

"People do stupid things when they're flustered, and Meredith was definitely flustered." Mike glanced back at the house. "She's going on the list. She lied to me—twice."

Jonathon laughed. "How could you tell which statements were lies? None of it rang true to me."

"Two things gave her away. She covered her mouth when she was speaking. That is classic. We all have a natural tendency to want to cover up a lie. And she said no, but nodded. We used to call that a verbal-nonverbal disconnect. Our brains are wired to make those match up, so when there's a disconnect, it's noticeable."

"Remind me never to try lying to you," Jonathon muttered. "So now what do we do?"

Mike had already considered that part. "We see if we can find out Aunt Barbara's cause of death and whether or not it was suspicious. But well done for remembering that Meredith was in the pub."

"I didn't." Jonathon's eyes sparkled.

"What?"

"I made it up." He rolled his eyes. "Come on. You saw how many people were in the pub. Even with my memory, I couldn't recall her."

"But… you mentioned her order. The gin and tonic and the sherry."

Jonathon nodded cheerfully. "And I did deliver an order like that. I only suggested it was to her after seeing a bottle of gin in her living room." He shrugged. "It was worth a try."

Mike chuckled. "And it paid off. We now know she was there. And if her aunt's death was suspicious, then next we look at the will. When it was written, more importantly, and whether the aunt changed it suddenly." He reached across and cupped Jonathon's cheek. "You are amazing."

"That's funny. I was thinking the same thing about you." Jonathon took Mike's hand in his and kissed his fingers. "Okay. Back to work. Where next?"

Mike snickered. "In case you haven't noticed, it's almost time for dinner. Paul will have to wait until tomorrow morning."

"Only if we can get to see him before Ruth and Clare arrive."

"We'll fit him in. Even if it's only to rule him out."

There was no way Paul Drake could be their killer. But then, Mike reasoned, he'd had the same thought about the last murder.

We can't rule anyone out.

CHAPTER SIXTEEN

"Is Ivy ready for the invasion?" Jonathon asked as he buttered a slice of toast.

Janet laughed. "She said last time your guests were here, she couldn't believe how much food you all got through."

"I blame Ruth," Jonathon said promptly, with a grin. He wasn't surprised when Mike guffawed.

"Ohh, I am *definitely* sharing that when they get here. I wouldn't like to be in your shoes. Ruth looks like she can pack a mean wallop."

"She does! She used to beat me up when we were children."

Janet's lips were twitching as she left the dining room.

Mike gave him a hard stare. "I am storing up every word you say, you know. I want to stay on their good side." He paused, his cup of coffee in his hand. "I hope they go for this. I've thought of little else all week."

Jonathon thought it adorable how badly Mike wanted to be a father. "We'll have to wait and see. We can only hope they like the idea as much as we do."

"What time are they arriving?"

Jonathon consulted his phone. "Ruth's last text said they'd been on the road for an hour, which means they set off very early." He laughed as his phone warbled. "Well, that answers your question."

"What does it say?"

He grinned. "Put the kettle on. We're gasping." He sent Ivy a text. "I've let Ivy know we'll need more coffee and two more cups." He quickly composed another. "And more toast. They'll be hungry."

"Aren't you excited too? You seem so calm."

Jonathon put down his phone. "I am so excited, I feel like I'm about to explode. But I'm tempering it with practicality." There was always the chance that this might not come off.

Janet poked her head around the door. "Your visitors have arrived," she said with a smile.

Jonathon hastily wiped his lips with his napkin and got up from the table. Mike followed him out of the room, through the house, and to the imposing entrance hall. Outside, Ruth was in the process of locking the car, while Clare carried the bags toward the house. She dropped them when she saw him and held her arms wide.

"Hey. It's so good to see you."

Jonathon gave her a tight hug, before being seized by Ruth. "I like my ribs the way they are," he grumbled. "Intact." He glanced over his shoulder at Mike. *See*? He mouthed.

Laughing, Ruth released him. "I echo what Clare said. It's good to see you, even if it does feel like you're up to something."

"I never could hide anything from you." Jonathon took her arm and led her into the hall. Clare and Mike followed, with Mike carrying the bags. "We have fresh coffee and toast waiting for you."

"Then do we get to hear what this is all about?" Ruth demanded. "Have you finally come up with the plan?"

"A plan," Mike said with a smile. "But I guarantee it's like nothing you've considered."

"Now you *have* intrigued me. But lead me to the coffee."

"You speak for yourself," Clare added. "I want toast."

"The wonderful Ivy does know we're coming, doesn't she?" Ruth's dark eyes sparkled with humor. "Especially after last time."

Jonathon squeezed her arm. "I really am glad you're here." The excitement he'd pushed down hard the last few days refused to stay down a moment longer.

Please let them go for this.

RUTH LET out a low cry. "That's wonderful news! Congratulations!" She hugged Mike first, then wrapped her arms around Jonathon. "I see you finally found the right moment," she whispered.

"Not exactly."

Clare hugged them both. "So when did this happen?"

"Six days ago." Jonathon stilled. "Was it only six days? It feels like so much has happened since."

"That wouldn't be the small matter of the death of a famous author, would it?" Clare sighed. "Tell me you're not looking into it."

"We *could* tell you that," Mike admitted, "but we'd be lying."

"You're not here to talk about the murder," Jonathon said quickly. When both women gaped at him, he held up his hands. "Yes, it was murder. Now let's get onto the real reason why we invited you."

Ruth frowned. "It wasn't to tell us you're engaged, then?"

Jonathon shook his head. "We're thinking about September for the wedding, but there's something we need to discuss with you before that."

Mike joined him on the couch, laying his hand on Jonathon's knee.

Ruth listened intently as Jonathon told them about what had led to his proposing to Mike, including the conversation with his father, before going through their idea, mentioning only the part that Ruth would play, as they'd agreed earlier. At one point she gave Clare a startled glance, and Jonathon's heartbeat sped up. When he'd finished, Jonathon took a deep breath, anxiously awaiting their reaction.

"I don't believe this," Ruth murmured.

"I know. This is incredible," Clare said from beside her.

Jonathon's heart sank. "Then you don't like the idea."

Mike sagged back against the seat cushions.

Ruth widened her eyes. "Oh God, that's not what I mean at all." She gave a chuckle. "It's just that… we were really happy that you invited us for the weekend, because we were about to invite ourselves to ask if… Mike would consider donating his sperm so that Clare can have a baby." Her eyes twinkled. "Great minds, eh?"

Mike burst out laughing. "We had the same idea."

Jonathon couldn't believe how things were proceeding. *This is actually going to work.*

"We do have one stipulation, however." Ruth grinned. "We do *not* want to be pregnant at the same time."

Claire laughed. "Two pregnant women in the same house? Hell no."

"Wait a minute." Jonathon looked from Clare to Ruth. "The same house? Is there something you want to tell us?"

Ruth held out her hand, and Clare took it. "You're not the only ones who got fed up. We decided a few months ago to start looking for a house together. Well, we found one. We're actually not that far from you, which is just as well, given the circumstances. And once everything goes through, I'm going to tell my family about Clare. Then it's full speed ahead with wedding plans." She leaned over and kissed Clare's cheek.

Jonathon couldn't be happier. "I think that's wonderful."

"Can I be practical for a minute?" Mike interjected. "What happens next?"

"Next is working out how to start proceedings for artificial insemination." Ruth squeezed Clare's hand. "Then we'll take it one day at a time." She gazed at Jonathon. "I'd suggest we get started ASAP, because it might take a while. I'll talk to my doctor after the weekend and let you know."

"There is one more thing I'd like to discuss." Jonathon looked at Ruth. "I'm not planning on having a best man, because I can't think of anyone I'd want standing with me. I was thinking, however, of having a best woman instead."

Ruth caught her breath. "Me? Oh, Jonathon." Her eyes glistened. "I'd be honored."

Clare handed her a tissue. "Look at you. If you're all emotional now, what on earth will you be like when you're pregnant?"

Mike glanced at Jonathon. "Be afraid. Be very afraid."

MIKE WAS in his favorite place in all the world: in bed with Jonathon, his chest against Jonathon's back, his arms around him. The sheet had been kicked off because of the night heat, and a breeze wafted over their bodies from the open window.

"Can I ask you something?" Jonathon sounded half-asleep.

"The last time you said that, it ended up with us deciding we were going to be parents. I'm not sure I can take another conversation like that," Mike joked.

"This week, while Abi's been looking after the pub… have you missed it?"

Mike hadn't expected that. "Why do you ask?"

"Because Janet asked me last weekend what you would do once we were married, and I didn't know. I suppose it's something we need to discuss."

"Do you want me to sell the pub?"

"God, no!" Jonathon sounded astonished. "You *love* that pub."

Mike wasn't sure what he wanted to do. The idea of traveling with Jonathon really appealed to him, especially as he'd hardly ever left the country. He'd envied Jonathon's lifestyle prior to living at the manor, and he knew Jonathon was keen to carry on with his photography.

"I rather like the idea of being married to a world-famous photographer," he mused.

"Even when that means your husband goes off all around the world?"

"Well, now. Will my husband want to go alone?"

Jonathon became so still in his arms. "Are you saying…?"

"I didn't really give you an answer before, but I'm giving one now. Yes, I'll go with you, but only until the baby is born. And we've no idea when that might be."

"And after that?"

Mike chuckled. "After that, both of us are going to have our hands full. That might be the time to consider selling the pub. Because I don't know about you, but I want more than one child."

Jonathon let out a long, contented sigh. "Me too." He wriggled until he was facing Mike, his arms around Mike's neck. "I don't think I've ever been this happy."

"I hate to throw a spanner in the works, but there's the not-so-small matter of your dad. We have to tell him of our plans. Wedding, surrogacy…. And sooner rather than later."

Jonathon sighed. "You're right. I'll invite him to stay next weekend. We have to do this face-to-face."

"Surely if he sees how happy you are, that will mean something to him."

Jonathon snorted. "Are we talking about the same man?" Then warm lips pressed against Mike's, and he lost himself in a slow, intimate kiss, Jonathon molding his body to Mike's. Jonathon broke the kiss. "Let's forget about my father, wedding plans, and murders. Let's leave it all outside our bedroom door." He rolled onto his back, taking Mike with him, wrapping his long legs around Mike's waist. "Make love to me."

Mike sighed. "I got it wrong. I thought my favorite place to be in the world was in bed with you, but that's actually my second-favorite."

"So where's your first?"

Mike kissed him, then brushed his lips against Jonathon's ear. "Inside you."

CHAPTER SEVENTEEN

JONATHON PLACED his napkin on the table. "I guess the girls are having a lie-in this morning."

Mike snorted. "In other words, Clare is making the most of the four-poster bed. You remember how much she raved about it the last time they stayed?"

Jonathon laughed. "I'll let Ivy know we're not quite done with breakfast yet." He cocked his head to one side. "What are your plans for today?"

Mike chuckled. "What you *really* want to know is, do I intend working in the pub, or will I be staying with you so we can do some more sleuthing under the nose of DI Gorland?"

"We-ell, I *was* going to pay Paul Drake a visit, and I thought you might want to come with me."

Mike said nothing, but it didn't take a genius to know what was going on in his head.

"I don't want to think him capable of murder either," Jonathon admitted quietly. "But I need to know if there's any truth to this story about his wife disappearing."

"I'm just afraid of the fallout."

Jonathon frowned. "What do you mean?"

"I mean, that if you ask Paul about this, there's the chance you could really offend him, especially if there's nothing to the rumors."

"And you'd lose a good customer," Jonathon concluded.

"Exactly. So this is going to require a lot of tact and diplomacy." Mike gave him a hard stare. "Think you can pull that off?" The twitch of his lips belied the serious question.

Jonathon gave a mock gasp. "I'm mortified to think you'd doubt me." He smirked. "I was more worried about you, charging in there with your size elevens."

Mike gaped. "How dare you? I'll have you know my feet are a dainty size nine." He grinned. "And don't worry. I'll be the soul of tact."

Jonathon gave that last remark the reaction it deserved—an eye roll.

PAUL LEANED over the rail and scratched the pig's back with a stick. "That's it, Bella. Eat it all up. Gotta feed those babies."

"Those piglets are really cute," Mike admitted, watching the tiny animals running around the pen.

Paul huffed. "I try not to think of 'em like that. Hard to send them off to…." He lowered his voice. "You-know-where, when you're attached to them." He handed Mike the stick. "If you scratch her belly, she'll gradually fall over. She loves it."

Mike glanced across at Jonathon. "Don't look. I remember how you were with Maisie."

Paul snickered. "Oh yeah." He peered at Jonathon. "I was surprised you didn't turn vegetarian after that." He straightened. "So wanna tell me what you're doing here? Not that I mind. I don't get many visitors." He arched his eyebrows. "I'm assumin' whatever brought you here couldn't wait until pub time."

"We got talking with some Teresa Malvain fans," Jonathon began, "and—"

Paul let out a derisive snort. "I dunno what people see in her books. Mind you, I never could stand that Miss Marple. Always pokin' her nose into murders. And the way someone always ends up dead when she's around. I swear, if I turned up someplace and *she* was there, I'd turn right around and get the hell out."

"Have you ever read any of Teresa's books?" Mike inquired.

Paul cackled. "Yeah, right. When I'm not taking care of this little lot, I'm in the pub. When do I have time to read?"

"Then you haven't heard the rumors?" Jonathon widened his eyes. "I was really shocked."

"Rumors? What about?" Paul shook his head. "When is there not a rumor circulatin' in Merrychurch?"

"Well, about you," Mike said frankly.

Paul blinked. "Me? What about me?"

"We were discussing one of Teresa's books, and someone—I forget who—said the plot reminded them of you. It was something to do with your wife." Jonathon kept his remarks purposefully vague.

Paul became very still. His face tightened. "You mean people are still spreadin' that muck around?

Some arseholes have way too much time on their hands."

"I didn't think to ask what they meant," Jonathon confessed, hating the lie.

"Before your time, nipper. And yours too, Mike, come to think of it." Paul sighed heavily. "But I guess now you wanna know what they're talkin' about, don't ya?" He indicated the farmhouse with a nod of his head. "Come on in. I'll give *you* a drink for a change, and then I'll tell you. Though it beats me what they wanna bring it all up for again."

They walked across the cobbled courtyard between the pigs' pen and the house. Jonathon felt an uneasy rolling in his stomach. He agreed they needed to know the truth, but he also knew Mike was right. They had to do this without causing offense.

Except how do you say to someone, "By the way, this gives you a really good motive for killing her— did you?"

Inside Paul's dark kitchen, they took a seat at the wooden table, while Paul reached into a cabinet and took out a bottle. "This'll put hairs on your chest," he said with a grin. "Made it meself."

"Do I dare ask what it is?" Mike peered at the bottle.

"Homemade elderberry wine. Laid this down about ten years ago. It was bloody awful until last year. Rough as dogshit. It just needed to age a bit more." Paul opened another cabinet and removed three glasses. "I won't give you a lot. I wanna keep you as friends." Another cackle erupted from him as he pulled the cork free of the bottle. He filled the glasses, then placed them on the table. "Cheers," he said, raising his own.

They copied him, and then Jonathon took a cautious sip. The red wine was surprisingly smooth and full-bodied. "This is delicious."

Paul chuckled. "You wouldn't have said that two years ago." He joined them at the table. "Okay, lads. Tell me the truth. I love it when you come by, but I've got a feelin' there's more to this visit than sayin' hi to Bella's piglets. You wanna know more about these stories you've heard."

"I got curious," Jonathon said simply. "When the subject came up of a plot from one of her books about a farmer's wife who goes missing, and then you were mentioned, I wondered what they could have in common. I didn't even know you were married."

Paul studied his glass. "April. Her name's April. And in 2005, she went out one day—shopping, I thought—and never came back." He scowled. "Of course, there were some idiots in the village who thought I'd done her in and buried her out in one of the fields. Someone even suggested I'd chopped her up into bits and fed her to the pigs. Morons. I told 'em, then what happened to her suitcase? The one that disappeared from her wardrobe the day she left. Or did I bury that too to make it look like she'd done a runner?"

"How long had you been married?" Mike asked.

"Twelve years. She married me at eighteen, bless her. We'd been courtin' since she was sixteen and I was twenty."

Jonathon gasped. "You cradle robber."

Paul smiled. "She was a rum lass. Told me at sixteen that she was going to marry me. I made her wait. By that time, I was working on me dad's farm, getting ready to run it when he retired. I kept tellin' her the life of farmer's wife wasn't for her, but she wouldn't listen. Give April her due, she stuck at it, but…."

"So she was thirty when she left?" Mike sipped the wine.

Paul nodded. "I knew she was finding it tough, but I had no idea she was that unhappy."

"She didn't leave you a note? She didn't call?" Jonathon couldn't believe she would just pack a bag and walk out, without a word.

"She left nothing. And there hasn't been a word from her, from that day to this."

"But surely…." Mike put down his glass. "You must've looked for her, right? Or tried to contact her through friends or family?"

Paul's expression hardened. "Look, if she wanted to leave that badly, I wasn't gonna make things worse by goin' after her. Maybe she'd found herself a fancy man, someone who'd show her a better time. Someone who wouldn't get her up at the crack of dawn to feed the pigs. Someone with more money than sense to spend on her. And if that's the case, good luck to her."

Jonathon wasn't fooled. "It still hurts, doesn't it? That she left like that?"

"Course it bloody hurts!" Paul retorted. "But what I wanna know is, why are people talkin' about it all over again? It was bad enough at the time. Why now?" Then he stilled again. "Wait a minute. Are you tellin' me that woman wrote a book about me an' April?"

Jonathon nodded. "It looks like it. Except in her book, the farmer had a son. But yes, the missing wife is finally found buried in a field. Everyone had thought she'd run off with a lover, and the farmer let them think that, but she never left the farm at all."

Paul looked from Jonathon to Mike. "Why are you really here?" His quiet voice was nothing like the raucous man they knew. "You nosing into her death? So what's that got to do with—" He widened his eyes. "Ooh. *I* see. You think I bumped off this writer woman 'cos she got too close to the truth? That doesn't make sense."

"That argument would hinge entirely on you knowing she was going to reveal all about her stories," Mike said quietly. "And on you being scared that people would start talking again and want to find out what really happened to April."

Paul gave an unhurried nod. "So rather than have people sticking their noses into my business, I killed her. Is that it?" He barked out a harsh laugh. "I can see it now. People trampling over my fields, looking for a potential burial site. Turning up with all sorts of gadgets for detecting bodies." His scowl returned. "Well, as I don't possess one of her books, and never have had, how would I know what she wrote? And if anyone turns up at the farm wanting a look, they're gonna get my pitchfork where the sun don't shine. No one sets foot in my fields, you hear me?"

"I don't think anyone will turn up," Jonathon said.

"Well, *you* did," Paul muttered. "And it's only dawnin' on me now that you must think I'm a suspect. Why else would you be here?" He stood suddenly.

"You know what? I've got work to do. So I think you'd best be on your way."

"We don't think you're a murderer." Jonathon's heart sank. This was terrible.

"Hogwash. You still came, though. And what's more, you didn't come right out and tell me why you came. You went all around the houses instead." Paul walked to the back door that opened out onto the courtyard. "Have a good day, lads. Don't be surprised if I'm not on my usual stool tonight. I think I'll do my drinking here." He opened it.

There was nothing to do but leave.

As the door closed behind them, Mike sighed. "I hate being right." They headed for the car.

"Well, you heard him. Do you think he was lying?"

"I think he's pretty pissed off right now." Mike's expression was gloomy. "But you know what? His re-action could be taken one of two ways. He's either angry that we could think of him like that, or he's angry to think someone may look into this. Because what came across loud and clear was him not wanting anyone in his fields."

"I don't blame him for throwing us out." Jonathon glanced back to the farmhouse. Paul was at the kitchen window, watching them.

"But you're not as sure of his innocence as you were, are you?"

Jonathon hated to admit that Mike was right. Paul's reaction could be anger or guilt. "I don't want to think of him as a murderer," he confessed.

"And that's because he's a friend." Mike unlocked the car. "You can't be objective." He got behind the wheel.

"And you can?" Jonathon got into the passenger seat.

"Maybe it's the ex-copper in me. I don't want to think of him killing Teresa any more than you do, but I'm not about to ignore the possibility."

As they drove away, Jonathon went over Paul's remarks in his head. "You know what would change everything? If April turned up."

"She's been gone since 2005. Why come back now?"

Jonathon considered the question. "Maybe it would be enough simply to find her. Paul told us he's never looked for her."

"So what if we look instead? Is that what you're suggesting?" Mike chuckled. "I love it when you wear your Mr. Fix-It head."

"But you will look into it? You're the one with the connections." The more Jonathon thought about it, the more he wanted to make it happen.

Besides, to his mind, Meredith seemed the more guilty of the two.

CHAPTER EIGHTEEN

MIKE PULLED up outside the village post office. "They close at twelve, so I won't be long. I'll see if we can trace where that package came from." Then he stiffened.

Jonathon followed his gaze and groaned inwardly.

DI Gorland was walking toward the car, scowling.

Mike lowered the window. "Good morning, John. Lovely day, isn't it?"

"It's DI Gorland to you." Gorland's scowl deepened. "How many times do we have to have this conversation? You are no longer a police officer. And that means you don't interfere with police inquiries."

Mike stared at him. "And what exactly am I supposed to have done that counts as interference?"

Jonathon was equally confused. All they'd done was spend a lot of time reading Teresa's books.

"We've had a complaint from a Meredith Roberts. Apparently, you've been harassing her."

Jonathon gaped. "She said that? We had coffee with her, that was all."

Gorland nodded. "And asked a lot of questions about Teresa Malvain. Well, she felt some of your questions were intrusive, and she came to the police station to make an official complaint. I was on my way to the pub to find you, until I saw your car. You've saved me the trip. So this is me *officially* telling you both to stay away from her. Got it?" He sneered. "Because if I find out that you've been bothering her again, I'll arrest the pair of you." He glanced in the direction of the post office. "And what are you up to here?"

"Posting something?" Mike said with such an innocent expression that it was all Jonathon could do not to burst out laughing.

Gorland narrowed his gaze. "Hmm. Well, just remember I'm watching you. *Both* of you." And with that, he strutted toward his car.

Jonathon waited until he was out of earshot. "It seems we really riled Meredith."

"I'm betting she didn't like the fact that we knew she lied to us." Mike watched as Gorland's car pulled away from the curb. "I'll be right back." He got out and closed the door behind him.

Jonathon reached into his jacket pocket for his phone. Now that Ruth and Clare were happy with the plans, he had to let his father know, and that meant inviting him to Merrychurch. Telling him of their impending marriage and their surrogacy plans was *not* a conversation to be conducted over the phone.

His father answered after three rings. "I assume you're calling to apologize for the way you ended our last conversation. Both for your tone and that rather cryptic final remark."

"Actually, I'm calling to extend you an invitation to visit us." Jonathon kept his tone even. It never ceased to amaze him how his father could irritate him with so few words.

"Us. As in, you and Mike."

"Yes. We were thinking of next weekend, if that's okay with you." Jonathon mentally crossed his fingers. He wanted this over with as soon as possible.

"I see." There was a pause. "That seems viable. I'll be there Saturday in time for lunch."

"Will you be staying the night?"

"That will depend entirely on whatever it is you have to tell me. Because that last phone call left me with the distinct impression that whatever your decision is, I'm not going to like it."

Jonathon had to admit, his father's usually sharp instincts were once again spot-on. "I'll have a room prepared for you, just in case." He said goodbye and disconnected as Mike got back into the car. "Well? Any luck?"

"Graham has already been to see the post mistress, but she only told him what we already knew, that it was posted in Winchester."

"If Graham is looking into this, then he might have dusted the book for fingerprints. He already has ours on file." Jonathon tapped Mike on the knee. "You need to call him."

Mike chuckled. "Er, you were here a short while ago when the mean-looking DI warned us about sticking our noses into police business?"

Jonathon snorted. "You don't mean you're actually going to pay attention to him?"

Mike's eyes gleamed. "Of course not." He got out his phone and tapped a few keys before putting it to his ear. "Hey. Is it safe to talk?"

Jonathon couldn't miss the explosive noise at the other end of the call. He smiled. "I'm guessing that's a yes."

Mike listened with an intent expression, nodding now and then. "Okay. Thanks. … Yes, I owe you a pint. I'll be there tonight if you want to stop by." He grinned. "Of course we'll share anything we learn. We said so, didn't we?" He disconnected the call, then put his phone down in the center console. "The only prints on that book were ours. Plus, he worked out how the sender knew where to mail it. Teresa posted on her Facebook page weeks ago that she'd found this charming old pub to stay in. Even shared the link." Mike shook his head. "Why do people feel the need to share everything like this?"

Jonathon stared at him. "You've just given me an idea."

"Uh-oh. Should I be worried?"

He whacked Mike on the arm. "I'm being serious. We need to check her Facebook page and other social media accounts. If she used them often, there might be clues we're missing. Graham's more on the ball than we are." Jonathon frowned. "Will her account still be up?"

Mike rolled his eyes. "You're kidding, right? Those sites are notoriously slow at closing accounts when someone dies. Unless she had an assistant who has already done it."

Jonathon widened his eyes. "An assistant. I didn't think of that. We need to contact them."

"Except the police will have done that right away."

Jonathon grinned. "In which case, we're not treading on anyone's toes, are we? I'll go back to the house and take a look online. You see if Teresa did have an assistant and if we can talk to them. Then we'll meet at the pub at four when it closes. That'll give us a couple of hours to compare notes and decide on a plan of action." Their lack of progress irked him. Teresa had been dead for over a week, and so far, they only had a couple of suspects, not that they'd investigated all possibilities. They still had Harold Tenby to see, for one thing. At least the police seemed to be as clueless as they were.

There had to be *something* of value online, given Teresa's propensity for sharing the minutiae of her life.

Something that would point to her murderer.

AFTER TWO hours of scouring Teresa's Facebook timeline and author page, Jonathon had had more than enough. Given the amount of posts she put online on a daily basis, he was amazed she ever found time to write a word. And that was *before* he'd managed to take a look at her readers' group, where she shared snippets from upcoming books, release posts, giveaways....

He was beginning to despair of ever finding anything that might help them, but then a post caught his eye.

Did they get away with murder—twice??? The spouse dies first, and everyone thinks it's a tragic accident—except for one relative. But when THEY get too close, they're found dead, apparently by suicide. But WAS IT??? My next book might be a huge departure

*from the norm for me, but I guarantee it is going to be
a book you'll want to read.*

Jonathon scribbled down a few notes before
calling Mike. "Listen, I think I may have found
something."

"That makes two of us. I've found Teresa's personal assistant."

That brought a smile. "Fantastic. And I think
there's another direction we should be taking. So
far we've looked at the books she wrote. What if we
should really be looking at the one she was going to
write?" He read the post aloud.

"Didn't she mention something about her next
book at the dinner?" Mike asked.

"Yes. Something about not only revealing the plot
of the next Summersfield novel, but also dipping her
toes into a new market."

Mike chuckled. "I love your memory. By the way,
I got a text from Graham. He said he's definitely coming to the pub this evening, and he wants to talk to us
about something."

"He said us? How intriguing." That could mean
only one thing—it was something to do with Teresa's
murder.

"I know we said we'd meet up at four to discuss
our findings, but Abi is running the bar right now, so
if you wanted to come over a bit earlier…." The way
Mike's words trailed off made Jonathon think he had
more than sleuthing on his mind.

Jonathon coughed. "I think you're forgetting
something. We have guests, remember?"

"Oh. Yeah. You're right. Oh well." The dejected tone in Mike's voice tugged at Jonathon's heart, and he couldn't bear to tease him a moment longer.

"Then isn't it a good thing that they called to say they're shopping in Winchester, don't expect them for dinner, and there's a damn good play on that they want to see while they're there?"

"You little sod."

Jonathon laughed. "Sorry. I couldn't resist. But I will come over, only if…"

"If what?"

"Only if you promise to make it worth my while," he teased.

"I just put fresh sheets on my bed. The ones I washed with that lavender and chamomile washing powder that you love so much. The bed smells wonderful." Mike lowered his voice. "But it would smell even more wonderful if you were in it."

That was enough to send Jonathon's mind off on a tangent that had nothing to do with murder and everything to do with Mike, naked, between clean, sweet-smelling sheets.

Sleuthing could wait.

BY NINE o'clock, the pub was filled with lively chatter as the locals gathered. Mike was surprised to see Professor Harcourt, who smiled as he sat on a barstool. "I've been having a very relaxing few days. Since we had tea with the Talbots, I've caught up on some sleep, done a lot of reading, even helped Melinda in the vicarage garden…. It's been great. Not that my wife is of the same opinion. She expected me home two days ago." He leaned closer. "I'm afraid I'm guilty of lying to her. I told her I was helping the police with their case."

Mike let out a dramatic gasp. "Oh, Professor." He grinned. "Okay, confess. What are you avoiding?"

"Is it that obvious?" Professor Harcourt sighed. "She recently put together a list of jobs she'd liked me to do around the house. Doors that need repainting. Locks that need fixing. In other words, DIY hell."

Mike snickered. "Now I understand. What'll it be?"

"A glass of brandy, please." Professor Harcourt glanced around the pub. "Where's Jonathon?"

"He's in the kitchen, talking to Constable Billings. It was too noisy out here."

Harcourt arched his eyebrows. "Nothing wrong, I hope."

"Oh, no," Mike assured him. "Graham had some information he wanted to share with us, and apart from the noise level in here, we thought it best if he wasn't seen talking to us. Word might get back to the wrong ears, if you get my drift." Mike placed the glass in front of him.

The professor's eyes sparkled. "Aha. You mean DI Gorland might think he's consorting with the enemy. Very wise."

"That you, Dr. Harcourt?" Seth Franklin approached the bar, smiling broadly, a half-empty pint glass in his hand. "I *thought* it was you earlier this week."

Professor Harcourt frowned, then returned Seth's smile. "Mr. Franklin. I haven't been Dr. Harcourt for a good few years now. How are you?"

Seth nodded, his cheeks pink. "Good. Why don't you come over 'ere, and we can have a good chat. I've been wantin' to see the quack about my bunions for a while. Reckon you might be able to give me some advice?"

Mike bit back his laughter at the expression on Professor Harcourt's face. "Oh. I see." He gave Mike a look that said plainly *help me*.

Just then, Graham and Jonathon walked into the bar. Graham gave Mike a wave as he headed for the door.

Mike beamed at Professor Harcourt. "It's not every day you get a chance to discuss someone's bunions. Don't let me stop you."

Professor Harcourt narrowed his gaze. "I shan't forget this, you know." His lips twitched, however. He followed Seth to a table at the far end of the bar.

Jonathon took the newly vacated stool. "What have I missed?"

Mike chuckled. "The professor is about to hear all about Seth's many ailments."

"Oh, the poor man. And you didn't save him?"

Mike leaned over the bar. "No, because I wanted to know what Graham had to say."

Jonathon's eyes shone. "Lots. And yes, I made notes."

"Forget the notes. Give me the gist." Mike laughed when Jonathon looked pointedly at the fridge containing the wine bottles. "Oh, I'm sorry. Does your throat need some lubrication? I'd have thought you'd gotten enough of that earlier." He loved the way Jonathon's eyes darkened a little.

"You are a wicked man."

Mike placed a glass of chilled chardonnay in front of him. "There. Now talk."

Jonathon took a sip. "Okay. A police officer contacted Graham, saying he knew Teresa. In fact, he was the one who recommended that she meet with Professor Harcourt for her research."

"Ah. Okay. So what did he have to say?"

"He mentioned Teresa's upcoming book, but this is where it gets interesting. This wasn't about the next Summersfield novel. This was for something new. Teresa was going to write books about real crimes, specifically about unsolved murders. And the reason he'd contacted her was because of a case he'd heard about when he was just starting out in the police force."

Mike let out a low whistle. "She wasn't kidding when she said it would be lucrative. That's a huge market."

Jonathon nodded eagerly. "Anyway, this guy's first inspector had told him a few details about a case he thought might be of interest to her. As far as I can ascertain, someone's spouse died in what looked like an accident, but a relative was suspicious. They went to the police and demanded an investigation, but nothing came of it. *Then* the relative killed themselves, apparently from grief." Jonathon locked gazes with him. "Does any of this sound familiar?"

Mike nodded slowly. "It's that post Teresa put on Facebook. So what was her angle? It wasn't really a suicide, but murder?"

"Yes." Jonathon's brows knitted. "But this is where I got confused. If this was the book Teresa was talking about with Professor Harcourt in their meeting, where does the untraceable poison come in that he mentioned? Is that what the relative took to kill themselves?"

Mike considered this for a moment. "Maybe we're talking two different books here—Summersfield number twenty-one, and the true crime one. Maybe she was researching the Summersfield book when she met the professor."

Jonathon's frown deepened. "That makes the situation worse. Which book brought about her death? That's if it was a book at all and not some other motive. Heaven knows, there are enough people out there who had reason to want her dead."

"It doesn't matter if there was one book or two," Mike told him. "The motive is the same—someone who didn't want Teresa shining a light on their past."

Someone who thought they'd gotten away with murder.

"So we're no better off," Jonathon mused.

"I don't know about that." Mike leaned forward, his elbows on the bar. "But I think I know what might help us get closer to finding out the truth."

"And what's that?"

He smiled. "We talk to her assistant. ASAP." She had to have some of the answers.

He hoped.

"By the way, Graham says he's going to see if he can find out anything more about this case. He'll get back to us when he does."

Mike arched his eyebrows. "And what does Gorland think of this development?"

Jonathon huffed. "Graham said he thinks it's not linked to her death."

"Well, that settles it." Mike grinned. "It almost certainly is."

"You're not implying that Gorland's a poor detective, are you?" That sparkle of good humor in Jonathon's eyes was very attractive.

Mike lowered his voice. "I'm implying he couldn't detect his way out of a paper bag."

Jonathon's attempt to stifle his laughter resulted in an epic fail when he sprayed white wine over himself.

CHAPTER NINETEEN

MIKE OPENED his eyes and rubbed them. Even without rolling over in bed, he knew Jonathon was awake. Mike had grown accustomed to the sound of his breathing, slow and even. Sometimes, when he woke up in the middle of the night, it was those comforting sounds that lulled him back into the arms of sleep.

I love it when he stays the night. Then he realized it was going to be a permanent feature, once they were married.

Now *there* was a thought to warm him.

"Morning." When Mike got no response, he turned over to find Jonathon sitting up in bed, a notepad in his hand. Mike sighed. "It's Sunday morning."

"And your point is?" Jonathon gave him a cheeky smile. "What can I say? I woke up thinking about the case. And what concerns me is some of the chief suspects are no longer around. Phil, Melody…."

"Is Fiona McBride on the list?"

Jonathon frowned. "Should she be?"

"I think after what Melinda and Lloyd told us, she—"

"They didn't *tell* us anything," Jonathon interjected. "They merely hinted. But you're right. They obviously know more than we do, so maybe we should take a closer look at her." He tapped the notepad with his pen. "And we mustn't forget Harold Tenby."

"Who?" For a moment, Mike was confused. Then the penny dropped. "Ah. The guy who rents Lily's house. Yes. We need to talk to him." He peered at the notepad. "And you've got Meredith." One name was conspicuous by its absence, however. "Why don't I see Paul's name?"

Jonathon heaved a heavy sigh and added Paul to the list. "There. Happy now? But I still don't think he's a murderer."

"What did I say about being objective?" Mike took the notepad and pen away from Jonathon and placed them on the bedside cabinet.

Jonathon smirked. "I'm getting déjà vu here. Because it feels like you've done this before."

Mike decided it was time to forget subtlety. He slowly pushed the sheets off his body, loving the hitch in Jonathon's breathing. "I am merely saying there's something here that needs your attention more than that list." When Jonathon shifted instantly across the bed to lie between Mike's spread legs, Mike let out a contented sigh and closed his eyes, his hands resting lightly on Jonathon's head.

Sunday morning sex was the best.

JONATHON PEERED at his phone screen and chuckled. "I think Janet has made Ruth and Clare's weekend. She took them breakfast in bed."

Mike scowled. "How come *we* never get breakfast in bed?"

"Because *I* don't want toast crumbs turning up in uncomfortable places, that's why." Except he wasn't thinking about breakfast. His mind had already returned to the case. "Do you think I should wait until Monday before contacting Teresa's PA?" Calling on a Sunday felt wrong, kind of pushy.

"If she's an assistant, she'll probably have an answer phone. You can always leave a message." Mike poured him another mug of coffee. "I thought I'd ask Abi if she wants to work today."

Jonathon regarded him intently. "Can I ask you something? Seeing as Abi is already doing so many shifts, why don't you make this a more permanent arrangement? You could make her the pub manager, giving her more and more shifts as we get closer to the wedding. Because if you're serious about traveling with me…."

Mike sat in the chair facing him. "I've been thinking about that too. If I go down that route, I might have to open the pub for more hours. Twelve till four, and six till closing is fine when there's only me to consider. But if I open from eleven until closing, that might improve the financial side of things." He smiled. "I should explain. The only time you make any real money with a pub or a bar is when you sell it. Until that point, whatever you make pays the bills. Employing Abi for a few shifts here and there has been okay, but if she's permanent, the salary I'd pay her would be income I'd lose."

"Then why the plan about opening more hours?"

"I want to increase the pub's profitability before I put it on the market."

Jonathon stilled. "Then you *are* going to sell it."

Mike shrugged. "I'm certainly considering it. I want to spend time with my husband, and then with our kids."

Jonathon chuckled. "Oh, so we're *definitely* having more than one? Better make sure Ruth knows." Something Mike had said struck home. "You know I have no money issues, right? What my grandfather left me is plenty for both of us, for the rest of our lives." Jonathon paused for a moment. "I've never been one to lie around all day being one of the idle rich. That is anathema to me. The photography allows me to do what I love, what I'm good at, *and* earn a living. The Vietnam trip would be my chance to get one more book out before our little family increases in size. When I asked if you would sell the pub, I wasn't suggesting for a second that you become a stay-at-home husband. It would be wrong of me." He reached across the table for Mike's hand. "I want to spend as much time as possible with you too."

Mike lifted his hand and kissed the knuckles. "We're both playing this by ear. Everything will work out, sweetheart. The key thing is, we're meant to be together. And we're going to be." His eyes twinkled. "Now call that PA."

Jonathon laughed as Mike released his hand. "Fine. I'll call her—as soon as *someone* gives me her name and number. Because I'm not going to get far without those."

Mike got out his phone, shaking his head. "Seriously rethinking this whole wedding idea. Not sure I want to be married to such a smartarse." He tapped the screen. "There. She's called Sharon Weston, and now you have her contact details."

Jonathon batted his eyelashes. "Thank you, *sweetheart*. Love you too." He opened the text and clicked on Sharon's number. He had to smile when Mike placed his notepad within easy reach, then left a pen on top of it before vacating the kitchen.

He thinks of everything.

"You've reached the voicemail for Sharon Weston. I'm sorry I can't answer your call right now, but please leave your name and number after the beep, and I'll get back to you as soon as possible."

"My name is Jonathon de Mountford, and I recently helped host the Merrychurch Literary Festival. I'd be grateful if you'd call me. My fiancé and I have been looking into Teresa Malvain's death, and—"

A click interrupted him in full flow. "Mr. de Mountford? This is Sharon Weston. I thought you might be getting in touch with me, although I had no idea you were an investigator of some sort."

Jonathon coughed. "That's because, technically, I'm not. My fiancé, however, is an ex-police officer, and we're helping the local police with their inquiries." Which was true—Gorland wasn't local.

Using the word fiancé sent a wave of pleasure through him. *I don't think I'll ever get tired of that.*

"Isn't that what they say about people who've been taken in for questioning? *Helping police with their inquiries*?"

In an instant he realized she was right. "Oh God. No. We're not suspects. We're just… helping them investigate, shall we say."

"Oh, I see. Well, as you can imagine, this has been a hell of a shock. It still doesn't seem real."

"I would have contacted you earlier, but we didn't know you existed until yesterday," Jonathon told her. "Mike—that's my fiancé—owns the pub where Teresa was staying, and we were wondering about a parcel she received." He told her about the book with the highlighted phrase. "Has she ever received anything like that before?"

"God, yes. There have been three or four anonymous letters too, and all the same—hinting at something she'd done in her past. Secrets she's been keeping."

"Did Teresa have any idea who was sending them?"

There was a pause. "If she did, she certainly didn't share it with me. The only reason I know about them is that I was with her one morning when she received one in the mail. When she didn't appear surprised, I asked her about it, and she showed me the others. I wanted her to contact the police, but she wouldn't." Another pause. "You know what? I think she had a good idea who was sending them. Like I said, she didn't name anyone—it's just a gut feeling."

"Did she have a diary of some sort?" There hadn't been one in her belongings.

Sharon laughed. "That notebook of hers. She wrote down everything in there."

"I know that's where she wrote notes for her next book. Could you share anything about that?"

"Feel free to look in the notebook. It's all in there. And it's not like she can complain about it, right?"

"But that's the problem. Her notebook is missing."

"Seriously? You mean, someone took it? Because I can't for one minute imagine her losing it. Was that after she died, because I think she'd have kicked up one hell of a fuss when *that* happened? That was her precious, truly."

"It was seen with her before the allergic reaction, but not since."

"But it's all still on the cloud."

It took a minute for the full import of her words to sink in. "She uploaded everything onto the cloud?"

"She didn't bother typing it all out and uploading. Teresa was way too lazy for that. But she did take photos of every page in her notebook before uploading them. That way, if she ever lost it, she still had the notes."

Jonathon's heartbeat raced. "Can I get copies of those photos?"

Another longer pause. "You said you're helping the police with their inquiries. Into what, exactly? Why would they be investigating death by anaphylactic shock?"

He sighed. "Because we have reason to believe she was murdered. Someone placed peanut oil in her coffee."

He couldn't miss Sharon's gasp. "Oh shit. Sorry, that just slipped out. So that's why you asked about the book and whether she'd received anything else. You think the killer might have sent them."

"It's a possibility we have to consider."

"Okay, to be honest? I never read the contents of her notebook. I wasn't given permission to do that. But... I can try to find the link and send it to you. Should I send this to the police too?"

"Haven't they already interviewed you? I'd have thought you would be one of the first people they'd contact."

"They probably contacted her agent first. I'm further down the pecking order. But doubtless I'll get a call soon."

"When you do, give them the link too. That's if you can find it." Not that Jonathon wasn't going to send it to Graham. Keeping on Graham's good side was high on his list of priorities. "How far back does this notebook go?"

Sharon laughed. "She was on maybe her tenth notebook. Everything went in them—research notes, plot notes, meetings, musings…. And if she saw a notebook that she liked, she bought it. There's a shelf in her apartment that contains nothing but notebooks—ones she's already filled, and others waiting to *be* filled." Sharon snickered. "I called it stationery porn. The present notebook has been going since January of this year." A slight pause. "The link should give you access to *all* her notebooks. Each one is in its own folder. I hope you have some spare time to read it all. You also have my sympathies."

"Why?" he asked, puzzled.

"Because you're going to have to wade through a *lot* of notes to hopefully find a few nuggets of information that might help you. I hope they *do* help, though."

"Thank you." Jonathon gave her his email address. "I'll be awaiting the link."

"Good luck." Sharon sighed heavily. "She was a pain in the arse to work for, I have to admit, but she didn't deserve this."

"Well, apparently *someone* thought she did." Jonathon thanked her again, then disconnected the call. He got up from the table and went into the pub in search of Mike. He found him checking the stock and making notes on a clipboard.

Mike glanced up as he approached the bar. "Well? I gather you were able to speak to her." Jonathon gave him a précis of what Sharon had said, and Mike groaned. "*More* reading? And we can't even ask Professor Harcourt to help us this time, because he'll be gone sometime soon."

"I'll go up to the house and grab my laptop. While I'm up there, I'll check my email to see if it's arrived. Then I'll download what I can and come back here." He grinned. "Besides, I need to put in an appearance. The girls have hardly seen us since they arrived."

Mike snorted. "The *girls* have been enjoying themselves, mark my words. Ivy is feeding them, they shopped till they dropped yesterday, they don't have to do anything today but relax…. And it sounds like they don't get that much time together, so they're making the best of things. That'll change when they move into their house, but for now, I'm sure a weekend of leisure is heaven for them."

"I suppose you're right." Jonathon gave Mike an innocent glance. "Is Abi doing the first shift?"

"Yes, why?" Mike narrowed his gaze. "I know that look. You're up to something."

"Do you know what would go well with reading notes? Cake. A lot of cake. And coffee. Specifically, Rachel's coffee and cake."

Mike laughed. "Elevenses at the tea shop? Why not? Only, be prepared to have Rachel looking over our shoulder."

Jonathon chuckled. "Teresa got it all wrong, you know, making a doctor's receptionist her amateur sleuth. She should have made her the owner of a coffee shop. They get to hear everything."

Mike reached into his jeans pocket, removed his keys, and tossed them to Jonathon. "Take my car. I'll meet you at Rachel's."

"Are you sure?" Then Jonathon widened his grin. "It's not like you didn't get enough exercise this morning. I get tired thinking about it."

And hot. He also got *very* hot.

CHAPTER TWENTY

MIKE SMILED as Jonathon strolled into the tea shop, his backpack slung over one shoulder. "I remember the day we met, when I picked you up near the train station. You were holding on to that backpack like it was made of gold. Later, of course, I understood. It contained your camera."

Jonathon sighed as he took the seat next to Mike. "Almost a year ago. The time has certainly flown by." He removed his laptop from the backpack and placed it on the table, then glanced around. "Why is there no coffee and cake? You're slipping." His eyes twinkled.

Mike indicated the rear door of the tea shop. "Rachel has just baked some scones." When Jonathon's eyes widened and he licked his lips, Mike laughed. "*Now* you know why I waited. You can't resist freshly baked scones. And yes, they come with butter, strawberry jam, and cream."

"I once started a small war in here," Jonathon confided. "I asked—very innocently, I might add—why some people felt it necessary to put the cream on the scone before the jam." He arched his eyebrows. "I had no idea emotions ran so high on the subject."

Mike groaned. "Of all the things to ask in a tea shop." At that moment, Rachel came into the shop, carrying a cake stand, and the aroma was mouthwatering. She placed it on the table before disappearing back into the kitchen to fetch the coffee. "Did Sharon send you that link? Did you download all the photo files?"

Jonathon nodded. "Yes and yes. Sharon was right. There were ten folders in the cloud. I haven't taken a peek at any of the contents yet, but I have taken the liberty of emailing them to you too." His phone warbled, and he removed it from his backpack with a scowl. "I don't want to answer calls or read texts right now. I want to eat—" He froze.

"Jonathon? What is it?" Jonathon's expression was one of displeasure.

"Change of plan. My father has a meeting tomorrow in Bath, so rather than visit us next weekend, he intends stopping at the house tomorrow evening and staying the night." With a sigh he composed a text, his fingers flying over the keys. "I'm letting Janet know. She hates last-minute changes."

"Look on the bright side," Mike suggested.

Jonathon stared at him in frank astonishment. "There's a bright side?"

Mike chuckled. "I can tell you never read *Pollyanna* as a child. If he comes tomorrow night, that's a whole week you *don't* have of dreading his visit. Plus, Ruth and Clare will be leaving tonight, so they won't run into each other."

"Good point." Jonathon's face brightened as Rachel approached with the coffeepot, which she placed on their table.

"Anyone would think you didn't like my coffee." Mike aimed a hard stare at him.

"You know when I *really* love your coffee? When you bring it to me in bed." Jonathon lowered his voice. "Of course, the best part is, you're naked."

Obviously his voice wasn't low enough, judging by the splutters that broke the tea shop's quiet. Rachel gave him a mock glare, her hands on her hips, but when she turned to head back to the kitchen, her shoulders were shaking.

Mike sighed. "Is nothing sacred?" He pointed to the laptop. "Boot it up. Let's get your mind on other things."

Jonathon bit his lip but complied. Mike poured the coffee, then split a warm scone for Jonathon before placing it on a small patterned plate next to the laptop.

Jonathon stared at the screen, deep in concentration. "This might take us a while. There's a lot to go through here. I mean, where do we start? These cover six years."

"Pick a year." Mike buttered half of the scone, then added the jam. "We have to start somewhere. However, Sharon said Teresa had received anonymous letters, so let's start with this year. We want to find out about the next book too." Then he realized Jonathon had fallen silent. "You've found something already."

Jonathon nodded. "From January this year. It's a note about Fiona McBride, actually." He scanned the screen. "Teresa thought she was the source of the anonymous letters."

"But why?"

Jonathon was still reading. "Okay, this is interesting. Teresa thought Fiona had found out about someone called Tessa Durban."

"Who on earth is Tessa Durban?" Mike got out his phone and opened a search engine. He typed in the name, then put down the phone and took a bite out of his scone. "God, these are good." He peered at the screen. "Ah. She's a writer."

"What does she write?" Jonathon helped himself to a bite of his scone and rolled his eyes. "Agreed. This is amazing."

"Correction—what *did* she write. Tessa Durban wrote three romance novels between 2008 and 2011, and hasn't written since." Mike clicked on a link and skimmed through the information. "Oh wow. Now I know why she stopped writing."

"Did she die?" Jonathon's eyes shone. "Was she killed by Teresa Malvain, and Fiona found out and was threatening to tell all?" He was clearly enjoying the thought.

Mike read aloud from the page. "On what planet could this be described as a romance? It's like the author delved deep into every romantic cliché, yet came up with something that has no soul, no plot, a heroine who isn't even likable, and a hero who obviously has no taste. I for one will never buy another of her books. Don't give up the day job, Tessa."

"Ouch. What is that?"

"That is a review of her first book. And there are lots more like it." He clicked on another book, then headed for the reviews. He grimaced. "Oh boy. She was an awful writer, if these reviews are anything to go by."

"I guess you were right about why she stopped writing. She couldn't have made any money at it. Who was the publisher?"

Mike searched for a name. "There doesn't seem to be one—oh, hold on a minute. Lulu."

"That's a platform for self-publishing," Jonathon told him. "So she self-published back in 2008? A pioneer."

"An unsuccessful pioneer, judging by her reviews. Obviously she was disheartened and never wrote again."

"Never mind that," Jonathon said with a hint of impatience. "The notes say Fiona had 'found out' about Tessa Durban. What exactly did she find out? That she was a dreadful writer? That isn't a secret. You only have to read her reviews." He got out his phone and tapped the screen.

"Who are you calling?" Mike asked as Jonathon put the phone to his ear.

Jonathon held up his hand for silence. "Hey, Sharon? It's Jonathon de Mountford again. Sorry to disturb you, but—" He smiled. "Thanks for picking up the call. I wanted to know if a name is familiar to you. Tessa Durban." He listened intently, one hand scrabbling in his backpack for his notepad and pen. "I see. You're sure? Wow. … Oh, course she didn't.…" He chuckled. "Who would want that on their CV? … Thanks. Yes, that helps a lot." He disconnected the call. "*Now* it makes sense," he announced triumphantly.

Mike sat back and folded his arms. "Let me guess. Teresa Malvain and Tessa Durban are one and the same."

Jonathon gaped. "How did you…?"

Mike buffed his fingernails on his shirt. "I wasn't a DI for nothing." He chuckled. "It's the only logical conclusion."

"Apparently those three books were her first forays into writing. She was still living in Merrychurch at the time. Then she wrote the draft of a murder mystery, got herself an agent, who in turn found her a publisher, and *voila*! She started writing the Summersfield series as Teresa Malvain and struck gold."

"So, no talent for romance, but murder was different?"

Jonathon smiled. "Sharon only found out because Teresa let it slip a few years back, when they were sharing a bottle of wine."

"That figures. She sure could drink." Mike rubbed his beard. "I'm assuming this isn't common knowledge."

"Absolutely not. Sharon said none of Teresa's fans have any idea that the romances were hers, and Teresa wanted it to stay that way."

Mike nodded slowly. "But then somehow Fiona finds out. And starts sending the letters, warning Teresa that her past would catch up with her. What was Fiona's plan? To expose Teresa? To humiliate her? And why?"

He gave a start when a loud cough erupted from behind them. Rachel stood there with a plate of cake. "Sorry, but I couldn't help overhearing what you just said."

Mike leveled a stern gaze in her direction. "What do they say about eavesdroppers never hearing any good about themselves? One of these days, you might be the topic of conversation."

Rachel pulled a chair from the next table and joined them. "Okay, you know I'm not one to gossip, but—" She glared at Jonathon when he stifled a chuckle. "Do you want my help or not?"

Jonathon bit his lip, and Mike smiled. "Please," he said, "do tell."

"You want to know why Fiona might have it in for Teresa? I'll tell you. It's all to do with Fiona's husband."

"Melinda mentioned something about her husband," Jonathon observed.

Rachel nodded. "Okay, this happened in 2003. Fiona's husband, Ken, was really ill, and she tried to get a home visit from the doctor, because there was no way Ken could make it to the surgery. Teresa kept telling her the doctor was fully booked, although Fiona tried for a few days, always getting the same answer. Then Ken has a series of mini strokes, and they ended up calling an ambulance. When he got to the hospital, he had another stroke, only this was a lot more serious. He died three months later."

"And Fiona blamed Teresa for his death," Mike concluded.

Another nod. "We could understand her reaction. That's why we were so surprised when she started Teresa Malvain's fan club. It didn't make sense."

"Maybe it was a cover," Jonathon suggested. "She acts all friendly toward Teresa, when in reality, she's biding her time, waiting for the right moment to reveal all."

The door chimes rang out, and Rachel left them to deal with some new customers.

Mike took another bite of his scone before speaking. "Okay, I get the letters and the book. But if she was doing all that, why kill her?"

Jonathon stared at his plate. "You're right. Without the letters and the book, I'd agree she could be the killer. She has a good enough motive, if she holds Teresa responsible for the death of her husband. But if she wanted to kill her, she'd simply do it and not bother with the letters."

"Unless…." Mike sipped his coffee. "Maybe she *wanted* Teresa to be fearful, off-balance. And this is all supposition, you know. We have no proof Fiona sent the letters or the book. We only have Teresa's suspicions." He pointed to Jonathon's laptop. "What we *do* have is a load of notes to go through. We need to know what was going to be in that next book. Because that might hold the key to her murder."

"Yes, it might," Jonathon agreed. "Although it might not have anything to do with her new book. We need to remember—someone took that notebook for a reason. There has to be something in it they didn't want anyone to know."

Jonathon was right. The notebook was clearly important.

Mike sighed. "And there I was, anticipating a quiet afternoon with you."

"Oh, it will be quiet." Jonathon smiled. "We'll both be reading."

Mike leaned over. "But who says we have to be clothed while we read?" he whispered. Then he straightened, his cup in his hand. "See? Every cloud has a silver lining."

Jonathon smirked. "Yes, Pollyanna."

CHAPTER TWENTY-ONE

JONATHON GAVE Ruth a hug. "Thank you for coming." They stood beside Ruth's car, the late afternoon sun warm on Jonathon's back. The chirp of birds could be heard all around them, and the faint odor of a fire drifted on the warm breeze. Ben had to be burning garden waste somewhere on the grounds.

She chuckled. "I still can't believe we all had the same idea." When he released her, she squeezed his hand. "I'll make an appointment to see my doctor as soon as possible, and then we'll talk logistics. It will probably mean you coming to a clinic to... do the deed, as it were."

He held on to her hand. "You're sure about this, then?"

Ruth nodded. "I wouldn't do this for just anyone, you know. And I like the idea that the four of us will be a family of sorts." She locked gazes with him. "Good luck for tomorrow with your father. I know you're probably looking forward to it with as much enthusiasm as you would have for, say, root canal work, but in the end, he can't argue. He's getting what he wants, after all, and I firmly believe he'll see that this is the perfect solution."

"I foresee one part of this arrangement that won't be so easy to swallow." Jonathon was hoping the surrogacy would soften the blow of a gay wedding, one that was sure to hit the headlines.

Ruth shook her head. "You are too good, do you know that? He's been a bigoted arse about all this, and yet you've tried your damnedest to keep him happy. He doesn't deserve to have you as a son."

"I only have one father, right? And I want our children to have a good relationship with their grandfather."

Ruth cocked her head to one side. "Where does your mother stand on all this? Does she have an opinion?"

Jonathon huffed. "Of course she does. She follows whatever my father thinks." At that moment, Mike and Clare came out of the hall, with Mike carrying their bags. Clare walked toward Jonathon, her arms outstretched. Jonathon found himself on the receiving end of an enthusiastic hug.

"We'll be back soon. And before the wedding too. Are you still aiming for September?" she asked as Mike loaded the bags into the boot of the car.

"Yes, although we need to set the wheels in motion for that." Such as applying for a marriage license, finding a suitable celebrant, planning the ceremony, organizing the reception…. Jonathon had a feeling the next two months would fly by. "When we have a definite date, we'll let you know."

Clare gave a nod before glancing at Ruth. "I'll drive, seeing as you got us here." She gave them a wave. "Take care, boys."

"Have fun storming the castle!" Ruth added with a grin as she got into the passenger seat.

Mike frowned. "Castle?" The car roared into life, and the girls drove away from the hall, the tires crunching on the gravel driveway.

Jonathon rolled his eyes. "I can see I have work to do if you don't recognize that line." He squinted at Mike. "You *have* seen the film *The Princess Bride*?"

"That sounds like a chick flick and probably not something I'd like."

Jonathon let out a loud gasp. "I may have to re-think this whole marriage idea."

Mike narrowed his gaze. "You *have* heard of ELO, Genesis, and Fleetwood Mac, right?" When Jonathon stared at him, perplexed, Mike smiled. "See? Two can play at that game, sweetheart. Now get that cute arse inside, and let's look at Teresa's notes before dinner."

As they walked into the hall, Jonathon couldn't resist. "I have a cute arse?"

"PASS ME your list, please." Mike held out his hand for Jonathon's notepad. He peered at Jonathon's neat writing. "Tasks yet to be done seem to be: interviewing Harold Tenby; seeing if we can find out anything about Meredith Roberts's aunt, and if there is anything to the rumors that Meredith had something to do with the change in her will and her subsequent death; seeing if we can definitely tie Fiona to the anonymous letters and the book parcel—"

"She was in the pub that night, remember. And she was near the bar where the coffees were," Jonathon reminded him.

Mike nodded. "So were Phil McCallister and Melody Richards, remember? We have quite a few suspects who could've put the peanut oil in the coffee, and they all have a reason for wanting Teresa dead."

"We know something else. Teresa had the notebook in the bar, because it was seen in her bag, but when the professor emptied her bag onto the bed, the notebook had gone. So that points to someone removing it in all the confusion."

"Something's occurred to me," Mike mused. "Remember at dinner, when Fiona introduced herself to Teresa? Well, Fiona asked if Teresa remembered her, and Teresa asked if they'd met. According to her notebook, she knew exactly who Fiona was—she already suspected her of writing the letters—which points to Teresa being a very cool customer, as well as a damn good actress. She fooled me, at least."

"Not an easy thing to do," Jonathon murmured, finishing his coffee. Not for the first time, the mention of the notebook struck an uneasy chord in his mind. Jonathon prided himself on his memory, and it irked him that there was something important he'd overlooked that remained out of reach.

Mike tapped his laptop. "Come on. We've got notes to read."

They sat on the couch, their feet resting on the coffee table, and Janet periodically brought coffee before informing them dinner was ready. Except Jonathon was in no mood to eat, and of course, Mike noticed.

"Want to tell me what's on your mind?"

Jonathon pushed his plate aside. "Something in Teresa's notes, about her meeting with Professor Harcourt."

"What's bothering you about that?"

"You remember what he said? Untraceable poison? Well... according to her notes, she wanted to know if a pathologist could tell if someone had blown his own head off, or if someone else had pulled the trigger. Apparently they discussed angles of trajectory, fingerprints on the weapon. Then she shared the outline for her new venture, the true crime series."

Mike stared at him. "So he knew about it? He didn't mention it."

"More importantly, he didn't tell us the real topic of conversation. But why would he lie?" Jonathon didn't like to think that the elderly professor who'd helped them with the reading and offered so much advice had lied to them.

"There is one possibility," Mike suggested. "Teresa hadn't shared what she was up to with anyone, apart from her PA. Maybe she swore him to secrecy."

Jonathon wasn't buying it. "But she's dead. What harm could it do to share the information now? And something else comes to mind. Maybe her question was related to her new book. Someone appears to commit suicide.... This grieving relative she mentioned in her post—supposing he shot himself? Blew his head off with a shotgun? How difficult would it be to fake that?"

"Maybe the person you should be talking to is Professor Harcourt," Mike said quietly. "But do me a favor? Ask him tomorrow. You've hardly eaten a bite."

Jonathon picked up his fork. "You're right. This can wait. Besides, we've got more important things to worry about. My father arrives tomorrow, remember?"

"Now that is enough to put someone off their dinner." Mike's eyes twinkled. "Eat. Then after dinner, we're going to put on a DVD and forget about this."

For a moment Jonathon was confused. "You want to watch a film?"

Mike chuckled. "I want to see what I'm missing out on. *The Princess Bride*?"

Curled up on the couch together watching one of Jonathon's favorite films sounded like the perfect way to end the day.

THE FOLLOWING morning, Jonathon awoke with a purpose. He wanted to tie up loose ends, and there was only one person who could help with that. As soon as breakfast was over, he sent Graham a text.

Are we okay to meet this morning?

Graham's reply was instant. *Your timing could be better. He's on the warpath. But I can meet you in the village. Churchyard, half an hour.*

It sounded an odd place to meet, but Jonathon agreed. When he'd finished sending his reply, he slipped his phone into his pocket.

"So what was that all about? Arranging to meet your other man?" Mike grinned.

"Yes," Jonathon responded promptly. "He's dressed all in blue, wears a pointy helmet, and carries a big stick."

"You're cheating on me with *Graham*? And I thought you had good taste."

Jonathon snickered. "Trust me, I have my hands full with you. I couldn't handle two men at once. I'm just popping out to meet him. I won't be long."

"Want me to come along?"

He laughed. "And how would that look if word got back to Gorland? Graham must be thinking along the same lines." He showed Mike the text.

"The churchyard? Ooh, that sounds kinky."

Jonathon rolled his eyes. "Make yourself useful. See that my father's room is ready?"

Mike nodded. "I'll make sure it's perfect." He leaned over and kissed Jonathon on the lips, a slow, lingering kiss that made him yearn to be back in their bed.

Then Jonathon pushed aside such delicious thoughts. He had to meet a man among the graves.

As soon as Jonathon entered the cool, leafy churchyard, he saw immediately why Graham had suggested it. Stone urns that had stood on gravestones and by headstones lay broken, their flowery contents trampled upon. Graham was standing by one of the graves, taking notes. He looked up as Jonathon approached.

"Morning. Now who does a thing like this? I'm thinking kids from that estate. Little buggers. Melinda reported it first thing this morning."

"And you thought you'd kill two birds with one stone."

Graham laughed. "Kind of. Okay, Watson. What's on your mind?"

"I was wondering if the police were investigating Phil McCallister, Melody Richards, Meredith Roberts, and Paul Drake for any possible involvement in Teresa's death."

Graham's eyes went wide at the last name. "Our Paul? What motive would he have for killing her?"

Jonathon ran through what they'd discovered, and Graham made notes. When he was done, Graham ran his hand through his hair.

"Let me get this straight. You, Mike, and Professor Harcourt read all of her books, looking for a killer?" He chuckled. "You'd have made a great copper." He sat on one of the headstones. "Okay. I agree there's motive where all of them are concerned. The problem is proving it. No one saw a thing. Sure, they saw the coffees on the bar, but as for seeing the killer add the oil? Not a sausage. We interviewed the authors, but they claim to have left the pub not long after Teresa first became ill. And no one saw them leave, the pub was so packed." He peered at his notes. "Meredith Roberts. Isn't she the one who complained about you two?" Graham grinned. "*Now* I get it. You got a little too close for comfort, didn't ya?"

Jonathon told him how they'd caught her out in a lie.

"So she went running to Gorland. Definitely fishy, I'd say. Yeah, I remember her. Folks around here were real surprised when old Miss Tremont died. We thought she was as fit as a flea. Not that there was anything suspicious about the cause of death. At least, I don't think there was. But that business with the will…."

"What business?"

"Well, according to the will left with her solicitor, the house and all her possessions were to be sold, and the proceeds were to go to different charities. But then her niece turns up, armed with a new will, a later version, that leaves it all to her. The solicitor checked it over, but it was all signed and legal." Graham rubbed his jaw. "So *your* take is Teresa puts all this in a book, and Meredith panics, thinking it'll make folks look more closely into Miss Tremont's death? You may have something there. I'll look into that."

"And what about Paul?"

Graham looked him in the eye. "You don't think he's a murderer any more than I do. But at least with his case, there's one thing we can do that'll clear all this up for good." He grinned. "*Cherchez la femme.*" He pronounced it *fem*. "If his wife turns up alive and well, that kicks *that* theory in the head, doesn't it? So let's find her. Because wherever she is, she's gotta be working so she can live, right?" He tapped the side of his nose. "You leave that with me. Tax records, bank records… if she's earning, we'll find her." Graham straightened. "Now, is that everything?"

There was only one thing left.

"Have you found out any more details about that crime Teresa was going to write about?"

Graham sighed. "I was looking into that when the DI got wind of it. So far, I've not pinned it down."

"Well, I might be able to help you. The apparent suicide? I think it was a shotgun incident." Jonathon told him about the notes.

Graham's eyes gleamed. "Now that is helpful. Yeah, that might help me narrow the field a bit." He gave Jonathon a broad smile. "Thanks, mate."

"If we turn up anything else, we'll let you know."

Graham grinned. "It's a good thing you're not like that Teresa's amateur detective. She ended every book the same way—making the local police look like bumbling idiots." He bit his lip. "Mind you, if you were to make the *DI* look like a bumbling idiot…."

Jonathon laughed. "I'll pretend I didn't hear that." He shook Graham's hand and left him in the church-yard to finish his notes. As far as loose ends went, it hadn't been a totally satisfactory meeting.

Phil, Melody, and Meredith were definitely staying on the list.

CHAPTER TWENTY-TWO

"YOUR FATHER has arrived, sir," Janet said in her quiet voice. "Shall I bring him here?"

"Yes, please." Jonathon gave the cozy living room a last glance, scanning it for anything they might have missed. He could still recall the look on Janet's face when she retrieved a bottle of lube from between the seat cushions. Jonathon hadn't known where to look. He wanted no such similar accidents while his father was around.

Mike entered the room. "I saw his car. You ready for this?"

"As ready as I'll ever be."

Mike came over and kissed him. "Just remember, I've got your back." When the door opened, he didn't move, but remained at Jonathon's side.

His father walked into the room with a cautious air that was quite unlike him.

Jonathon gestured to the couch. "Good evening. Please, sit. Would you like a drink before dinner? Mike is playing bartender for us."

Father smirked. "How apt. A Scotch and soda would be good." He sat, his arm draped elegantly over the end of the couch. "I must admit, I'm curious to hear about this decision of yours. I half expected to see Ruth here."

"She left yesterday."

His father blinked. "Then she *was* here? This does involve her?"

"Most definitely." Jonathon noted his father's satisfied expression. It was the look of a man used to getting his own way in all things.

Not this time, Father.

Mike brought over the glass of Scotch and a vodka and Diet Coke for Jonathon. "Pleased to see you again, sir." He left them to pour himself a drink.

Jonathon sat in the armchair next to the fireplace. "Dinner won't be long. We thought we'd have a talk before eating."

Mike joined him, perching on the arm of the chair, his arm around Jonathon's shoulders.

His father settled back against the cushions. "Now, supposing you tell me your news. You *do* have news for me?"

"Indeed I do. Father, allow me to introduce Mr. Mike Tattersall." When his father's brows knitted, Jonathon smiled. "My fiancé."

"Your—" That frown hadn't budged. "I don't understand."

Jonathon's smiled widened. "You know, fiancé? I proposed, he accepted?"

Mike held up his left hand, the ring glinting around his finger.

"But Ruth… you and Ruth…."

"Ah, yes. Ruth. Actually, I must thank you for your part in this."

His father's eyes bulged. "*My* part?"

Jonathon nodded. "When you suggested Ruth would be a good match, you *were* thinking about future children, weren't you?"

"Well, yes, but—"

"Mike and I decided you were right. So we approached Ruth to ascertain if she'd be willing to be our surrogate, and she agreed." Jonathon beamed. "Hopefully it won't be long before there's the pitter patter of tiny feet, and you'll be holding your first grandchild."

His father stared at them before taking a long drink from his glass. "I had assumed you and she would marry."

"Ah. Yes. Well. There's a slight problem with that. She's already in love with someone else. Fortunately, her future partner is more than happy for her to carry our child. Not to mention the tiny but extremely significant detail that I am gay, as you very well know, so marrying Ruth is out of the question, however much you may want that. Nor am I single." He didn't need to know the rest. Two shocks were more than enough for now.

When his father gaped at them, speechless, Jonathon softened his voice.

"Father, you're getting everything you wanted, just without the wife part. The family line will continue. We're hoping for a couple of children, but if things don't work out the way we've planned, then we'll adopt. Rest assured, a de Mountford will occupy this house for many years to come."

His father cleared his throat. "Can I ask… who else knows about this… engagement?"

"Seeing as he got down on one knee in the middle of the pub, virtually the whole of Merrychurch," Mike informed him cheerily.

"You proposed… in the pub?" His father's pained expression was almost comical.

Mike nodded happily. "And I believe I have you to thank for that. He proposed immediately following his phone conversation with you."

"And how did the villagers react to this proposal?"

"Why don't you come to the wedding, and you'll see for yourself?" Jonathon said with a smile.

Father took another drink. "This is one battle I'm not going to win, isn't it?"

Jonathon had played nice long enough. "It shouldn't *be* a battle. Not if you want me to be happy. Let me ask you something. How would *you* have felt if you'd been in love with Mother, but Grandfather demanded you marry someone else? And don't tell me you'd have gone along with it for the sake of the family." He sighed. "Father, I know. What irks you is not that I'm not marrying Ruth, but that I *am* going to marry a man. Isn't it about time you accepted the fact that you have a gay son?"

"You make it sound so simple," his father said, his eyes wide. He gazed at Mike. "Can you honestly tell me your parents are happy that you're gay?"

"My parents have known I'm gay since I was a teenager. They're happy I've found someone who completes me. And they can't wait to have him as their son-in-law." Mike tilted his head to one side. "Did you ever stop to think that publicly acknowledging you have a gay son might do wonders for your street cred?"

Father blinked. "My… street cred?"

Mike nodded slowly. "You're a high court judge with an impressive record. I'm not suggesting for a moment that you hang a rainbow flag in your courtroom or walk in the Pride parade, but having a positive attitude toward the LGBTQ community would do you no harm."

His father gave Mike a look of frank amusement. "Why should anyone care about that?"

"Because we're living in the twenty-first century. Because LGBTQ rights are big news. Because LGBTQ rights are human rights. And because people are watching what you do. Who wants to be portrayed in the media as a homophobic asshole?"

Jonathon listened with both amazement and pride. Mike couldn't care less about his father's status, and he wasn't afraid to speak his mind. And judging by his father's contemplative expression, Mike had clearly given him something to consider.

The door opened, and Janet came into the room. "Dinner is ready, sir." She withdrew.

"As I recall, you have a very good cook," his father said as they made their way to the dining room.

"Ivy is a treasure." Jonathon glanced at Mike with a half smile. "When Mike's living here, I'm going to have to work hard at watching his weight." He waited for the explosion.

"*My* weight? How many portions of Ivy's lasagna did you eat last week?"

"I'm thinking of turning one of the rooms into a home gym, just to keep him in check." Teasing Mike was a joy Jonathon never tired of.

To his surprise, Mike's eyes widened. "Could we? Because right now the basement of the pub is where I store my weights and other stuff."

Jonathon came to a dead stop at the door of the dining room. "How come I didn't know that?"

Mike's eyes twinkled. "I don't exercise when you're around, that's why." What was implicit in his glance, however, was the unspoken sentence: *I get my exercise in other ways when you're there.*

Thank God he kept his mouth shut. Jonathon didn't think his father was ready for *that* much information.

As they entered the room, his father shook his head. "You already sound like an old married couple. I suppose that bodes well for the future."

A few words grudgingly spoken, but to Jonathon's ears, they were the beginning of a thaw, and inwardly he rejoiced.

He might not dance at my wedding, but there's every chance he'll be there.

"THAT WAS a smart move of yours," Mike murmured as he slipped between the cool sheets. The window was open, and the air that wafted through was redolent with the scent of night-blooming jasmine that grew in the garden below.

"What was?" Jonathon lay beneath a thin covering that hid very little.

"Putting your father in a room at the other end of the corridor. Although…." Mike grinned.

Jonathon narrowed his gaze. "You already gave him enough of an education this evening. Trust me, the last thing he needs is to hear his son having sex."

Mike molded his body to Jonathon's. "Then we *are* having sex?"

Jonathon smirked. "Was there ever any doubt?" He enfolded Mike in his arms. "Can I be serious for a minute?"

"Of course."

"I loved what you said to my father earlier. You spoke your mind, and you were honest." Jonathon caressed his cheek. "I was so proud of you."

"I did it for his benefit. I intend on being around a long time, and he needs to know what to expect right from the outset. I see no point in sugarcoating things. He has to learn what he sees is what he gets where I'm concerned." Mike hadn't realized how strongly he felt until he saw Thomas's reaction to their news. He couldn't drag the man kicking and screaming into the twenty-first century, but he could point out a few truths.

"I really think he'll be at the wedding. He might attend with a lot of trepidation because, hey, it's a gay wedding and he won't know what to expect, but he'll be there."

"Oh." Mike chuckled. "I've just had a great idea. I know a few bars in London where they always have drag acts. What if we asked a load of drag queens to the wedding? We could fill up half the seats with them. Think of the look on his face!"

Jonathon grabbed his jaw and held it firmly. "Wipe that idea from your brain. I mean it."

Mike laughed softly as Jonathon released him. "Sweetheart, I wouldn't do that. This wedding is going to attract a lot of media attention because of who your father is and who you are. I wouldn't do anything to spoil our day. Even if the idea is *really* tempting." He relished Jonathon's arms around him. "What do you want to do tomorrow, once he's left?"

"I'd like to continue reading Teresa's notes. Do you need to go back to the pub?"

"Only to pick up some clothes and do some laundry." Mike covered Jonathon's hand with his. "We could have morning coffee at Rachel's, if you'd like."

"Would you mind if I invited Melinda? She's invited us to tea so many times, I'd like to return the favor."

Mike thought that was a lovely idea. "I'm sure she'd love to come. Call her first thing." He paused. "Have you given any thought as to what you'd like for the wedding day? I know you mentioned the garden, but we need to start moving on this."

"Can we talk about this in the morning?"

"Don't you want to discuss our wedding?" Mike stilled as Jonathon shifted away from him, then smiled as he opened the drawer in the bedside cabinet. Mike knew what that meant. He caught his breath when Jonathon eased him firmly to lie facedown, and cool, slick fingers explored him. "I guess I'm not driving tonight." He spread his legs wide, welcoming the intrusion.

Jonathon's breath tickled his ear, his warm chest pressed against Mike's back. "Not initially. Your turn comes later."

Mike let out a happy sigh. "I'm all for equal opportunities."

CHAPTER TWENTY-THREE

"THIS IS very kind of you." Melinda took a small bite of her scone, and her face lit up. "Oh my. Rachel has a very light touch. These are delicious."

Jonathon poured her another cup of Earl Grey. "It seemed only fair to invite you, after all those afternoon teas at the vicarage." He bit his lip. "Did you ask Lloyd to come along?"

Melinda rolled her eyes. "Lloyd has other things on his mind right now, such as a visit from the bishop. I left him to it. He probably won't even notice I'm not there." She added lemon to her tea, then sat back in her chair. "So… on to more important questions. Have you decided on a date yet?"

Mike guffawed. "I wondered how long it would be before you mentioned the wedding. And the answer is, no, not yet. When we do, you'll be one of the first to know about it."

She gave them a knowing smile. "Aha. Then it's sleuthing business. Any closer to discovering Teresa's murderer?"

Jonathon sighed. "Well, we have some suspects." He told her about Phil McCallister and Melody Richards. "They're still on the list, although I'm not sure how we can find out more about them, seeing as neither of them are around."

"Rest assured, if the police feel there are grounds for investigating them, they'll pursue them," Melinda said sagely. "Now, what's this I hear about you two harassing Meredith Roberts?" Her blue eyes twinkled, the skin crinkling around them.

"Now she is definitely suspicious." Mike relayed how she'd lied to them. "I want to know more about how her aunt died."

Melinda's brow furrowed. "Meredith was never a frequent visitor, at least not until the last few months before Barbara Tremont died. But those final weeks, it seemed every time I walked through the village, she was on her way to or from Barbara's cottage."

"Was her death expected?"

Melinda's frown deepened. "She was old, but her health had been reasonably good, I think. We were all a little surprised by the swiftness of her passing, if I'm being honest. It never crossed my mind that she may have had a little help." Her face tightened. "And if that *is* the case, I hope the police—how does the phrase go?—throw the book at her." She sipped her tea. "Any other suspects?"

"We need to talk to Harold Tenby," Jonathon informed her.

Melinda sighed. "That poor man. It pains me to say this, but you might have something there. I have never seen a man so radically changed. And I know he blamed Teresa, with good reason."

"You think he's capable of murder?" Mike asked.

Melinda studied him closely. "Who knows what any of us are capable of when pushed to the extreme?"

"We've made some headway with the missing notebook." Jonathon told her about their discovery of the cloud. "And so far, it's turned up one anomaly— how Teresa describes the meeting with Professor Harcourt, and how he described it. Though we can't work out why he would lie about it."

"Professor Harcourt?" Melinda's face fell. "That poor man."

Jonathon blinked in surprise. "Why such sympathy for him?"

"Because tragedy has certainly dogged him." Melinda leaned forward, her voice low. "His wife drank, you know. Oh, everyone knew about it, but it was one of those things you didn't discuss in polite company. Well, one day she was in her bath, she'd drunk far too much, and she electrocuted herself with a hair drier."

"That always sounds like something from a film or a TV show," Jonathon commented. "Does that really happen?"

To his surprise, Mike nodded. "Not as often as it used to. I suppose wiring has improved in recent years."

Melinda's eyes shone. "And there you have it. Theirs was an old house, with faulty wiring. It was due to be rewired later that year. And the hair drier was ancient too. An accident waiting to happen, the coroner ruled."

"Then it was an accidental death?" Jonathon inquired.

"Oh yes, no doubt about that. Doctor Harcourt— as he was then—was distraught. None of us were particularly surprised when he sold the house and moved to London a little over a year later. He couldn't stand living in the house where she died." Melinda smiled. "As it turns out, that was the best thing for him. He went back to school to train to be a pathologist. And look at him now."

"That does sound tragic," Mike agreed. "When was this?"

"Let me see. It would have been the late eighties, maybe 1988. Professor Harcourt would have been in his early thirties then." Melinda gave a slow nod as she took another bite from her scone. After swallowing, she sighed. "Unfortunately, the tragedy didn't end there. His brother-in-law committed suicide a year or so after her death. They were so very close, Professor Harcourt said. They had no parents alive, no other siblings. It was obvious his brother-in-law had never recovered from the loss of his sister. He shot himself with a pistol that had belonged to their father—a war souvenir, I believe—the night of his sister's birthday."

Jonathon stared at her. "That's awful. At least the professor found happiness again. He said he's been happily married for twenty-seven years." What Jonathon didn't share was the wave of disquiet that washed over him. *What the hell?*

Melinda's face lit up. "Then I am happy for him. If ever a man deserved some good fortune, it's Doctor—Professor—Harcourt." She glanced at Mike with a half smile. "And what about Fiona McBride? What have you concluded about *her* motives for killing Teresa? Her husband died in 2003. Not *that* long to be harboring a grudge."

Mike took a bite of cake before responding. "There's some evidence she might have been conducting a little campaign against Teresa. Whether that was as far as she took it, or whether she progressed to murder, we don't know. What we *do* know is Phil, Melody, Meredith, and Fiona were all in the pub that night. Any one of them could have poured peanut oil into the coffee."

"Except how would they know which coffee was destined for Teresa?" Jonathon wanted to know.

"Maybe they added it to both cups to be on the safe side," Melinda said with a graceful shrug. "That's what *I* would do." When both Jonathon and Mike stared at her, she widened her gaze. "I was trying to put myself in the murderer's shoes, that's all."

Jonathon grinned. "Be thankful you weren't there too, in that case. Except you have no motive for killing her."

"That you know of," Melinda corrected, her eyes twinkling. "But here's a question for you. How many of those suspects knew about her allergy?"

"If they didn't know about it before the dinner, three of them certainly knew about it after. The subject came up during the meal, and Phil, Melody, and Fiona were all on Teresa's table," Jonathon confirmed.

"Yes, but consider this. They would have *needed* to know before then to come prepared. Because where would they find peanut oil between the dinner and the pub? On a Friday evening in Merrychurch?" Melinda wiped her mouth with her napkin. "And now, I must finish my tea and be on my way. I'm meeting with the ladies who help me arrange the church flowers to decide on who is doing what during the next few weeks. This has been delightful, boys."

"Thank you for coming." Mike leaned across and kissed her cheek. "Say hello to Lloyd for us."

Jonathon kissed her other cheek, and Melinda flushed. She collected her handbag, then after patting them both on the shoulder, she left the tea shop.

As soon as she was out of sight, Mike rested his chin on steepled fingers. "You know when she was talking about Professor Harcourt?"

Jonathon stilled. "I think we might have had the same thought. Did that remind you of anything?"

"You mean, like the plot Teresa outlined for her true crime book?"

He nodded. "Except for one thing. Teresa was asking about a shotgun, and Professor Harcourt's brother-in-law used a pistol. That doesn't sound like the same case."

"There's one way to find out." Mike gestured to the table. "Finish your coffee and cake. We're going to pay Graham a visit."

"You think he'll know anything about this? This happened before he was born."

"We're going to see him because if anyone can find out what happened, *he* can." Mike declared emphatically.

"Yes, but can he do it without incurring Gorland's wrath?" Jonathon said with a grin. "I agree, though. There's a limit to what we can discover. Just try to ask him when Gorland isn't around?"

Mike huffed. "Yeah, right. I swear Gorland has a klaxon in his office that goes off whenever we're in the vicinity. Because wherever we don't want him to be, he shows up."

"I hate to state the obvious, but we're going to the police station. It's a foregone conclusion that he'll be there." Jonathon didn't want to run into him either.

One, Gorland was a nasty piece of work, and two, he clearly had it in for Mike.

Jonathon avoided nasty people, especially those who were homophobic to boot.

As soon as they entered the quaint village police station, Mike groaned inwardly. Gorland was standing behind the main desk, talking with Graham. He scowled as they approached.

"You'd better be here to report a crime and not scrounging for information," he said with his familiar sneer.

"What about helping police with their inquiries?" Jonathon asked with an innocent air that had Mike fighting to stifle a snort.

Gorland opened his mouth, clearly about to give them a piece of his mind, but then another uniformed officer came out of the rear office. "A call for you, sir," he said quietly. "It's the Met."

Gorland scowled. "You'd better not be here when I get back." He left them in a hurry.

Graham rolled his eyes. "Mate, your timing is way off. Quick, tell me what you want before he gets off the phone."

"Can you see what you can find out about the death of Professor Harcourt's wife and then his brother-in-law's suicide?" Mike asked quickly.

Graham gaped at him. "You don't suspect Professor Harcourt, surely."

"No, we don't," Jonathon replied, "but we need to check it out." He reeled off the bare details of Teresa's plot and the similarities between the two.

Graham made some hasty notes on a nearby pad. "Gotcha. I still think it's a wild goose chase, but you're right, it needs investigating, if only to dismiss it. I'll call into the pub tonight if I've heard anything."

"Call in even if you haven't," Mike told him. "There'll be a pint with your name on it, as usual." He coughed. "Not that I'm bribing a police officer with the offer of a pint, you understand."

Graham cackled. "Yeah, right. Like I'd do all this for a measly pint." He grinned. "Three, at least." He tapped his notepad. "I'll get to work on it right away." He cast a furtive glance in the direction of the office. "Well, as long as he leaves me alone for five minutes." He shook his head. "I hate the way he talks to you two. It's not like you haven't helped us solve a couple of cases, right? Personally, I think you accomplish a lot, but *he* doesn't see that."

"He doesn't like us," Jonathon said simply. "And I think we all know why that is."

"Yeah." Graham's face darkened. "Well, an attitude like that will not get him an invite to the wedding of the decade."

Mike had to laugh. "I take it *you* want one."

"Too right, mate!" Graham gave a grin, and his bad mood evaporated. "I can't wait." A noise from behind him had Graham twitching. "Okay, get out of here. I'll see you later. And I'll find out what else I can dig up on those other suspects too. Sod Gorland. I know which side *my* bread is buttered. I'll stick with the guys who've helped me solve two cases."

They left him to it and headed back to the 4x4. "Let's see what Graham can find out."

"He's not a murderer," Jonathon muttered as he fastened his seat belt.

"Professor Harcourt? I'm with you," Mike agreed, "but you know we have to check it out, right?" He pulled out of the police station car park and took the lane that led to the manor house.

"What are we doing now?"

"*We* are going back to your place, where we will read some more of Teresa's notes. Maybe there are even more people out there who need investigating."

God, he hoped not. They had way too many suspects as it was.

CHAPTER TWENTY-FOUR

JANET WAS clearing away the coffee cups when Jonathon's phone buzzed into life. He waited until she'd withdrawn from the room before answering. Jonathon smiled when he saw Ruth's name. "Possible baby news," he told Mike as he connected the call. "Good evening."

"I'm just calling to see if you two are around this weekend. We need to visit."

Jonathon didn't miss the note of urgency in her voice. "Is something wrong?"

"Not… wrong, exactly. I went to see my doctor yesterday, and it proved very informative." Ruth paused. "Now, you're not going to turn into a delicate little snowflake if I mention ovulation, are you?"

He laughed. "Definitely not."

"Oh, thank God for that. Okay, the upshot is… we don't need a doctor or a clinic. We do this ourselves. We work out when I'm at my most fertile, and then we do the deed. Well, not you and I, you understand. But it turns out this coming weekend is the best time. You do have a turkey baster in that enormous kitchen of yours?"

For a moment Jonathon was stunned into silence. "Turkey baster? You don't mean…."

Across the room, Mike's eyebrows shot up.

Ruth giggled. "Well, not an *actual* baster, but the principle is the same. And I'm joking. We don't need yours. There's one in the kit."

"There's a kit for this?"

She laughed. "I know! We were amazed too. But it explains everything. All we need from you is the… er… donation. Clare will do the rest. Then I spend a day doing absolutely nothing but lying down, to give it the best chance of catching, as it were." Her voice softened. "You do realize it might take a few tries, don't you?"

"I know." That didn't matter. The idea that they were going to do this thrilled him to the core.

"That's why we thought no time like the present. So… is this weekend okay?"

"Of course. I'll have your room ready. And Ruth? I told my father."

There was a pause. "I bet *that* conversation went down like a lead balloon. You can tell us all about it when we see you. Enjoy the rest of your evening, and give my love to Mike."

Jonathon assured her he would, then disconnected the call. He gazed at his phone in silence, until Mike laid a gentle hand on his shoulder, and Jonathon looked up. "I didn't even hear you move."

"That's because I'm part ninja." Mike smirked. "Turkey baster? I can't wait to hear this." Then he glanced at his watch. "But you'll have to tell me on the way to the pub. It's time to open up." He grabbed his jacket from the arm of the couch and held out a hand to Jonathon. "That's if you're coming with me?"

Jonathon smiled as he took Mike's hand and got to his feet. "Graham is going to stop by, isn't he? You might be too busy to talk to him."

"Good point."

As they headed out to Mike's car, Jonathon relayed Ruth's news. Amusing though it had been, their conversation had lit a fire in him.

We're really going to do this.

MIKE SCANNED the bar, his chest tight. The pub was reasonably busy, but his mind wasn't on task. For the third night running, there was no sign of Paul Drake, and it pained him that they might have irrevocably broken a good friendship. In the far corner, Jonathon sat with Graham, their heads together as they talked, Jonathon scribbling notes.

"Glad to see you haven't given my stool to anyone else."

Mike blinked. Paul stood by the bar, his hands stuffed into the pockets of his jeans. Mike pulled himself together. "As if."

Paul bit his lip. "I'm here 'cos Graham called. Said I might learn something useful if I came along." He nodded toward the pumps. "Well, get a move on. Beer won't pour itself, y'know."

Mike reached up for a pint glass and slowly filled it. "You do know we never thought that—"

"Not gonna talk about that, all right?" Paul's face darkened slightly, but then he sighed. "I get it. I know how it looked. And then I got to thinkin'. Me staying away… how did *that* look? Like I had something to hide? Screw that." He sat on the stool, one arm resting on the bar while he reached for the peanuts with the other. "You wanna be careful. Some folks are allergic to these, y'know."

Mike rolled his eyes. "You don't say." A thought occurred to him. "Paul, you remember the coffees I poured for Teresa and Professor Harcourt that night?"

Paul nodded.

"Well, you were in the perfect spot to see anyone who was nearby. To see anyone who might have had the opportunity to put something in the cups."

Paul's lips twitched. "I wondered when you'd get around to askin' me. Some ex-copper *you* are."

Mike stilled. "Then you do remember who you saw?"

"Sure. Not that I saw anyone do it, you understand. I'd have said if that were the case. But I remember who was here." Paul counted off on his fingers, his forehead creased into a frown. "Them writers, for one. Him with the glasses, and her, a tiny little thing. Then there was that Fiona." He grimaced. "Lord, her perfume was so strong, it reached you before she did. Then there was Harold, and—"

"Harold Tenby? He was here that night?"

Paul nodded. "Not for long, mind you. In fact, I was surprised to see him. Not a social drinker, our Harold. Not surprisin', when you think about it. But yeah, he was around. Barbara Tremont's niece was here too, with her pal." Paul scowled. "That was a rum business, and no mistake."

"You're talking about her inheriting the house?"

"And the rest. Heart attack?" Paul huffed. "She was a walker, was Barbara. Used to go for long rambles with that walking group from Lower Pinton. You've seen 'em, those folks that walk with them ruddy long staffs, like ski poles?"

"The power walkers, you mean?" Mike saw them in the village sometimes.

Paul's face lit up. "That's them. Now tell me this. How does someone who goes on power walks drop dead from a heart attack? But no one said a word when she died." His eyes darkened. "You mark my words, that niece of hers had a hand in it."

The irony of the situation struck Mike. "And that was also the plot of a Teresa Malvain book."

Paul widened his eyes. "No kidding. Did she write *anything* original?" He took a long drink from his pint.

"You still like your ale, I see." The voice came from behind Paul. A short woman with long red hair stepped into view, her gaze focused on Paul.

Paul froze before spluttering beer onto the deep red carpet. "Bloody 'ell!" He almost fell off his stool, whirling around to stare at her, wiping his mouth with the back of his hand. "What the…?"

She smiled before addressing Mike. "A gin and tonic, please." Then she sat on the stool next to Paul's. "And get him another. He seems to have spilled most of his."

Paul put down his glass on the beer mat before looking her in the eye. "Did you get lost? 'Cos it's only taken you thirteen years to find your way back."

With a start, Mike realized who she was. "You're April."

She smiled. "So he does still mention me."

"Mention you?" Paul's eyes bulged. "Half the village thinks I chopped you up into little bits and fed you to the pigs."

April burst into raucous laughter. "So it's true, what that copper told me on the phone. I thought he was joking."

"Copper?" Paul squinted at Mike. "You?"

Mike shook his head and pointed to Graham, who was walking over to them. "Him."

Graham held out his hand. "Mrs. Drake. Good of you to come."

She shook it. "Well, it all sounded so intriguing."

Paul gaped at her. "That's all you have to say after thirteen years?"

Graham coughed. "I think this is a conversation best taken elsewhere, don't you? I'm sure you two have a lot to talk about."

"Just as long as he knows I'm not coming back," April flung out.

"And as long as *she* knows I wouldn't have her," Paul fired back. "She'd only upset the pigs." He jerked his head toward the door. "Come on. We can talk at the house." He raised his voice. "Now that this lot have seen you're alive and in one piece, of course." And with that, he marched her out, his hand at her back.

Mike stared after them, stunned.

Jonathon came over to the bar. "Never a dull moment around here, is there?"

"Was that April Drake I saw outside?" Fiona McBride leaned on the bar. "A G and T, please, Mike." When he placed a glass in front of her, she chuckled. "Wow. Fast service around here."

Graham cleared his throat. "Another pint, when you've a minute, Mike." He peered at Fiona. "Mrs. McBride. Glad I ran into you. Saves me the trouble of paying you a visit tomorrow."

"Me?" The word came out as a squeak. "Why would you want to see me?" Fiona stared at him in undisguised panic.

"It's the little matter of a parcel you sent to Teresa Malvain. Not to mention some letters. You know, the ones you didn't sign?" Graham's eyes gleamed.

Mike was impressed. So far it was only supposition that she'd been the one who sent the anonymous letters, but he had to admit, Graham was a superb bluffer.

"L-letters?" Fiona took a drink from her glass. "I've no idea what you're talking about."

"Teresa did, though. She knew it was you." Jonathon kept his face straight. "We know this from her notes."

"And then there's the small matter of your fingerprints," Graham added, his gaze flickering briefly in Mike's direction.

Fiona's mouth fell open. "And how would you know they're mine? You haven't got mine on file, have you? Plus, I wiped the book clean before I packed—" Her eyes widened. "Oh shit."

Graham beamed. "I love dealing with amateurs. They always get flustered." He sighed happily as Mike handed him a pint glass. "Cheers."

Fiona glared at him. "You tricked me."

Graham peered at her over the rim of his glass. "Er, excuse me? You sent anonymous letters. You sent a book containing a highlighted phrase designed to intimidate her. And you knew all about her allergy, didn't you? In fact, of all the people at that dinner table, you knew her best."

"And you were here the night she died," Jonathon remarked.

"Close enough to drop peanut oil into her coffee, in fact," Mike said quietly. "And unlike the others, you knew about the allergy *prior* to the dinner, so you could have come prepared."

"You... you think I killed her?" Fiona paled. "But... I ran her fan club."

Mike nodded. "Perfect cover." He tilted his head. "After all, you've had fifteen years to plan this, haven't you? It was 2003 when your husband died, wasn't it?"

It was as if his words took all the fight out of her. Fiona crumpled visibly. "Yes," she said simply. "But I was only going to humiliate her. I wanted her to suffer, the way she'd made *me* suffer all those months, while he...." She swallowed hard. "I didn't kill her."

Graham placed his hand on her shoulder. "You can tell me all about it. Down at the police station."

"Am I... am I under arrest?"

"Right now, you're helping the police with their inquiries," Graham said in a low voice. He gave a nod in Mike's direction. "We can talk another time."

"Sure." Mike watched as Graham guided Fiona toward the door. He leaned on the bar and shuddered out a long breath.

"Are you okay?" Jonathon covered Mike's hand with his.

"Yeah. I didn't expect that. Not to mention Paul's wife showing up." He imagined she and Paul had a lot to discuss.

Jonathon's lips twitched. "When he said she'd upset the pigs…." He gazed thoughtfully at the door. "Do you think Fiona did it?"

"I think she had the motivation and the opportunity. Just because she says she didn't kill Teresa doesn't mean she's telling the truth." Mike inclined his head to the corner where Jonathon and Graham had been sitting. "So what did Graham have to say before April showed up? It looked like a riveting conversation."

Jonathon nodded. "It was. And I have a lot to tell you. But not here. Later." He smiled. "You have pints to pull."

"And I have things to tell you too." Mike leaned closer. "We need to look at Meredith and Harold."

Jonathon stilled. "Did they know about her allergy?"

The words stopped Mike cold. "You know what? I have no idea. I was so busy thinking about the fact that they were here and they both have motives, that I didn't think about that part."

Jonathon nodded slowly. "Then that's what we have to work on."

"When you two have finished gasbaggin', I'll have a pint." Seth grinned. "A man could die of thirst in this pub."

Mike laughed and reached for a clean glass.

Sleuthing would have to wait.

CHAPTER TWENTY-FIVE

JONATHON PAUSED as he got out of the car. "So…
are you just dropping me at my door like a gentleman, or…?"

Mike grinned. "Trust me. My thoughts of what
I want to do with you tonight are *not* those of a
gentleman."

"Thank God for that." Jonathon opened the front
door quietly. It was past midnight, and he didn't want to
make too much noise, for fear of disturbing Janet.

Mike followed him into the house. "Anyone seeing your bathroom would be convinced I already live
here."

Jonathon chuckled. "I could say the same about
yours. I think that's what I'm looking forward to the
most after the wedding. Having you under the same
roof, permanently." Whether Mike sold the pub or not,
they were both in agreement on that score—they'd had
enough of spreading themselves between two homes.
He paused in the entrance hall. "I was going to make
some tea before bed. Do you want some?"

Mike stilled. "Tea? Since when do you drink
tea?" He peered closely at Jonathon. "Okay, where is
the real Jonathon?"

He laughed softly. "Idiot. Ivy was talking about this tea she'd found that was great for drinking before bed. It's called CatNap, and its ingredients are supposed to calm you before sleep. I bought some, but I haven't tried it yet."

Mike shrugged. "I'll try anything once."

Jonathon led him down the stairs into the large kitchen. The air was filled with the scent of bread, and Jonathon sighed happily. "Ivy's been baking." He went over to the whistling kettle, filled it, and placed it on the range to heat before opening the cabinet to find the box of tea. He sniffed at the contents. "I smell something lemony."

"Never mind the tea." Mike sat at the huge wooden table in the center of the kitchen. "How about you tell me what Graham said?"

Jonathon placed a couple of heaped teaspoons of the mixed leaves into a china teapot. "That story the police officer told Teresa? It *was* about Professor Harcourt." When he caught Mike's sharp intake of breath, he turned around, the spoon still in his hand. "And before you get carried away, there was absolutely no evidence linked to his wife's death to suggest foul play. Everything Melinda said was true. There had been other incidents of bad wiring in the house, which was why it was going to be sorted out. And the alcohol level in her blood was high enough to show she was very drunk."

"And what about the brother-in-law? Was that bit true too?"

Jonathon nodded. "He went to the police about a year after she died, demanding they investigate."

Mike stared at him. "A year? He waited that long?"

Jonathon leaned against the worktop. "I know. Surely if he was suspicious, he'd have gone earlier than that. He claimed Professor Harcourt had wanted to make a change from GP to pathologist for some time, but that his sister had refused both to move nearer to London and to provide him with the money to study for a further five years."

"I take it the wife had all the money. So the brother-in-law thought money was the motive."

Jonathon nodded. "Then, on what would have been his wife's birthday, Professor Harcourt organized a dinner at a restaurant with a few of her closest friends and her brother. According to the guests, during the meal, the brother-in-law drank far too much and starting repeating his accusations."

"How did that go down?"

The kettle started to whistle, and Jonathon quickly took it off the heat, then waited a moment before pouring the water into the teapot. "According to the witnesses, Professor Harcourt was really gracious and very understanding about the whole thing. He'd had a bit to drink too, they said, but he didn't appear to bear his brother-in-law any malice, despite the drunken accusations he kept firing at the professor." Jonathon sighed. "One woman said she felt really sorry for him. The brother-in-law kept asking why Professor Harcourt hadn't managed to save her—him being a doctor, after all—and how it wasn't over. He said one day he'd prove Harcourt did it."

"Had the police already investigated by this time?"

Jonathon gave another nod. "But it seems the brother-in-law wasn't going to accept their findings. Anyway, when the meal ended, Professor Harcourt apologized profusely before calling a taxi. The police questioned the taxi driver when the brother-in-law was found dead. He confirmed they were both drunk. He'd dropped off the brother-in-law first. In fact, he helped Professor Harcourt get him into the house. Then he dropped off the professor. They discovered the body two days later when Professor Harcourt grew concerned after repeated calls with no response."

"The brother-in-law did shoot himself?" Mike asked.

"With their father's pistol, just like Melinda said. He was found on the couch, with photo albums on his lap and beside him. Photos of him and his sister as children. There was also a copy of the eulogy he'd given at her funeral in his hand. The inquest ruled it as suicide. Everyone said how close he and his sister had been, and with it being her birthday…. His doctor testified that he suffered from depression and had never really gotten over her death." Jonathon took two cups from the cabinet and placed them beside the teapot.

Mike rested his chin on his laced fingers. "Then what on earth was Teresa talking about? This can't be the true-life murder case she was going to write about. There's nothing to suggest it was murder."

"I agree." Jonathon stirred the leaves in the pot.

"Did anyone hear the gunshot?"

"No one around *to* hear. He lived in a remote area, with woodland behind the property and no other houses nearby. The coroner estimated the time of death as having taken place early in the morning, maybe three or four o'clock."

"So why would Teresa think this was anything other than a suicide? She must have had some reason to pursue this."

Jonathon poured the tea through a strainer into the cups. "You know what I think? This is a wild goose chase, just like Graham said. There's no evidence to suggest either of those deaths was murder. And why a police officer would put her onto this, suggesting there was, is…." He shook his head as he put down the teapot. "I don't understand any of it."

Mike got up from the table, walked over to him, and enfolded Jonathon in his arms. "Then let's not think about it anymore tonight, okay? Let's drink this… interesting-smelling tea, and get some sleep."

Jonathon bit his lip. "I thought you had designs on my body."

Mike grinned. "That part comes after the tea. Don't worry. You always sleep well after a good… finish."

Jonathon smirked. "My, how delicately put."

"I'm practicing for when we're parents." Mike's eyes sparkled. "Things not to say in front of the children."

Jonathon chuckled. "I can see it now. 'Daddy, you and Papa must be very good dancers, because you do a lot of dancing.'"

To his surprise, Mike's face lit up. "Until just now, I hadn't given a thought to what our kids will call us. But Daddy and Papa… I like that." He cocked his head to one side. "Which one am I?"

"That's easy." Jonathon stroked Mike's face with a gentle hand. "With that beard? You're Papa Bear." Then his breathing caught as Mike lifted him into his arms. "Papa Bear is strong. I like that."

Mike kissed him languidly, his hands easily supporting Jonathon's weight, and suddenly Jonathon didn't want to be in the kitchen. He wanted softness beneath him, and a hard, lean body curled around him.

Sleep could wait.

MIKE ROLLED over to find Jonathon sitting up in bed, his laptop already open in his lap. "Phone not enough for you?" He rubbed the sleep from his eyes.

"Listen, I've found something." Jonathon scrolled down the page. "Remember at the meal, Teresa said her investigations were more thorough than those of the police?"

Mike huffed. "I'm hardly likely to forget that remark."

"Well, she was investigating the brother-in-law's suicide, and I don't know how she did it, but she found something they missed."

"Like what?" Mike sat up in bed, running his fingers through his hair.

"A witness."

Mike frowned. "A witness to what?"

Jonathon peered at the screen. "Apparently there was a tramp in the woodland. He'd made himself a den out there, catching rabbits, birds, squirrels—whatever he could get his hands on."

Mike grimaced. "Lovely."

"Yes, but the important part is… that night, he saw something near the brother-in-law's house."

Mike had heard enough. "Okay, I'm not buying any of this. The police would have found him and questioned him."

"Teresa's notes say they did, but they dismissed what he had to say because he'd been off his head on cheap cider or whatever he'd managed to buy. And it did sound a little… strange."

"What did he see?"

Jonathon clasped his hands in his lap. "A blue angel."

Mike stared. "A blue… angel. Did he specify what shade of blue?"

"Actually? Yes. Pale blue. It was walking through the woods."

Mike threw back the covers and sat on the edge of the bed. "Yeah, well, now I see why they dismissed it. What makes you mention it?"

"The fact that Teresa thought it worth noting. It must have meant something to her."

"She doesn't say what in her notes?"

Jonathon shook his head. He closed the laptop carefully. "I've been thinking."

"Should I be worried?" Mike teased. But when Jonathon's thoughtful expression didn't alter, he shifted across the bed and took Jonathon's hand in his. "What is it?"

"Do you want to know what bothers me? The missing notebook. That points to the murderer not wanting anyone to know what was in there. So where is it? We know it was in her bag down in the pub, because Professor Harcourt saw it. And she took her bag upstairs. No notebook. But it has to be there. No one went up there and removed it, because we'd have seen. It wasn't exactly small, right?"

Mike had to agree. "But we've been over that room several times. There's nowhere it could be." He sighed. "You want to take another look, don't you?"

Jonathon leaned back against the pillows. "For a while now, I've had the feeling I've missed something, and I think it's connected to that notebook. Something I've seen, something I've heard, or something someone said to me…. And it eludes me."

"You think it's back at the pub?"

"I don't know!" Jonathon scowled. "All I *do* know is, it's driving me crazy."

"Then let's have some breakfast and go over there. Two pairs of eyes and all that." Privately, Mike didn't think there was anything to find, but at least he could help alleviate Jonathon's nagging doubts.

"Thanks, Mike." Jonathon leaned over and kissed him on the lips. Then he pulled back a little, as if seeing Mike for the first time. "Good morning," he said softly.

Mike laughed. "I know that look, and I'm not going to let you get sidetracked. Shower. Breakfast. No sex."

Jonathon snickered. "Spoilsport." He moved the laptop out of the way, climbed out of bed, and sauntered across the room toward the bathroom, giving a little arse wiggle as he went.

"And you can cut that out too. I'm not falling for it," Mike called after him. He lay back against the pillows, his mind on Jonathon's words.

What on earth could he have missed?

As Mike approached the pub, Jonathon caught sight of a car pulling up in front of it. "Oh dear. You have an unwelcome visitor."

Gorland leaned out of the window, his perpetual scowl in place.

Mike drew alongside him. "Good morning. In need of a drink already? I'm afraid we don't open until midday."

"I suppose you're feeling pleased with yourselves," Gorland said with a sneer. "Not that you had much of a hand in it."

"I don't have a clue what you're talking about," Mike said pleasantly.

"Well, she might have been in your pub when she gave herself away, but it's police procedures that will nail her. *If* she's guilty."

Jonathon caught his breath. "Fiona McBride?"

Gorland opened his eyes wide. "Don't act like you're surprised. Although, I'll admit, your instincts were spot-on when it came to Meredith Roberts. Turns out the aunt's new will was posted to her solicitor, with an accompanying letter. The two witnesses who signed it… no one's ever heard of them. So it looks like we have at least two people who could have done this. There's going to be an exhumation of the aunt's body, of course. They must have missed something the first time. But we'll get our man—or woman, in this case." He smiled, his eyes glinting. "I guess this means I won't be seeing you hanging around the police station anymore. Oh dear, how sad."

"Does this mean you can prove either of them put peanut oil into Teresa's cup?" Jonathon demanded. "Especially as no one saw them do it."

Gorland frowned. "According to *your* pathetic, amateurish investigations, maybe. I think you'll find a witness will turn up. They always do. Someone saw something, and it will come to light." Jonathon had to admire his confidence. "And now that I've delivered my good news, I'll go back to work. Sorry you didn't catch the perpetrator this time, boys, but you can't win every time." With a wave of his hand, Gorland drove away.

"I have never wanted to hit someone so hard in all my life," Jonathon ground out as they entered the pub.

"You think he's right?" Mike bolted the door behind them.

Jonathon's mind worked furiously. "I think he's forgetting something very important. The missing notebook. The EpiPens. Her phone. When did either of them manage to remove them from Teresa's bag without being seen? Because they *are* integral to this case." And with that, he dashed over to the door that led upstairs, with Mike behind him.

Inside the room, Jonathon scanned its contents. Mike was right about one thing—they'd been over that room with a fine-toothed comb. He took a deep breath and looked again. "There is one place we didn't look, you know." Jonathon pointed to the old oak wardrobe in the corner.

"Wait a minute. We looked in there. *And* we used a mirror to check the top. Nothing up there either." Mike went over to it. The wardrobe stood away from the two walls. "Plus, we checked behind it and at the side. Nothing."

"Then what about underneath?"

Mike blinked. "You can't get underneath. That plinth goes all the way around the base. There's no room to slip a cigarette paper under it, let alone a notebook."

Jonathon gazed at the wardrobe for a moment. Then he went over to it, placed his hand on the side, and pushed it toward the wall, tilting it. "Look under while I hold it. But be quick. This thing is heavy."

Mike got down on the floor and peered underneath.

His gasp told Jonathon all he needed to know.

"It's here. The notebook is here. And so are two EpiPens. And Teresa's phone." He paused. "And a tiny glass vial."

Carefully, Jonathon let go and eased the wardrobe back down to the floor, where it landed with a thud.

"What are you doing? That's evidence. We need to remove everything." Mike sat back on his haunches, staring up at Jonathon.

He nodded. "And the only people who know what's under there are you, me and the murderer. They're going to want to retrieve them. And soon too. They can't risk leaving them. Because who knows when you'll decide to repaint the room, update the furniture…?" Jonathon smiled. "Trust me. They'll be back."

"So what are we going to do? Hide in the wardrobe in the hopes of someone turning up? Set up cameras?"

Jonathon laughed. "Nothing so hi-tech. But we'll need backup."

And he knew exactly whom to ask.

CHAPTER TWENTY-SIX

JONATHON WAS helping Mike by collecting empty glasses when Professor Harcourt strolled into the pub. "Professor!" Jonathon laughed. "You're still here? I'm surprised your wife hasn't started divorce proceedings for desertion by now."

Harcourt chuckled. "Far from it. She said on the phone last night that I must go away more often. Something about having complete control of the TV remote…."

Mike snickered. "A brandy for you?"

Professor Harcourt tut-tutted as he sat on the nearest barstool. "It's bad when the bartender knows your usual tipple. But yes, please. One last brandy before I have to leave." He glanced around the pub. "Despite the murder, this has been a most pleasant stay. I'd forgotten how peaceful it is in Merrychurch. A couple of weeks here was just the tonic I needed. Unfortunately, real life rears its ugly head." He gave a heartfelt sigh.

"You don't sound like you want to leave us," Mike commented.

"I don't, and that's the honest truth. Unfortunately, the B and B where I'm staying needs my room for a prior booking, so I have to go home." Professor

Harcourt smiled. "And in spite of my jokes, it will be good to see my wife. Our son should be home by now for the summer too."

"Why not stay one more night?" Jonathon suggested. "There's a room here. Unless you'd feel awkward about staying in the room where Teresa...."

Professor Harcourt let out a wry chuckle. "After all the things I've seen in my career? I'm not *that* delicate." He sipped the brandy Mike had placed in front of him. "But I can't deny I like the idea." His expression brightened. "Hang real life. One more night can't hurt." He put down his glass. "I'll go and collect my bag, and then I'll be right over to finish my brandy." His eyes twinkled. "After I've called my wife and told her I'll be home tomorrow."

"Look at it this way. She gets one more night of the TV remote," Mike said with a grin.

Harcourt nodded eagerly. "Which is precisely the tack I intend to take." He got off his stool and walked to the door.

Mike gave Jonathon a speculative glance. "What are you up to?"

"Giving the professor the opportunity to eliminate himself from our investigations," Jonathon declared emphatically. "Because come tomorrow morning, we'll know, one way or another. Right?"

Mike shrugged. "I guess." He stilled, and Jonathon turned to see what had caught his attention.

Fiona McBride was walking toward them.

"Good afternoon." Fiona's cheeks were pink. "I wanted to talk to you both, after the way things ended yesterday." She sat on the stool the professor had recently vacated. "I've told the police everything—the book, the letters, all the stuff I found about Teresa's early writing career—all of it. And yes, I was going to tell the world. Like I said yesterday, I wanted her to suffer." Her face reddened. "I didn't intend on killing her."

"The fact that you're here now and not in a police cell tells me something." Mike regarded her keenly. "Either they believe you, or they don't have enough evidence to arrest you for her murder."

Fiona's eyes darkened. "Oh, they're still looking. That Detective Inspector assured me of that. But my lawyer tells me—"

"You got yourself a lawyer. Very wise." Mike placed a gin and tonic in front of her. "You didn't get the chance to drink this last night, so here's a fresh one. On the house."

"Thanks." Fiona took a long drink. "I didn't kill her, okay? You need to believe me."

"We're not the ones you need to convince," Jonathon reminded her quietly.

She shivered, then glanced around the pub. "I don't come in here that often. Where are the toilets?"

Before Jonathon could point her in the right direction, Mike cleared his throat. "Actually? They're out of order at the moment. But as it's you, I'll let you use my bathroom upstairs. Go through that door marked Private. At the top of the stairs, you'll see three doors on your left. The bathroom is the middle door."

"Thanks." Fiona got off the stool and headed for the door.

Jonathon arched his eyebrows. "Okay, now it's my turn. What are you up to? There's nothing wrong with the toilets." Then he stiffened. "You're letting her go upstairs because you want to see if she—"

Mike nodded slowly. "And as soon as she comes back, I'll go check." He smiled. "I wonder how many of the people on our suspect list will pay us a visit over the next few days. Maybe the toilets need to stay out of action for a while longer."

Jonathon shook his head. "Is being sneaky a requisite for being a copper?"

Mike snickered. "It's on the application form. 'Do you consider yourself sneaky? Give examples.'"

Jonathon wouldn't have been in the least bit surprised.

Minutes later, Fiona was back, rejoining them to finish her drink. Mike excused himself and disappeared behind the door.

"So, are you going to continue with the fan club?" Jonathon inquired.

She sighed. "Mike was right. It was just a cover. Maybe I should start a new fan club, for a writer who's actually nice to their readers." Her eyes lit up. "Melody Richards. She could do with a positive fan base, right? And she's a good writer. Maybe now that Teresa isn't getting her fans to post dreadful reviews, everyone will get to see what Melody's work is really like."

Jonathon thought it sounded like a step in the right direction. He looked up as Mike reentered the bar, giving him an inquiring glance. When Mike shook his head, Jonathon let out an internal sigh of relief.

Fiona wasn't the murderer.

Fiona finished her drink. "It's not a nice feeling, knowing the police think me capable of murder."

"It doesn't matter what they think, if you didn't do it," Jonathon said gently. "And sooner or later, they'll find the real killer."

Mike nodded in agreement.

"They could still charge me, couldn't they?" Fiona swallowed. "I mean, I did send those letters. I haven't denied it."

"That will be up to the police to decide," Mike told her. "Let's see the way things turn out."

She nodded and got to her feet. "Thanks for the drink, and the use of your bathroom." Fiona gave them a tentative smile before walking out of the pub.

"I'm glad it wasn't her." Jonathon gazed at Mike. "Did she go in the room, though?"

Mike nodded. "The old James Bond trick worked. The hair I placed across the door crack had gone. But everything was still in place." He stared at her empty glass. "Maybe she needed to see for herself where it happened."

"Possibly." Jonathon shivered. He gave himself a mental shake. "How about if I see to some lunch for us?" And before Mike could respond, he headed for the kitchen.

Teresa's death had brought home one thing to him with startling clarity. Jonathon did not like looking at his friends and neighbors as potential murder suspects.

Maybe I'm not cut out to investigate such things after all.

MIKE WAS having the most wonderful dream. It was slow and sensual, filled with heat and—

He opened his eyes, and the delicious sensations came to an abrupt halt.

Jonathon's chuckle reverberated through him. "I wondered how long it would take to wake you up. I've always wanted to try this."

"What made you try it this morning?" Not that Mike was complaining.

"We need to be up early. We don't know when Professor Harcourt will leave, and we need to check the room before he does."

Mike glanced over at the alarm clock beside the bed. "Well, seeing as it's six a.m., I don't think he'll be checking out right this minute." He lifted the sheet and stared at Jonathon, who was grinning. "And who told you to stop?"

Warm breath wafted over his erection. "Bossy," Jonathon said with a snicker. Then all words became superfluous as he went back to his erotic task, only this time with more enthusiasm.

Mike had a feeling his alarm clock had just been put out of a job.

"THIS IS a marvelous breakfast," Professor Harcourt declared before taking his last mouthful of toast. "I shan't want lunch at this rate."

Jonathon poured himself another cup of coffee. "I'm glad you enjoyed it." He glanced at the kitchen door. No sign of Mike. "What time is your train?"

"Oh, not until midday. I shall be out of here before you open. That's if I can arrange a taxi to take me to the station." Professor Harcourt smiled. "Knowing how unreliable taxis can be in this village."

"Mike or I will take you there," Jonathon assured him.

"In that case, I can go for a last stroll. My bag is all packed." Professor Harcourt gave a sigh of contentment. "This was a marvelous idea. At least I'll know where to stay, should I ever return here."

The door opened and Mike stepped into the room. One look at his expression of dismay was enough to send Jonathon's heart plummeting. He didn't need to see the single nod that followed. When Mike took his phone from his pocket, Jonathon knew.

"Well, I shall go upstairs and perform the necessary ablutions, and then I'll be off on my walk." Professor Harcourt pushed back his chair and stood. "Thank you again." He gave Mike a cheerful nod as he left the room.

Jonathon waited until the professor was out of earshot. "No doubt?"

"The tape's torn. So unless he bumped into the wardrobe with an almighty thump, it's been moved. I haven't touched it, like we agreed." Mike gestured to his phone. "But I have called him, just in case. He'll buzz me when he gets here."

Jonathon sighed heavily. "Then we'd better get up there and find out for certain."

As he reached the door, Mike laid a gentle hand on his back. "I know, sweetheart. I don't want to believe it either."

In silence they left the kitchen and headed for the door to the upstairs part of the pub. As they neared the guest room door, Jonathon could hear Professor Harcourt moving about inside.

Mike rapped on the door. "Professor?"

After a moment, it opened, and the professor stood there, his jacket over his arm. "Did I leave something downstairs?" When Mike didn't respond, he stepped to one side. "Please, come in. It *is* your room, after all."

"Everything was okay?" Mike asked. Jonathon followed him in.

"Everything was excellent." Professor Harcourt's eyes sparkled. "Would you like me to leave a review online? That's *the* thing nowadays, I know. It doesn't matter where I go, five minutes later there's a message on my phone, asking me to rate my visit." He sighed. "Everyone wants feedback. At least I don't get that from the people who find their way to my table."

Mike's phone buzzed, but he ignored it.

"Before you go," Jonathon said in as natural a manner as he could manage, "did you see a notebook in here?"

Professor Harcourt frowned. "Notebook?"

Jonathon nodded. "Teresa's. It went missing."

"Oh, I see. I'm sorry, but I haven't seen it."

Jonathon walked over to where the professor's bag sat on the floor near the door. "Then you wouldn't mind if I took a look in your bag?"

Professor Harcourt frowned. "Looking for what?" Then he widened his eyes. "Her missing notebook? Why on earth would *I* have it?"

Jonathon held up his hands. "Actually, you're right. I don't need to see in here."

Professor Harcourt smiled. "I'm glad you trust my word. For a moment there, I was beginning to feel like a suspect."

"I don't have to take your word." Jonathon inclined his head toward the door and called out, "You can come in now." He studied Professor Harcourt's face as Graham stepped into the room. Without looking away, Jonathon pointed to the wardrobe. "It's all yours. You're looking for a handprint." In silence, Graham walked over to the oak wardrobe, a pot in one hand, a brush in the other, his hands gloved.

"Handprint?" There was the faintest tremor in Professor Harcourt's voice.

Jonathon nodded. "If there's nothing? You'll have our sincerest apologies. But if there is? It'll be from where you tilted the wardrobe to get underneath it. Because we already know you did tilt it." He glanced at the bookcase below the window, with several fat volumes sitting on its shelves. "I figure you could have propped it up with these while you removed them."

Graham got on with his task, dusting the surface of the wood. Mike stood beside the bed, his expression watchful.

"Removed... them?" Professor Harcourt paled slightly.

Jonathon gave another nod. "The notebook. The EpiPens. Teresa's phone. I'm guessing the glass vial is where you kept the peanut oil that you slipped into her coffee. You had to hide them, right? Unfortunately for you, I found them yesterday."

"And like I said that night in the pub," Graham chimed in, "that means it was premeditated, because who just happens to have peanut oil on them?"

And there it was, the missing piece that had eluded Jonathon's mind.

He stared at Professor Harcourt. "Yes," he said slowly. "Those were Graham's exact words. And now I remember what you said after them. 'If you add to that the missing notebook, EpiPens, and phone, it all points to murder.'"

"Of course it does!" The professor's face reddened. "But they have nothing to do with me!"

"Only one problem with that." Jonathon regarded him sadly. "The only people at that point who knew about the missing notebook were myself, Mike, and Graham. So if we hadn't told you, Professor, there was only one way you could have known—if you were the one who'd taken it."

Professor Harcourt stared at him, his mouth open.

"Of course, you didn't know about the cloud," Mike added. "Where Teresa sent all the photos she took of her notes? That meant we didn't need the notebook after all."

"She took… photos?" Harcourt's face fell.

"Got one," Graham called out. "Only one print here."

"And it's Jonathon's," Professor Harcourt flung out. "He just told you he looked under there yesterday."

Jonathon sighed. "Yes, but that was before I sprayed furniture polish all over it and cleaned it up."

"But anyone could have come up here since then and removed them," the professor remonstrated.

Mike shook his head. "We know it was you." He pointed to the top of the wardrobe. "I placed a piece of masking tape on top, securing it to the wall. Only one other person came in here, and I checked immediately after. The tape was undisturbed, so I knew they hadn't looked under the wardrobe. But when I checked while you were having breakfast…."

"Plus, that explains the thud we heard the night Teresa died. We all thought it was the sound of her falling to the floor, or something like that." Jonathon gazed at him steadily. "It was the wardrobe landing back on the floor after you removed the books propping it up." He glanced at the bag. "So I already have a fair idea of what I'm going to find when I look inside, but why don't you show us instead?"

Chapter Twenty-Seven

Professor Harcourt stared at them in silence before slowly walking over to the bed and sitting on the edge. "Open it," he said in a low voice.

Graham put down the pot and brush, picked up the bag, and placed it on the bed next to the professor. Still wearing his gloves, he opened it and peered inside. He carefully lifted out a shirt, placed it on the bed, and then nodded. "They're here. Notebook, EpiPens, vial, and phone."

"What made you think of me as a suspect?" Professor Harcourt asked. "Stupid question. If you've read her notes, you already know."

"Actually? What started us off was you lying about the research meeting," Jonathon told him. "You assumed that with the notebook missing, we'd never know what she really wanted to talk about. You didn't reckon on her uploading photos of her notes."

"When did you realize she was going to write about your case?" Mike asked.

"I didn't kill my wife!" Professor Harcourt blurted out.

Jonathon remained silent, but Graham looked up. "I'd advise you not to say anything else until we get you to the police station and you have a lawyer present."

Professor Harcourt waved his hand dismissively. "Actually? It's such a relief to tell it all. Don't worry, young man. I'll say exactly the same thing when you're recording it. I'm just glad that it's over. I've lived with this for nearly thirty years."

"Your wife dying in the bath? The hair drier? That was a genuine accident?" Mike dragged an armchair across and sat facing the professor.

He nodded. "Where I went wrong was not helping her. I *could* have saved her, of course, but I didn't. Eric—her brother—kept saying that I should have been able to save her. He was right."

Jonathon's heartbeat increased. "Did he kill himself?" When Professor Harcourt shook his head, Jonathon gaped. "But... you had an alibi. The taxi driver who took you home. You were too drunk to do anything."

Professor Harcourt gave a sad smile. "Two things to note here. My first wife was an alcoholic, but her brother could get drunk on one pint of beer. I made sure he had more than that. As for me, I can drink quite a lot before my faculties are impaired. I can also play the drunk when I have to."

"What really happened the night of that meal?" Jonathon perched on the arm of Mike's chair. "After you'd dropped off Eric at his house."

"The taxi driver took me home, helped me out of the car, saw me to my door, and even helped me unlock it, because I was apparently too drunk to get my key in the lock. Once he'd gone, however, I got changed into my autopsy scrubs, grabbed a pair of surgical gloves, got into my car, and returned to Eric's house in the early hours of the morning. I parked the car some way from the house and walked through the wood."

Jonathon gave a start. "*Now* it makes sense!"

"What does?" Mike asked with a frown.

"Teresa's note. What the tramp saw that night. The blue angel. He saw you in your scrubs, didn't he?"

Professor Harcourt nodded. "That little detail convinced Teresa she was on the right track."

"Keep going, professor." Graham hadn't moved from beside the bag.

"I had Grace's key. Eric was still in the chair where I'd left him, passed out. The photo albums were already beside him on the couch, the ones from their childhood. I went to his desk to look for the eulogy he'd given at her funeral. I knew he'd kept it." Professor Harcourt sighed heavily. "He'd talked for fifteen minutes on the phone the previous night about how much he loved her, and how he wasn't sure he could go on without her. He used to call me up and read it to me."

"Why did you go looking for it?" Mike asked.

"I figured it was the closest I'd get to a suicide note."

"Then you went there with the purpose of killing him, intending it to look like a suicide?" Graham wanted to know.

Professor Harcourt gave a slow nod. "I knew before the meal that he wasn't about to let this go. He wasn't going to stop until he got someone to believe him."

"But you hadn't killed her," Jonathon remonstrated.

"Hadn't I?" Professor Harcourt's eyes were full of pain. "I stood there and did nothing while she screamed. By not helping her, I as good as murdered her. Oh, not according to the law, I know, but…. Living with that knowledge was proving to be a burden. Besides, Eric was right. With Grace's money, I was able to pursue my dream. His death made it even easier."

"I don't understand. How did you benefit from Eric's death?" Mike asked.

"When we married, Grace drew up a will. In the event of her death, all her money was to go to me, but if I was deceased, it would pass to Eric. He had a similar will: Grace was his beneficiary, but in the event of her death, all monies would revert to me. They had no one else, only each other."

"You knew about their father's pistol," Jonathon surmised.

Professor Harcourt nodded. "I knew where Eric kept it, and I also knew he kept it loaded in case of intruders. Intruders! He lived out in the middle of nowhere."

"Did he know what was happening?" Mike asked softly.

Professor Harcourt shook his head. "He was still unconscious. I positioned his hand on the gun, supporting it as I aimed it up under his chin and pulled the trigger, my hand around his. That way, his prints were on the trigger, and if they wanted to test for gunshot residue…. The blood spatter would be on the eulogy and the photos. What little was on my scrubs would be gone when I destroyed them. Then I walked back through the woods, got into my car, and drove home."

"And the combination of his behavior during the meal, the eulogy, and the photo album was enough to convince the police that he'd taken his own life," Graham concluded.

Another nod. "I'd made sure I didn't react to his drunken insinuations during dinner, so our fellow guests' sympathies were with me, rather than him. I made apologies for him, but by the end of the meal, they were apologizing for him too."

"So when did you first know Teresa was on to you?" Mike asked.

"When we met that day to discuss her research. She told me she only had the barest details of the case, but I knew it had to be mine. She had more research to do, she said. That bit about how to fake a suicide shooting? That shook me. It really sounded like she knew it was me." Professor Harcourt gazed at Jonathon with agonized eyes. "But if she did know, why didn't she say anything? I had to conclude that she was lining me up for a future blackmail ploy, or else an exposé. And I couldn't risk that. It wasn't until the literary dinner that I realized what she intended doing with the information." Professor Harcourt stared at the carpet. "When we got to the pub, she let it slip about the scrubs and the tramp's testimony. And then I knew I had to stop that book coming out."

"But why? Your career is virtually over. So what if she wrote a book about it? She had no concrete evidence."

"I wasn't thinking of her harming me. I didn't want any of this to touch my son. He's brilliant—far more intelligent than I ever was. His professors speak so highly of him, and they expect great things of him. I didn't want his future career blighted by the discovery that his famous father was a murderer. I didn't think anyone would find out."

Mike leaned forward. "That all sounds very noble, but I think it's probably more likely that you did it firstly to save your own skin. And this wasn't a spur-of-the-moment thing."

Jonathon nodded. "The peanut oil suggests premeditation."

"You're right, of course. I came to the festival prepared to kill her if I had to. I knew about the allergy—everyone did—so I brought along the vial of peanut oil. I was hoping I wouldn't have to use it, that she hadn't made the connection between her new book plot and my past. But that comment about planning to base one book on a real-life case—that was aimed at me. When we sat in the pub waiting for the coffee, she said we needed to talk. We never got the chance, beyond her letting slip about the scrubs. There were all these people, clamoring her for autographs, asking questions...."

"And by then you knew she was going to write the book, come what may," Jonathon concluded.

Professor Harcourt nodded. "I noticed when the coffees were placed on the bar, but I said nothing. I wanted them to stay there for a while, because the longer they did that, the greater the opportunity for 'someone' to add the oil. And with all those people, it was easy to add it unnoticed."

"But how would 'someone' have known which cup to put the oil in?" Jonathon asked.

"Social media strikes again. I drink my coffee black, but that woman posted about *everything*, even to complain about there not being enough cream in her bedroom for the coffee you'd laid on for her." He shook his head. "She really was a bitch. So if anyone commented that I could have easily ended up with the doctored cup, I could simply drag out her recent posts and show how *anyone* could have known which cup was hers." He huffed. "Stupid. I should have put the oil in both cups."

"Was it an accident, her cup falling to the floor and breaking?" Mike asked.

"Let's call it an 'engineered' accident."

There was something Jonathon had to know. "Did she guess at the end? That you'd done something?"

Professor Harcourt met his gaze. "I don't know. When it hit, she immediately found it difficult to breathe. Her speech slurred, and she was dizzy and confused. I doubt she had the presence of mind to know it had been me. I'd managed to slip the EpiPen up my sleeve when she first reacted and asked me to take it from her bag. When I couldn't find the spare—which, of course, was there all the time—she panicked, trying to find her phone, but I'd already removed it from her bag on the way up to the room. Then I simply waited for the cardiac arrest that I knew would result." His face fell. "I didn't have to wait long. When she was dead, I yelled for you, then made it look like I'd been trying to help her. I didn't think for one second that you'd find the items."

"Lionel Harcourt?" Graham placed one hand on the professor's shoulder. "I am arresting you for the murder of Teresa Malvain. You do not have to say anything. But it may harm your defense if you do not mention when questioned something that you later rely on in court. Anything you do say may be given in evidence." He placed the shirt back in the bag and zipped it up.

Professor Harcourt smiled. "Nicely done, constable. And I think I've said everything I need to, don't you? I'm ready to go when you are." He rose carefully, then gave Mike a nod. "You obviously haven't lost your touch, ex-DI Tattersall. And your future husband is clearly as talented an investigator as you are." Then Professor Harcourt gave Graham an appreciative glance. "I'm glad it's you and not that irritating DI Gorland." His eyes twinkled. "Not that you have to repeat that."

Graham coughed loudly, and in spite of his churning stomach, Jonathon chuckled.

Graham gazed at Mike. "I'll be back later to take a photo of the handprint. *After* I've made sure the professor is comfortable." He led Professor Harcourt from the room, holding his bag.

Jonathon went over to the window and gazed down into the street, his heart heavy. "I know he killed her, but—"

"You felt sorry for him." When Jonathon nodded, Mike sighed. "I know. He's an old man. But he killed two people. With forethought."

"But he looks so… nice. Sweet. Harmless." Jonathon couldn't marry the two images in his head. The sweet elderly man and the premeditating killer.

"At least Graham gets the credit for the arrest." Mike snickered. "I wish I could be there to see Gorland's face when he finds out where Graham arrested him and how it all came to light."

Jonathon laughed. "I don't think we need worry about Gorland wanting an invitation to the wedding, do you?"

Mike came up behind him and slipped his arms around Jonathon's waist. "Speaking of which…. Now that we know everything, do you think we could concentrate on a certain event?"

Jonathon leaned back, safe in Mike's arms. "Oh, I think we can manage that. As long as you realize there'll be no sex for the rest of the week."

Mike stiffened. "Why not?"

"Because I want to be sure of providing the girls with a really good sample this weekend."

Mike's breath tickled his ear. "Who says *I* have to give up sex? All we need is a chastity device for you, and we're sorted."

"Chas—" Jonathon turned around slowly, and Mike beat a hasty retreat. As he ran down the stairs laughing, Jonathon called after him, "Remember I know where you're sleeping tonight."

Revenge was going to be sweet.

EPILOGUE

September 2018

JONATHON TOOK one last look in the mirror. The cream suit had been his first choice ever since the assistant had pointed it out, despite Mike making jokes about the likelihood of him dropping food onto it during the reception. Jonathon hadn't been fooled for an instant. The look in Mike's eyes when Jonathon had emerged from the changing room….

I made the perfect choice. A thought which applied equally to his future husband.

The knock at the door startled him out of his musing.

"Thought you should know. The parents are here. Both sets." Mike sounded amused.

Jonathon laughed. "Well, I'm sure yours are in fine spirits as usual. How are mine?"

"Your mum looks kind of… surprised. As for your dad, he looks like he's sucking on a lemon. Either that, or a bee flew into his mouth and stung him."

"That sounds about right."

"Do I get to see you, or do I have to talk to you through this door?"

Jonathon let out a dramatic gasp. "It's bad luck before the wedding."

"Excuse me?" Mike's tone was indignant. "Who was that in your bed this morning? Because he looked a lot like me. And I'm not the only one who wants to see you. Your best 'man' is here too."

"Actually? I want to see both of you. So open the door." There was something in Ruth's voice that piqued Jonathon's interest.

He opened the door and caught his breath. Mike looked incredible in his dark blue suit, his beard neatly trimmed, his tan visible against the white shirt. Beside him, Ruth wore a gold-and-cream dress, with a matching hat.

"Will we do?" she asked with a smile.

"You both look amazing." Jonathon had always thought Mike was a good-looking man, but the sight of him in his suit was breathtaking.

"Well, I don't *feel* amazing," Ruth grumbled. "I am, however, puzzled. I thought you two were the ones who were supposed to receive gifts. Because I got one this morning."

Jonathon frowned. "What did you get?"

Her apparent bad mood disappeared, and she grinned. "Morning sickness."

For a moment Jonathon was stunned into silence. Mike stared at her, as if the words hadn't sunk in. Then they threw their arms around her as if synchronized, hugging her tightly. Jonathon's vision blurred. He glanced at Mike, only to find Mike's eyes in a similar state.

Carefully, he broke the hug, glancing down to her belly. With a tearful smile, Ruth took his hand and placed it there, then kissed his cheek.

"When are you due?" Mike asked at last, his arm still around her.

"The doctor says May. And once you have your little bundle of joy, we can start work on ours. Clare is already buying things for the baby's room." Ruth's eyes shone. "She's going to make a great mother."

"I hope the baby looks like her," Mike said earnestly.

Ruth kissed him on the cheek. "Hey, if he or she looks like you? That's no bad thing." She wiped her eyes. "Now you two need to get out there and get married so this little nugget has a set of dads."

"Nugget?" Mike's eyes gleamed. "Hey, that's a great name for the baby. We'll have to remember that one."

Jonathon glared at him. "Let's not."

Ruth kissed them both on the cheek. "I'd better get out there and look like I'm expecting you." She flashed them a grin. "As opposed to just expecting." And with that, she left them at the bedroom door.

Mike held out his hand. "Time to make it official. And you were right about the venue. It looks perfect." They'd set up the chairs in the Italian garden. The ceremony was to take place beneath an arch built by Ben Threadwell, and white roses covered it. Ben had been growing them since June. Not only that, the fountains in the long pool were working, to add the tinkling soundtrack of water to the proceedings.

"You're still okay with us walking out together?"

"Seeing as we couldn't make up our minds which of us got to wait at the front for the other, it was the only solution. By the way, Melinda and Lloyd are here, plus Sue and Andrew, and most of the village." Mike smiled. "I can't wait for the party once we get the official stuff over."

"Hey, I want to remember every second of the official stuff. I only plan on getting married once, so I'm going to etch it into my memory." Jonathon wanted everything to be just right.

Mike regarded him warmly. "Glad to hear it. Then let's get out there." He held out his hand, and Jonathon took it.

Time for two to become one.

"THIS IS my favorite part." The celebrant grinned. "I now pronounce you married. You may kiss your husband."

Jonathon let out a happy sigh. "Finally." He leaned in and kissed Mike lightly on the lips, but Mike was apparently having none of it. He took Jonathon in his arms and kissed him fully as the guests cheered and applauded. Ruth showered them with rose petals, and Sue tossed handfuls of confetti.

The celebrant cleared his throat, and reluctantly they broke the kiss. He turned them gently to face the seated guests. Jonathon spied so many happy faces staring back at them. Rachel sat next to Lily Rossiter, and Graham sat at the end of a row, grinning. Melinda had tears trickling down over her wrinkled cheeks, and Lloyd gazed at them with a proud expression. Jason Barton stood to one side, his camera aimed at them. He gave Jonathon the thumbs-up before taking more photos. Clare had joined Ruth and was helping her scatter yet more petals.

He scanned the faces for their parents. Mike's father beamed at them, and beside him, Mike's mother was crying. His own mother seemed overcome by the guests' enthusiasm, as though she hadn't expected such a rapturous reaction or so many people. His father appeared to be suffering from similar emotions.

The celebrant gave another slight cough. "Ladies and gentlemen, may I be the first to introduce to you, Jonathon de Mountford and Mike Tattersall."

The applause that followed took even Jonathon by surprise. Everyone rose to their feet, their faces alight as they clapped and cheered. Mike curled his hand around his and squeezed.

At Jonathon's side, Ruth murmured, "You're keeping your names?"

Mike nodded. "Jonathon has to keep his, and there is no way I'm going to be Mike de Mountford-Tattersall. That's far too much of a mouthful." Then he was engulfed in a hug from his parents, who pulled Jonathon in as well.

When they parted, Jonathon caught sight of his parents, standing only a few feet away.

"Do you think they'll ever be happy for us?" Mike said quietly.

Jonathon smiled. "Wait till they're holding their first grandchild next year. I guarantee we'll see a thaw." He looped his arms around Mike's neck and kissed him, taking his time. "Love you," he whispered as they broke the kiss.

Mike's eyes sparkled. "Love you too." Then he grinned. "Now lead me to the champagne." Around them, guests came forward to congratulate them, and the air was filled with excited voices.

"I hope you're wearing your dancing shoes," Jonathon commented. "You're going to need them." The ballroom was all set up for the reception, and the party to follow promised to go on long into the night.

Mike leaned closer. "Not only that, I'm wearing my dancing foot."

Jonathon blinked. "You have a dancing foot?"

Mike nodded. "And a bionic foot too." When Jonathon gaped at him, he laughed. "Did you know, in the dictionary next to *gullible* it says, 'See Jonathon de Mountford.'"

"I wouldn't joke if I were you," Jonathon warned. "Otherwise, when we're exploring the tunnels in Vietnam, I might decide to accidentally lose you."

"I'd find my way back to you," Mike said confidently. "Trust me, sweetheart, nothing could ever part me from you. Besides, I was a detective, remember? I have skills." He buffed his fingernails on his jacket.

"And I'm looking forward to being on the receiving end of your *skills* tonight," Jonathon whispered.

Mike groaned. "Don't say things like that, not when we're in public. Because you *know* what I'm thinking about."

"Later," Jonathon assured him. "We have a party to attend, and friends to greet."

And the rest of their lives to enjoy each other.

K.C. WELLS lives on an island off the south coast of the UK, surrounded by natural beauty. She writes about men who love men, and can't even contemplate a life that doesn't include writing.

The rainbow rose tattoo on her back with the words 'Love is Love' and 'Love Wins' is her way of hoisting a flag. She plans to be writing about men in love - be it sweet and slow, hot or kinky - for a long while to come.

If you want to follow her exploits, you can sign up for her monthly newsletter: http://eepurl.com/cNKHlT

You can stalk – er, find – her in the following places:
Email: k.c.wells@btinternet.com
Facebook: www.facebook.com/KCWellsWorld
KC's Men in Love (my readers group): http://bit.ly/2hXL6wJ
Blog: kcwellsworld.blogspot.co.uk
Twitter: @K_C_Wells
Website: www.kcwellsworld.com
Instagram: www.instagram.com/k.c.wells
BookBub: https://www.bookbub.com/authors/k-c-wells

K.C. WELLS

TRUTH WILL OUT

A Merrychurch Mysteries Case

Jonathon de Mountford's visit to Merrychurch village to stay with his uncle Dominic gets off to a bad start when Dominic fails to appear at the railway station. But when Jonathon finds him dead in his study, apparently as the result of a fall, everything changes. For one thing, Jonathon is the next in line to inherit the manor house. For another, he's not so sure it was an accident, and with the help of Mike Tattersall, the owner of the village pub, Jonathon sets out to prove his theory—if he can concentrate long enough without getting distracted by the handsome Mike.

They discover an increasingly long list of people who had reason to want Dominic dead. And when events take an unexpected turn, the amateur sleuths are left bewildered. It doesn't help that the police inspector brought in to solve the case is the last person Mike wants to see, especially when they are told to keep their noses out of police business.

In Jonathon's case, that's like a red rag to a bull….

www.dreamspinnerpress.com

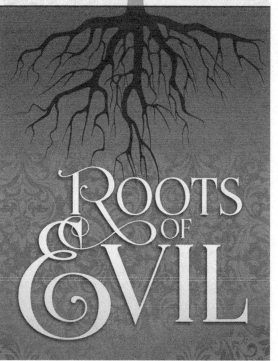

Sequel to *Truth Will Out*
A Merrychurch Mysteries Case

Many consider Naomi Teedle the village witch. Most people avoid her except when they have need of her herbs and potions. She lives alone on the outskirts of Merrychurch, and that's fine by everyone—old Mrs. Teedle is not the most pleasant of people. But when she is found murdered, her mouth bulging with her own herbs and roots, suddenly no one has a bad word to say about her.

Jonathon de Mountford is adjusting to life up at the manor house, but it's not a solitary life: pub landlord Mike Tattersall sees to that. Jonathon is both horrified to learn of the recent murder and confused by the sudden reversal of public opinion. Surely someone in the village had reason to want her dead? He and Mike decide it's time for them to step in and "help" the local police with their investigation. Only problem is, their sleuthing uncovers more than one suspect—and the list is getting longer….

www.dreamspinnerpress.com

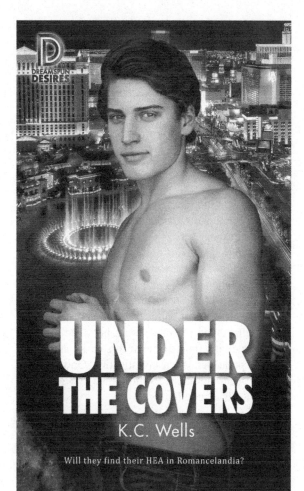

UNDER
THE COVERS

K.C. Wells

Will they find their HEA in Romancelandia?

Can they find their HEA in Romancelandia?

Chris Tyler loves his job. He photographs some of the hottest guys on the planet, but none stir him like Jase Mitchell. He'll never let Jase know – he values their friendship too much to spoil it.

Jase is looking forward to the Under The Covers Romance convention. It's a great opportunity to connect with readers who want to meet their favorite cover model, but more importantly, with agents who could advance his career. Too bad the only person he yearns to connect with is Chris.

What Chris wants is Jase in his life, but he's afraid that's sheer fantasy. What Jase desires is a Hollywood dream, but that will mean leaving Chris behind. What both crave is a real-life romance and their own Happily Ever After.

www.dreamspinnerpress.com